FEB 1 1 2017

This is a work of fiction. Names, characters, places, and incidents
either are the product of the author's imagination or used
fictitiously. Any resemblance to actual persons, living or dead,
localities, businesses, companies, and events is entirely coincidental.

THE SECOND LETTER

ROBERT LANE

We are all of us born with a letter inside of us, and that only if we are true to ourselves may we be allowed to read it before we die.

Douglas Coupland

I want to splinter the CIA into a thousand pieces and scatter it to the winds.

John F. Kennedy

THE
SECOND
LETTER

CHAPTER 1

West Coast of Florida, April 14, 1961

The day the letter arrived Dorothy Harrison heard the song for the first time and thought it was one for the ages.

She twisted the ribbed knob of her car radio in an effort to eliminate the static and noise that crackled through the speakers of her pearl fawn 1959 Buick Electra 225. A deuce and a quarter of fins, steel, and chrome that the world would never afford the luxury to construct again. Machine, time, and a woman forever joined in a singular stylistic statement.

She drove down the beach road and swung onto a green-canopied street. She turned into her drive and parked on the packed white sand next to the trimmed oleander bush with its tropical red flowers. Angelo, her young Cuban gardener, dragged branches to a brush pile. She knew he would wait for a west wind before igniting the dry sticks. The oleander bush was toxic and its smoke dangerous to inhale. A black sedan rested across the street. She wondered what they wanted this time and why they just didn't leave her alone. Beyond the sedan in the park, old men played cards, read newspapers, and smoked cigars.

"Morning, Miss Dorothy," Angelo said. He faced her with his hands at his sides and his shirttail tucked in. The shirttail was always tight within his trousers.

"Good morning, Angelo. Beautiful day, isn't it?"

"Yes, ma'am. When the Lord wants, he can make a sweet one. I'll be here just a couple of hours if that will be all right with you."

"That's fine. You really do have everything looking very nice."

"We have a visitor," Angelo said. "He came by himself in that black car. Said he knew you. He's inside right now and all dressed up."

"I'm sure he's just an old friend." She knew of none, though, who would be casually driving around the west coast of Florida.

She had been listening to WTSP 1380 AM on her in-dash radio playing the Shirelles' "Will You Still Love Me Tomorrow." The question swirled in her head. Dorothy, Dottie to the friends she'd abandoned in Washington, DC, liked the song and wondered what Jim would have thought of it. He always admired the big swing bands of Dorsey and Miller, and he eventually grew to appreciate Ellington's style, but you didn't hear much of that music anymore. Although it had only been a few months, it was almost as if that era had slipped out with him. Dorothy thought the world was changing at an accelerating pace and in the process, redefining time.

Her Northeast friends could not fathom why she and Jim had relocated to Long Key, a mile-and-a-half strip of untrimmed subtropical foliage, crushed seashells, and small cottages on the extreme southern tip of St. Petersburg Beach. A few extra feet of water could obliterate it all, and nearly did in the unnamed storms of the 1920s. But her friends knew that Dottie always did things on her own terms, and besides, it didn't matter where she lived. The party followed her.

She had spent her childhood years in India and China as the only child of missionary parents. In 1925, when she was twenty-eight, she married Jim. He was a dashing Secret Service agent before such men even existed. On the DC socialite circuit, Dorothy was a svelte blonde of physical and intellectual energy. Thanks to her father, who wanted to tell the world about Jesus, and her physician mother, who wanted to tell the world about the importance of clean drinking water, Dorothy possessed a greater knowledge of world affairs than the bottom half of the Department of State.

Dorothy had once confided to her mother that she thought clean drinking water did more good for the world than Jesus. "Don't tell your father," her mother had replied with a smile.

While Jim served as chief of the White House Secret Service detail under Presidents Harding and Coolidge, Dorothy became an expert in historical preservation. She was credited with reviving much of Alexandria, Virginia's, historic district. His interest eventually migrated to covert operations, and in 1947, he joined to the newly formed Central Intelligence Agency. An invitation to one of their fanfares was a quick ticket up Washington's slippery social ladder. But it wasn't the life they wanted.

They moved south to an island.

They initially bought a house on Boca Ciega Bay, but when the old stone church just three blocks away faced demolition—— the post office passed on its option to purchase the building—— Dorothy couldn't let the small 1917 building go. They handed over $1,385, unloaded the bay front property, and renovated the church into their home. They discovered the warm waters of the Gulf were an ideal place to make love, just as the falling sun split itself between the sky and the water and was level with their bodies.

Jim was away on business when the first black sedan had arrived. Dorothy knew by the look on the driver's face before his foot ever touched her front porch.

Jim died January 5, 1961. One hundred and one days ago. The sun rarely penetrated the leaves that shielded her expansive side yard. A constant breeze, like a lover's memory, blew through her property and caressed her home with the scent of the sea and a hint of the exotic places that had landed her there. Harbored under long-needled Australian pines with the Gulf of Mexico on one side and the bay guarding the other, Dorothy Harrison held court for the relentless stream of visitors anxious to escape the nation's capital as well as new acquaintances eager to engage her company.

She entered her house and saw him as he stood underneath the stained-glass window that depicted a cross on a shield. Dorothy always thought it looked like a map of Ohio with a crooked *X* in the middle.

"My goodness, Ted, you're a pleasant surprise. What brings you to my 'God-forsaken piece of sand'? I believe that was your comment when you viewed it on a map."

Theodore Sullivan placed a copy of *Vogue* magazine on a table next to a bright blue-and-white Pan Am luggage tag. Dorothy noted his summer beige suit and wondered if he had purchased it solely for this trip. He was a man who was rarely seen in public unless charcoal gray or deep blue cloaked his body. His hair, as always, was closely cropped. He greeted her with a kiss on her offered cheek. "I spoke too hastily then; it's a beautiful home, shows you what I know. It's good to see you, Dottie. The town's not the same without you. The parties, always a bore, you know, are even more so. All serious business now."

"Certainly seemed serious at the time." She glanced at the magazine. It had arrived yesterday and she hadn't the time to read it. The cover featured a woman in a rainbow-striped dress and short hair under the banner "The new enticements." Is that what's in? Things certainly are changing rapidly.

"I suppose you're right," Sullivan said. "There're just so many more players now."

"Did you fly yourself down?"

"Yes. It is the one element that I still enjoy."

"You know you can take your tie off here. I won't tell." She imagined that he piloted his plane with his tie and suit coat on.

"I really do like your place." He glanced around. "It looks like an easy place to walk into and a hard place to leave."

"Those are the best. Can I get you an iced tea or lemonade?"

"That'll be swell."

"Which?"

"Oh, a lemonade would be great."

"How's Maureen?" Dorothy moved off to her side kitchen and poured a large glass of lemonade from the hand blown pitcher she kept in the refrigerator. She had just purchased it from Nancy's gallery down the street and was using it for the first time. She wanted to share that with Ted, but she knew that despite his ulterior politeness, Ted Sullivan harbored no interest for anything but his work.

Nor did he engage in social visits.

"She gives you her best," he said. "Still planning to come down and see you in the fall. I believe that Betty is joining her as well. They think DC is hot." Sullivan took a handkerchief across the back of his neck.

"I'm glad Betty's coming. Maureen and I discussed them visiting in early November and I was so hoping Betty would join her. Let's move to the porch. There's a nice breeze there."

They sat next to each other, and Sullivan drank half of his lemonade in one long, slow, appreciative act. "It really is a remarkable bit of sand you have here," he said. "You can practically spread your arms and touch water on both sides. You always had a knack for style. You found that perfect perch, no matter where you were."

"'The symbolic spot' is what Jim would say."

Neither of them spoke for a moment. Two fishermen holding lines with a dozen fish strewn on them ambled down the road. She assumed they were headed to the restaurant with the pine walls on the bay where the fish would become the two-dollar catch of the day.

"You still have your tie on," she said.

Sullivan glanced at her. "I envy you, down here. The game has so much more money, so many strata. We used to sit at a round table and we knew the enemy was on the other side of the pond. Now we sit at the same round table and hide our notes from each other, disguise our thoughts, and measure our words. Where there used to be one agency, there are now five. Where there used to be three divisions in an agency, now there are a dozen, bumping into each other on foreign corners and in embassy basements. You can't fathom the money that goes into it all."

"Why do you do it?"

Sullivan blew out his breath, hung his head, and looked down at his polished tan tied shoes sticking out from his cuffed pants. Dorothy thought they seemed so out of place on a wood porch swept with sand. "A few more years," he said. "A few more years."

"I don't think so, Ted." She looked hard at him, not letting him get away with it. He brought his head up and met her stare with an emotionless gaze.

"It's a battle, and we line up three deep on both sides of the ball. Even after Korea, there's still a growing contingent that's salivating to get entwined in French Indo-China. Heaven forbid that some third-rate country has a civil war and we stand idle. We always have to put a spin on how it threatens our very democracy and how our indifference is akin to shunning Almighty God himself. Why all the muscle, they contend, if we're never to use it. The world is a domino, they say. But where is that written? Department of Defense——what a sick Goebbels twist. Call it the Department of Offense and see what type of public support you'd garner." Sullivan broke eye contact and looked again across at the park. "And now we've bedded with Satan to export our righteousness south of the border.

"I do it to be heard," he said, his eyes still lost in the park, "to sleep at night, to sleep forever, and know that I voiced what I believed, and to have done it in a manner that exceeded what I thought I was capable of. I'm afraid that's as good as I can come up with."

"Pretty heady stuff for island conversation," Dorothy said. "Jim always said you were too good for the CIA."

"I left an envelope on your coffee table."

"I saw it. Does it have anything to do with Jim's death?"

"We've been over that."

"I know." His evasive answer did not escape her.

"I can walk out with it. But I'd rather not. It brings no harm to your door. It contains an official letter that I, and others, would like preserved, but not in Washington."

"The safes are getting too full up there?"

"We don't know whose safe to trust anymore. I mean that in both semantic senses. In the wrong hands the letter could be used as leverage against the US. It shows how far our madness has gone."

"Angelo is torching the brush pile when the wind is right. Why don't I just toss it in with the pine needles?"

"The wind is never right. We need to preserve it to remind us of who we are. Perhaps it can be used someday to help turn the tide toward saner times."

The Shirelles' song still massaged her head. WTSP used to play polka, but she woke one morning and they were broadcasting something called "Top 40." Jim used to be in her life, but she woke one morning and he was gone.

That airwave remained silent.

"You would like me to keep it?" Dorothy asked.

"Do you mind? You were always topnotch at preserving things. I could use a bank box, but I'd rather have it where, if necessary, I am not beholden to banking hours."

She let out a laugh and it surprised her. She was not a woman who laughed merely to bridge awkward conversational moments. She saved it for humor, and found heaps of the real stuff every day. "You and your cloak-and-dagger games. I'd be happy to keep it on one condition: that you and Maureen come visit at least once a year and that you walk away from that game you're drowning in." She thought "drowning in" was a little harsh, but there it was.

"We have a deal."

"Shall I tell you where I hide it?"

"Matters not to me, only to you."

"Are you certain?"

"All this sand," Sullivan said as he surveyed the park, "reminds me of Shelley, 'Round the decay of that colossal wreck, boundless and bare the lone and level sands stretch far away.'"

"Oh, Teddy, it can't be that bad." She surprised herself by reaching over and lightly touching his shoulder.

Theodore Wayne Sullivan III, Skull and Bones like his father before him, and valedictorian of the class of 1920, said nothing. He watched the men across the street in the park and then turned his head toward Dorothy. He shifted his weight away from her.

"What?" she asked.

Sullivan hesitated. "Nothing. I really must be going."

Dorothy watched his eyes look above her own and she thought his voice betrayed a tint of self-contempt. No, she thought. Finality. Within the minute, he drove away.

"Where do you want to hide it, Miss Dorothy?"

Angelo held the 8½" x 11" yellow letter-sized envelope. They stood in the middle of her home. The slight young man had appeared on her front porch grasping remarkably good English and a garden rake the day after she moved in. He had held the rake as if it was the proudest thing he'd ever possessed and he knew that he would accomplish great tasks with his simple, crude tool. His parents had moved to the United States when he was young and wanted their two sons to speak as well as Hemingway wrote. They considered the great fisherman, coming down to Havana from Key West to stalk marlin around the time Angelo was born, to be a bridge between the two countries. He took care of several properties on the island, but he was soon spending his extra time under the soft pines of her residence. *We* have a visitor.

"I haven't a clue," she said.

"Don't you want to know what's in it, what the letter says?"

"No, I'd really rather not. In fact, I don't even want it in the house."

"The salt air and rain will have to be kept out, Miss Dorothy. They just eat everything. How long do you think you need to hide it for?"

The challenge seemed to perk him up a bit. He was so despondent since his terrible loss and she fretted about him.

9

That part hadn't worked out for her and Jim and she knew she was leaning on Angelo and his wife to fill the void and now that, too, was gone.

Dorothy let out an exasperated breath. "You're right. We need to wrap it and then seal it in a container."

"I got an old tackle box, tighter than anything I know."

"I'd hate to have you use that."

"It's old, Miss Dorothy, and I don't use it anymore. We can wrap it in oilskin and put it in the box. You know those loose stones out back, corner of the house? I think that hole's large enough. Been thinking for some time how to fill that hole. It'll be good in there for a long time."

"That'll be fine. That hibiscus is going to take over that corner anyway. Go ahead, but better not tell anybody where you put it. That will be our secret."

"How long do you think you need to hide it for?" Angelo asked for the second time.

"I don't know," Dorothy said. "I guess until someone comes looking for it."

Angelo went out the back door with the envelope, and she appraised herself in front of the living room mirror. She noticed wrinkles around her mouth and wasn't sure if some of them weren't new in just the past few days. Really, she thought. That fast? She took consolation in what she did have some control over wasn't half bad. Not a new pound in forty years, still a slim waist, bright eyes, and erect shoulders. Flat-out impressive. I don't know about the new style, she thought, recalling the cover of *Vogue*. Not right for me. She adjusted the collar of her shirt and pretended it had not been crooked while Ted was there. Then her shoulders gave an involuntary slump at the same time her chest let out her breath. What can it all possibly matter, she thought. As if anyone will ever remember, will ever know.

The question from the song, though, really boils it down. There will never be any doubts. Not even when the sand renders it all boundless and bare. I will love you until I have no more tomorrows.

That evening, as she often did, she took a swim just as darkness came, and the glow from the pink hotel softened the bottom of the night. The water was the one place where time's lost days were returned. She imagined Jim, her lifeline, being the water itself and wrapping himself around her.

She wondered if Ted had held back at the end. Was the letter about Jim? So silly to think so. He had died in a CIA plane crash. The driver told her that the shroud that covered his mission forbade any detailed information, but it seemed such an empty ending to such a full life. What had Ted said? He always chose his words so carefully. Such a meticulous man.

Matters not to me, only to you.

Only to you.

Only to me.

CHAPTER 2

Present Day

Kathleen's arm was draped over my chest and her head rested against my shoulder. For a half hour, I had been awake and holding that position. I gently unraveled myself and left her in the previous night, tangled in white sheets with her blonde hair tossed on the pillow. I needed to run. I laced my shoes tight and set out to pound the packed sand beaches of the Gulf of Mexico.

I locked the door behind me. Not everyone in the world is as fond of me as I am.

I ran thinking of the two weeks in the Keys that we had just returned from, living aboard *Moon Child*, my neighbor Morgan's forty-two-foot Beneteau. I ran until the Florida heat jolted me from my trance, my body's temperature rising, my muscles breaking free, my lungs screaming at me. My world back in order. Running is one of two things I know in which I can so effortlessly push myself to dangerous extremes. The other is drinking. I need both to live. One nearly killed me.

I sprinted the last hundred yards to my house and doubled over, hands on my hips, and wondered what the hell was chasing me. I thought of rinsing myself under the outdoor shower, but decided to hit the back screened porch and see if she had crossed over to the new day.

She sat in a brown-cushioned chair and wore tan shorts, no shoes, and a white silk T-shirt with a deep V neck. Her thick hair rested on slender shoulders. The steam from her cup of coffee wasn't that much different from the muggy air into which it dissipated. Bryan Lee came through my floor speakers telling me it hurt him too. It put me in the mood for Taittinger Champagne in the morning, which is one of my favorite things. I make damn certain I rarely indulge.

"I've got to remember to keep shoes and shorts here so I can run in the morning," she said when I lowered the blind to block the sun that assaulted our bodies like white bread in a toaster. "I had *way* too many rum runners and buttered lobster the last couple of weeks, and it's time to start burning it off."

I sat next to her and propped my feet on the glass table where her pale pink toes rested against my calves. A twin engine Edgewater with a hardtop and double antennas rocketed across the bay at the end of my dock and out toward the open waters of the Gulf of Mexico.

"I thought we decided that we could never have too much moonshine," I said while I scanned the bay's surface searching for dolphins. I took a deep drink from my bottled water. I had consumed a whole bottle prior to the five miles.

"You weren't paying attention. We did muse whether we could live without it or not."

"Apparently I misunderstood that whole conversation."

"I think you're selective on what you understand."

"I struggle with musing."

That earned a slight smile. "I see. By the way, Garrett called."

"Key West to Cleveland a little more than he could handle?" I glanced at her. Her bright gaze awaited me. And I had been dolphin hunting. Incredible.

"I think he can handle all he wants. He said to give him a ring."

"Would you like breakfast?" I asked.

"No."

"A hug?"

She glanced at me. "You're a sweaty mess. Not even suitable to be around people after you run."

"Then I'll start running twice a day."

"Take me home, James."

"It's Jake, and we've been over that a dozen times."

"Really," she drew the word out until it became stuck in the thick air. "I don't know why I keep missing that."

Despite her breakfast denial, I scrambled eggs with diced onion and tomato. A few minutes later I placed the eggs, toast, and grapefruit in front of her on the glass table on the porch. I ate all the eggs and toast. Half the grapefruit. We got into my truck and crossed three bridges—I live on an island off another island—and arrived at her house on the island across the bay. When you live on an island, you cross a lot of bridges.

While I atrophied in traffic on my return trip—they were building a higher bridge that would irritate the hell out of me for at least two years—I dialed Garrett's office phone instead of his cell. I wanted to see if I could get Mary Evelyn, his middle-aged, devout Irish Catholic secretary, to address me by my first name. It was our special time together. Talking with her is as close as I ever get to a church.

"Good morning, Mr. Travis," she answered. Bright and cheerful. Always. Some people are like that. Maybe I should consider being a nonspecific-aged Midwest female Irish Catholic secretary. Maybe the whole world should. Wonder how that would fly in Sandland?

"I know you can do it. I feel it within you."

"I understand you all had a very enjoyable time in the Keys, Mr. Travis."

"What if it was my last wish, like one of those wish foundations, would you then, could you?"

"Mr. Travis—"

"Jake on three. Ready? One, two—"

"It's such a relief when you call. I do tire of talking to adults all day."

"And I look forward to the voice of an angel." But she was gone, and I don't know how much of that she got. Three seconds later Garrett's voice filled the air in my truck.

"Colonel called, he wants you to go to church," Garrett said. Not bright and cheerful. Not Irish. I already missed Mary Evelyn.

Garrett and I had left Special Forces after five years, and Colonel Janssen had retained us to perform contract work. Key West was nice, but on one level, it was boring as hell. Garrett's cover job was being an attorney in Cleveland. The one on Erie's shore. I don't know how he did it. Janssen certainly hadn't dialed Garrett's cell. He either utilized a SCIF (Sensitive Compartmental Information Facility) or a multifunctional phone where both ends followed procedures to ensure a secure connection.

"You tell him I'm busy?"

"He knew we were sailing."

"Perhaps he needs a reminder that I have his address."

While Janssen tried to recruit me after I left the army, I'd come home one day and his ass was planted at the end of my dock. Sipping my last Heineken. I didn't mind him helping himself to the bottle, but I did mind his unannounced presence. To reciprocate, I had Mary Evelyn track down his unlisted home address. I sent him a Christmas card of an olive-tone

Jesus, Asian angels, white sheep, and black wise men all on recycled paper with a portion of its cost going to charity. It declared that the prince of peace had arrived.

I thought that was important information considering the line of work he was in.

"He was just showing off," Garrett said.

"What'd he really want?"

"Wants you to go to church."

That caught me.

Garrett said, "There's a museum in your neighborhood that used to be an old church."

"I know it. A bike ride from my house."

"Someone recently hacked the outer walls and dislodged some stones."

"Tell him to call a mason, they're free."

"He wants us to retrieve a letter that they believe, but aren't positive, was held in those stone walls."

"It's in my neighborhood and he's going through you?"

"I think the event pushed him to the limit. Probably be best if you two don't communicate for a while."

The colonel had granted me a personal favor a few months back. Kathleen's wealthy womanizing husband had ties to the Outfit in Chicago. The Cook County DA was prepping him to sing, and the Outfit caught wind and buried him. They decided that she might know too much and thereby constitute a threat.

They dispatched four guns with the intent to kidnap and kill her. They went one for two, which is not bad at Fenway, but fatal that night. We located her, and Garrett and I dropped four hit men on a not too distant beach. We were lucky; a bullet passed clean through Kathleen's left shoulder. It left a scar, a reminder that some things never heal. Janssen orchestrated the cover-up. A Jane Doe was dropped on the beach, given

Kathleen's identity, and Lauren Cunningham became Kathleen Rowe in hopes that the Outfit would cease their relentless pursuit. Her parents were early cancer victims—not the big door prize they hoped for—and only a few friends and her investment-banking brother in New York knew the truth. Janssen didn't tolerate loose ends and even sanctioned a headstone for Lauren Cunningham.

I never told her about the marble. But I knew how it all ended, what that last chapter looked like. It was a cold stone above Lake Michigan where even the wind ran from winter.

"Tell him I swung by, asked around, and nobody saw the perp," I said. "What else do we need to discuss or muse upon? I understand I need to work on musing."

"That's doesn't even break the top hundred. Mary Evelyn's sending you a file. The letter was never supposed to be there, although someone certainly knew of it. Janssen says it's imperative that we recover it."

"Always is."

"He sounded even more."

"Someone could make copies," I said.

"They couldn't be authenticated. The real deal is damaging," Garrett said. "Raydel Escobar, a carpet guy that runs skin joints and lives on the island across from you, contacted the government. He's suggesting a quid pro quo arrangement while maintaining that he came across the letter purely by luck."

"What would he like in return?"

"Forgiveness."

"His transgression?"

"A sizeable bill with the IRS."

"We both know there are more pleasurable sins than screwing the IRS," I said. "Let's broker a deal and be done with it."

"We don't negotiate."

"We certainly encourage others to."

"When instructed to return the letter, he claimed, despite his previous assertion, that he didn't have it. Check the e-mail and let me know what you think."

"That's not on the agenda today," I said.

"Or any day. If you need me——"

"I need you like I need a new——"

He hung up.

I didn't *feel* like looking at an e-mail that particular moment. Besides, it took eternity to go through the encryption process. I parked my truck in the driveway, pumped my bike tires until they were hard with air, and headed down the street.

The old stone church was on a side street under large Australian pines with a prominent sign proclaiming it the Gulf Beaches Historical Museum. I wondered if you could have a museum that wasn't historical. Natural history, perhaps. The side yard was a carpet of coarse hard sand and pine needles. Small tables with metal chairs looked out toward the tropical green park across the street. A white picket fence with small gray dolphins on it outlined the front and side yards and an old man was picking up twigs. I got off my bike and realized that I could see both the Gulf and the bay. It was a hell of a spot.

I couldn't imagine what I was doing there.

CHAPTER 3

"We think it happened three nights ago," said the man who served as the museum's volunteer docent for the day. "I opened up at noon; we're closed Monday through Wednesday. Elissa came and told me."

"Who's Elissa?" I asked.

I had asked him one question and received four answers. He wore wire glasses, a green vest over a short-sleeved white shirt, flowered shorts, and sandals. He was pushing eighty. It was as if his top half was still up north and his bottom half had migrated to Florida.

I took that all in before I realized he was missing his right arm.

"She's an older lady who lives behind the museum. Said when she got up a few mornings ago she noticed the stones were scattered all around. She never heard a thing, though, but she doesn't hear much of anything anymore. Says she doesn't mind—not too interested in all the noise."

"Missing anything?" Besides your arm?

"Well, I suppose. But that's her intent, isn't it?"

"I mean in the museum."

"Oh. No, not that I know."

"Any damage done inside?"

"What's your interest again?" It came out pretty gutsy for a one-armed old docent.

19

We were the only people in the museum. There was a large black-and-white photograph on the wall to my right of the pink hotel when it was an army hospital during the war. About a quarter of Florida's hotels had been confiscated by the government during World War Two to serve as administrative and convalescent centers. There were pictures of men in long pants holding lines of fish and pictures of old buildings that might not have been so old at the time. I recognized some of the buildings as still being upright, but others were long gone. That's a better deal than the men received.

The middle of the room held glass cases that housed a hodgepodge of mementos. By virtue of being placed under glass, however, they gained a new life and historical standing. The old church had a high ceiling above a stained-glass window—damn thing looked like a map of Ohio with a pirate's *X* in the middle—and off to my left, an alcove with a clear window revealed an untrimmed hibiscus bush on the other side. I stood next to a display rack that held pamphlets on area attractions as well as several self-published books about the history of the small community in which I lived. I picked up a card that listed various levels of donations to keep the museum operable. The top level was $25. They don't aim high. There was also a line thanking the "anonymous donors who make a difference." A sign advertised an annual fund-raiser to be held at the museum next week.

"I've been meaning to come here for some time. I heard someone vandalized it. Can't imagine why. What do you think they got?" I asked.

"Why do you keep insisting something's gone? Just some old stones knocked off the exterior. Don't know why anyone would even bother. Probably just some kids."

A couple with all their limbs came in and he greeted them. They said they were down from Maryville, Tennessee, south of Knoxville. They commenced a peripheral self-guided tour.

"How long's it been a museum?" I asked. I had faded over to the alcove to allow him some room when the Volunteers arrived.

"Little over twenty years." He adjusted the guest book. I wondered if he was a natural southpaw or he had lost his good arm. He joined me in the alcove.

"Did the church relocate then?" I asked.

"Heavens no. The church was long gone. This was Dorothy Harrison's house." He proclaimed it as if it was the most apparent fact in the world and my lack of knowledge was inexcusable.

"Of course. Begging your pardon, but who is Miss Harrison?"

"Was." He blew out his breath. It's not easy dealing with the ignorant public. "She died in '89 when she was ninety-two, just like the song."

"The song?"

"You know, 'The Christmas Song,' kids from one to ninety-two; no reason to live past ninety-two if you can't celebrate Christmas. Supposedly she always said she wanted to go at ninety-two."

"A goal to die?"

"Well, you could say her goal was to live to ninety-two."

"I like that better."

"She bequeathed her home to the town, and it became a museum a year after her death. You're standing in what was her bedroom. Take a look around, son, and meet her." He pointed with his one hand toward the display case. Then he said, "But she's been watching you the whole time." He moved away from me.

He said with his back to me, "And it's 'Mrs.' Not 'Miss.'"

I glanced up, and centered high on the opposite wall from the front door and cluttered on both sides with black-and-white photographs, hung a color portrait of a lady. She gazed straight ahead, south, and wore a soft red dress. Her blonde hair was pulled back behind her neck. Her warm smile and confident eyes seemed unaffected by the exposure of light and age that washed the painting. I wondered what shade of red the dress originally was, but I couldn't imagine her eyes or smile ever looked any different than they did in her portrait.

I peered into the display's case glass, tried to recall the last time I'd heard someone say "bequeath," and sank in time as the items in the case pulled me in. There was a picture of Dorothy as a young woman. Another black-and-white photograph showed President Harding's swearing-in ceremony, with the same striking lady three people to his right and beaming at the president. Another picture was of her and a stud, her husband, the cutline indicated. An article about Jim Harrison indicated that he was in charge of Secret Service presidential protection. I knew the service had started in 1865 to combat counterfeiting and at the designation of Congress after the assassination of William McKinley in 1901, it was charged with full-time protection of presidents. McKinley was the third president to be assassinated in a thirty-six-year period.

Three out of ten. Thirty percent of US presidents from 1861 to 1897 were gunned down.

Jim Harrison, the article said, joined the CIA after its inception in 1947. There were no more articles referencing his professional life until a terse paragraph on his death. He died on a business trip in a "tragic plane crash." Like a museum that wasn't historical, I wondered if a plane crash could be anything else. There were no details. Jim just stopped appearing in the photographs.

That's what death is—you no longer show up in pictures.

I flipped through a photo album, and even late in her life Dorothy rose up to greet me. She was tall and confident and held her trim shoulders erect. Her energy burned the photograph, its toast-brown Kodak corners curled. The alcove, her bedroom, had been transformed into a shrine to her. I read every word. I viewed every picture.

I thanked the docent and strolled around the outside of the building. In the back, several large stones lay dislodged on the ground. They left a sizeable cavity, but there was nothing else to see. Someone had attacked Dorothy Harrison's house over twenty years after she died.

I left my rusted bike inside the white picket fence, walked across the street, and claimed the end of a bench that wasn't covered with baked-on bird shit. Dorothy had moved here at the height of the cold war. What was chasing her? Who did she know? A horrific combination of words. Cold. War. It's always the short ones that pack the punch. They slug way above their weight limit.

A turquoise convertible from a few decades past crept by at a speed that allowed me to count the rotation of the tires. An older man drove and a woman with large white sunglasses rode shotgun, and everything in the car shone bright and new with the sun. I left the park to the old men smoking cigars and playing chess with discarded newspapers off to the side. I pedaled back to my house. Key West, only a few days ago, was suddenly shelved with events far more distant in the past. Yet things from that distant past hung in my mind like yesterday.

Time, in many ways, is just another ugly four-letter word.

I like print. By touching paper I save myself from becoming a computer with two legs. Who wants to make love to that?

Mary Evelyn had sent the email encrypted U//FOUO, unclassified, for official use only. I printed the fourteen-page dossier on Escobar, brushed a gecko off my seat, and settled into one of the soft chairs on my screened porch. An osprey flew by with a sheepshead in its talons—you don't see that very often. It was stupid hot. I got up, turned the ceiling fan on high, sat back down, and held the pages with both hands so the fan wouldn't whip them away. I skipped around for the salient facts.

Raydel Escobar, age forty-three, wanted to give the US government, actually return to the government, a letter. A letter, our government believed, that was hidden in the exterior walls of the museum. In appreciation, he would like the IRS to stop pestering him. Escobar was seven million in arrears.

The letter was classified and I wasn't cleared to know its contents. *I was certainly cleared to risk my life to retrieve it.* Escobar claimed it dropped on his lap—he had no hand in securing the letter—and while he would dearly love to simply hand it over, he could fathom no reason to do so as long as the IRS was crawling up his ass.

Escobar operated a successful carpeting and rug business and owned three Tampa gentlemen's clubs. The Welcome In was his first club, and he kept them under a different corporate umbrella. Not enough there to be seven mill behind. He had participated in a land deal for a new interchange, and depending on his cost basis, he might have struck gold with that. Escobar was known to associate with Paulo Henriques, a building contractor from Palm Beach who miraculously escaped the '08 meltdown. No way was he clean. Henriques was linked to Walter Mendis, a Palm Beach mobster. The FBI circled Mendis for years, but had never gotten him in their talons.

We caught a break when the contractor who built Escobar's mansion, Stuart Shramos, in return for leniency with his own IRS difficulties—see, we *do* negotiate—supplied the blueprints and nonpublic commentary on Escobar's compound. It was across the bay at the tip of Kathleen's island.

Escobar's twenty-four-by-thirty-foot study overlooked mangrove islands and the Gulf of Mexico. Its two-inch bulletproof glass faced west and was specifically designed to withstand UV radiation. Apparently bulletproof glass came with an SPF rating. In the eight-foot-wide hallway leading into the study, one of the walnut panels secretly doubled as a door that led to a safe room. The room was designed to hold his family and permanently house the security equipment. Shramos claimed that Escobar inquired if one layer of Kevlar built within the paneled door would be sufficient to deflect machine gun bullets. Shramos had informed Escobar that he had no experience with Kevlar or machine guns.

They put in two layers.

I couldn't get excited about breaking into some Cuban's bay front compound surrounded by hombres with itchy fingers who would have every right to unload on me. And there I am scrunching around for some envelope that could be anywhere; the bilge of his boat or behind a double Kevlar-reinforced wall. I wanted to get the lay of his property and then infiltrate his life. I already knew the ugly truth. We'd compose a COA—course of action—and by the end we'd wing it, hour by hour, minute by minute, until the split second when infinite divisibility disproved its theory. Garrett and I adhered to a simple dogma:

Operate at one level under your opponent.

An hour later I stepped around the end of the treated-wood fence by the sea wall that separated our properties, but not our lives, and entered Morgan's house.

It was time to engage Raydel Escobar.

CHAPTER 4

"Let's hook some trout," I said.

Morgan sat on his porch with a tablet on his lap. He wore faded yellow swim trunks, a moon talisman around his neck, and nothing else. His sandy, frayed hair was tied in a ragged ponytail. Morgan never participated in a minute's worth of exercise in his life, yet he carried not an ounce of fat on his bony frame. Hopping on and off boats, he claimed, was far better for your body—and mind—than any prescribed workout regime. A rotating fan in the corner behind him attached to a hose blew even more water molecules into the humid air.

"It's early afternoon," he said.

"Doesn't that mist get on your pad?"

He closed the cover. "No. It hits me from behind."

"I need to scout a house in shallow waters I'm not familiar with."

"Not real fishing, right?"

Morgan knew I carried a Florida PI license and recovered stolen boats for insurance companies—that became public knowledge after two drug runners pulled a gun on me and bought the farm—or in this case, the Gulf—on a stolen Donzi about forty-eight nautical miles northwest of Key West. But after Garrett and I ambushed the posse of mob men, left the bodies on the sands of the state park, and then switched identities for Kathleen, he knew the boat business was a sidebar.

Morgan was with us that night and was instrumental in finding Kathleen.

"I've got frozen shrimp on the boat and a few rods. It's as legit as we need to be. Let's go."

Thirty minutes later, Morgan navigated my twenty-seven-foot Grady White center console, *Impulse*, around several mangrove islands to places I had never been to, although I could only marvel why. The flat surface, as still as the sky, reflected the mangroves, and mullet swam in the clear water above the sand and grass floor. He eased back on the throttle and *Impulse* drifted, with her twin Yamaha 250s raised, in about two feet of water. We were a few hours past low tide and had good enough water to get as close as we needed.

"This will do," I said.

Morgan lowered the anchor into the water without the water even acknowledging its entry. I took a pole down from a gold rod holder, ran a hook into the bottom side of the shrimp, and cast a few times toward the mangroves.

The house towered above the flat land and presented a face of dark glass reflecting all it saw. I knew from the aerial photograph that it was the only house on a cul-de-sac—Escobar had purchased the surrounding property to ensure his privacy. I placed my pole in a launcher and retrieved the Steiner marine binoculars from the radio box. I stood under the hardtop so I was partially blocked in the event someone was looking at me looking at them. There wasn't much to see.

"Let's take her around the mangroves for different angles," I said.

I lifted the anchor, and for the next hour Morgan took the boat in and out of mangroves while I tinkered with my rod and viewed the house from different angles. A low chain link fence ran across the shoreline of the property. It was partially submerged, and I didn't know what purpose it served in its present state. A stucco wall that matched the terra-cotta color of the house bordered both sides. It was tiered so that it was lower as it approached the water's edge. I'd had enough and told him to head home.

He had a better idea and we ended up at Dockside, a waterfront tin roof shack that hadn't seen a coat of paint in fifty years. We both ordered grouper salads with a dozen oysters on the side and iced tea. No booze. When I lived on Fort Myers Beach for a year, I kicked off my weekends on Monday morning and never looked back. I was lucky to escape. Now when I feel myself slipping, I place an old alarm clock—I bought it at a neighborhood garage sale—on my porch and set it to 5:00 p.m. No drinking until Tinker Bell, with her double silver bells on top, gives me the all clear. When Barbara, my ninety-something-year-old neighbor, inquired about the alarm, I spilled a full confession. She smiled and said it usually coincided with her second glass of wine and not to reset it any earlier. She didn't want to be playing catch-up.

Morgan started each day with half a beer, and after that nothing alcoholic graced his lips until late afternoon.

"She had some quiet moments, you know," he said as we sat on high wood stools facing the narrow channel. A weathered gray plank served as a table and a damp roll of paper towels sufficed for napkins. "I'm glad you insisted on Kathleen. Tough call to make when she was under, but she's fine with it. Although I did like Maritana Rowe," Morgan said.

"You never told me where you got that from."

"No, I didn't."

"Not going to, are you," I said.

"You're a bright guy."

"And how did you know she'd like 'Kathleen'?" Morgan asked.

"I didn't."

We were quiet, both of us comfortable with silence. A center console went by pushing the tide and a woman stretched out in the front exposed as much of her body as possible to the sun. The captain stood behind the wheel under the hardtop and wore a long sleeve shirt and a wide brimmed hat. I finished my salad and the oysters were gone, although I wished they weren't. I was still hungry so I opened a pack of crackers, but the Florida humidity had beat me to them. We hadn't discussed the events that preceded Key West—the four bodies left on the beach or the contents of his old red spinnaker bag. I wanted to make sure he wasn't waiting for me.

"I know it got pretty ugly on the beach, but it's not always like that. We really try to avoid——"

"Jake." Morgan rarely interrupted people. "Never justify yourself to close friends and certainly not to yourself."

I was often uncertain as to what my friend was talking about, and in such cases I'd learned to defer to him. I was trying to unlearn much of what I had been taught or assumed about life and was discovering that unlearning is a far more difficult task than learning. It takes a concentrated effort to realize the baggage you carry is largely the unnecessary byproduct from being dragged through society. Like a wet dog, you need to shake it all off. Morgan carried no such baggage and personified Twain's adage to never let schooling interfere with your education.

Morgan and his sister were raised and homeschooled aboard a forty-four-foot Morgan charter sailboat. His father wanted to christen him "Jib" and his mother insisted on "Winston." The issue was never resolved. His sister got "Catalina" and still ran the business. Morgan and Catalina didn't know their own ages. Their parents didn't want them, especially at the bookends of life, to be burdened with the expectations and then the limitations that numbers imply. They were permitted to leave their vessel, *Solar Wind*, and venture into the world only after they read one hundred books selected by their parents. But there were gaps in his resume that one can naturally expect after cruising the Caribbean for decades.

His uncommon calmness under fire that night on the beach warranted its own set of questions.

I took a sip of iced tea and said, "I didn't see enough today to really help me."

"I figured as much."

"I'd like to see it at night."

"My favorite time to be on the water."

"I thought around nine would be a good time."

"Eleven thirty will be better. The moon sets at 10:13, and high tide is 11:08. A dark night and high water." Morgan measured time by the synodic month, or moon phases, and was acutely aware of the position of the earth's sole satellite and the largely unheeded effect it cast over all living things.

"Meet you at the dock at eleven?" I asked.

"Looking forward to it. After being on the water the last two weeks, I was feeling a little down today. My natural state is to float."

"It was sweet," I said as I drained my iced tea. I allowed a couple pieces of ice to slide into my mouth.

Morgan said, "Every man has a part of him that wishes he lived in Key West."

"Or is Key West a part of every man?" I countered as I split the ice and heard it crack.

I picked up the tab, and we untied *Impulse* and headed around the corner, past the big white Contender with the blue bottom and a single blue canvas that covered her twin outboards, and back to my lift.

We headed out at eleven o'clock, but with no guise toward fishing.

I brought along my night goggles, wore a black warm water wet suit, and painted my face with liquid latex black paint. My five-inch serrated knife was strapped to my left thigh. I wore Vibram FiveFingers water shoes. Morgan cut the engine well before sight of the house, and we poled our way up tight against the mangroves. He again slipped the anchor soundlessly into the shallow sand, and I slipped over the starboard freeboard—into two feet of water.

I crept to the corner of the property where the low chain link fence that bordered the front of the property stopped and settled next to mangroves. *Rhizophora mangle* are pretty from a distance, but their root structure makes it nearly impossible to get up under them. Plus, they stink. Birds use them for a crap house. My feet were on solid ground, although my right foot rested on a root. In front of me was the terra-cotta stucco wall that ran down both sides of the property. It was four feet high by the water and stepped up to six feet as it got closer to the house. From the home's rear, the occupants had a sweeping view of the mangroves and Gulf of Mexico.

He rose out of the darkness, standing at a window.

Raydel Escobar stared dead ahead, as if he couldn't tell where the sky started and the water ended. He wore beige pants and a black shirt and held a cell phone to his ear. Doing business at midnight. His frame filled the large window and then he was gone. As I started to leave, a man with a shotgun appeared from the corner of the house and made his way toward me. The guard was slow and looked bored and passed not more than ten feet in front of me. My right foot suddenly slipped off the root and I made a perceptible splash as my body settled. He stopped and peered in my direction. I stopped breathing.

He must be afraid of the dark, for he suddenly pivoted and left. Escobar wasn't getting his money's worth.

Lights, an armed guard, and high walls. I wasn't going to fight this battle on Escobar's terms.

"Let's go," I said quietly to Morgan when I returned to the boat.

"What's next?"

"Let's get close to his boats."

The aerial photo of Escobar's compound in Mary Evelyn's e-mail revealed two boats, a yacht and a fishing boat. The yacht was bigger than my house. That's not saying much.

Morgan grabbed a pole and pushed *Impulse* around to the front of the yacht so that the yacht's massive bow blocked us from the house. He switched to a paddle when he lost the bottom. We were in the channel, in all likelihood dug out for Escobar's toys. I put on my flippers and slipped overboard into the food chain, but this time my feet found no support.

I moved silently through the dark water, in and around both boats, passed under the dock, and rubbed against the large, crusted pilings. I maneuvered behind the smaller boat that was on a lift that barely cleared the water. It was a forty-foot center console Intrepid powered by four 350-horsepower Yamahas. Fourteen hundred horses on forty feet of fiberglass. I'd be surprised if her forward hull even got wet with the throttle shoved down. I got out my Intova LED flashlight from its Velcro strip that I jerry rigged onto my wet suit and kept the beam low. No name on the side or transom. No registration numbers. The stainless steel props were in good shape, but not new. Escobar could have recently purchased it and not gotten around to putting the hull numbers on, but my bet was he didn't want the boat to be traceable.

There were faster boats, but a four-engine forty-foot center console was about as fast as you could go without screaming that speed was your intent. Put five engines on a similar boat, or have a juiced-up Fountain, and everyone knew it was all about speed. Law enforcement heads would turn. If I wanted to be unnoticed, yet be able to outrun 99 percent of the boats on the water, Escobar's power pack on the Intrepid would be the ticket. What did he need her for?

The yacht, a deep blue fifty-five-foot Carver Voyager, was a different matter. *Chica Bonita* was prominently scrawled across her stern and she carried Florida registration numbers. She hadn't left the slip for a while—she displayed a prominent water line. I couldn't make out the name on the tender, it was too high and my angle wasn't right.

I made my way back to *Impulse* and pulled myself over her transom.

"We're leaving?" Morgan asked.

"*Si.*"

I paddled until we were well clear of the house and then Morgan turned the key, flipped on the running lights, and banked hard starboard into the black. I watched the house fade behind us, its lights giving in to the night. I was left with one a simple assessment.

In such a massive structure, an 8½" x 11" envelope could be anywhere and would be impossible to find.

Search and destroy was off the menu. I was going to have to find something on Escobar to gain leverage and force him to hand over the letter.

"Leverage" is polite nomenclature for "blackmail." Anyone who owned three strip clubs, tooled around with mobsters, and, here's the clincher—owned a carpet business—had to have some serious dirt swept under his rugs.

I just had to find it.

CHAPTER 5

Sunrise the next day was at 6:35. It is not that simple or precise, but we like to believe it is.

I drove over to the hotel that was a few minutes from my house. The pink Moorish-style hotel was built in the 1920s by an Irishman from Virginia, named after a character in a play from a French dramatist that was turned into an English opera, and is set in a city named for its Russian counterpart.

I have no idea what all that means.

A membership allowed me to utilize its facilities, and I kept a locker in the health club. At the pool Jaffe sprayed the paver brick deck with a thick red hose. He inquired where I'd been the past few weeks. We chatted a few minutes about his family in Jamaica, which delayed my entry into the warm water until 6:40, according to the hands on the tower clock. I swam for forty minutes, then sprinted barefoot on the beach in my wet trunks for three miles.

After my run, I stood under the outdoor shower on the boardwalk by the edge of the sand and let the water rapidly reduce my feverish body temperature. Water displaces heat about twenty-four times faster than air—it's not that simple or precise either. After a hot run, seventy-two-degree water will instantly chill you, while wandering into a seventy-two-degree room is a waste of time. Water's edge, the narrow strip of sand that is never dry or wet, was dotted with walkers and joggers, seashell collectors, coffee mug holders, hand holders, and children with plastic buckets gleefully sprinting out to greet the sea. A small yoga class stretched on the high and dry sand, and its participants stretched their arms toward the high blue cloudless sky.

At its best, life is a real winner.

In the locker room, I put on cargo shorts and a short sleeve buttoned shirt. In the members lobby I made a cup of Colombian dark and snatched a banana a day before its prime. I asked Joan, the attendant, if she was still doing her systems check every morning. She lived alone and had suffered a stroke a few months back, but didn't realize it until later in the day when she first attempted speech. Nothing she would normally be concerned with, but on that given day, it just didn't kick in. She staged a full recovery, and her children bought her a cat. They insisted that she verbally greet her feline companion every morning as a method to ascertain if everything was operational. But when she showed me pictures of her grandchildren on her phone, her hands trembled. Full recovery. Really—the crap we believe in.

At its worse, life constantly reminds us that it's a short-term lease. A one-way ticket, and when they hand it to you, you have no idea at what stop you're getting off.

I took the outdoor stairs and claimed a white wood rocking chair on the second-floor porch. I peeled the banana, opened a newspaper, and watched two guys below me in the courtyard give each other a kiss. A corporate crowd wearing nametags, storm troopers of the business world, made their way out to the southern pool where breakfast on round tables with black tablecloths awaited them.

The sun would turn into ice crystals, the Republican Party would embrace the EPA, and the marines would adopt Lennon's "Imagine" as a theme song before I went to breakfast with my name hanging around my goddamned neck.

My phone rang. I tossed my banana peel at a seashell garbage can.

"I changed my mind," I said without salutation to Garrett. "Upon further consideration, I believe that contentment has finally found me."

"Where are you?"

"Floating on the edge of the Milky Way."

"Bring it in, Jake."

"The hotel."

"You're not compatible with contentment."

"Depends what she looks like."

"Nothing you'd be interested in."

"Still might give her a try one day."

"What have you discovered?"

"That inner peace is knowing that you'd rather see a church burn than spill a martini."

"Can we talk now or do I need to wait till you come off your exercise high?"

"Let's roll."

"Stone churches don't burn," Garrett said.

"And I would give up a week of martinis to preserve this old dame, but there's nothing there but a one-armed old docent who still uses the word 'bequeath.' Morgan and I scouted the house; the photos don't do it justice. It's a guarded compound. How'd this guy know the letter was hidden in the wall at the back of the church?"

"'Bequeath'? Really? How many points is that?"

"Twenty-two."

"I thought it'd be more."

"Q carries it."

Garrett said, "Ask him when he hands it off. Almost has to be some local connection, but it doesn't matter. Janssen called again. Pushing the heat. Said the pressure's coming from the State Department and it's related to the World Fairness Bill. We continually knock other countries for human rights violations, or at least our interpretation of human rights, and there is some concern that the letter, if exposed, will make a mockery of our sanctity for human lives, let alone third world working conditions. My bet is the letter is a damaging relic from the Vietnam era."

"Johnson's war," I added.

"Killed him too."

"We win that one?"

"Don't think so."

"Should have nuked them all."

"Maybe that's in print."

"Why's he bleeding it to us?" I asked.

"Maybe that's how he's getting it, maybe to put a fire under us, maybe because he gets his rocks off stringing us along."

"That's a barge load of maybes." The two guys below selected lounge chairs and moved them tight up against each other so that there was no space between them. They each had a cup of coffee. For a moment I thought I was back in Key West.

"Jake?"

"Yeah?"

"Got a plan?"

"I'd eventually like to procreate and enter that whole chain of life thing." Garrett didn't respond to that. "I got a good feel for the place last night, what might work and what might constitute a suicide attempt. I need to get close to Escobar and figure how to introduce myself to him. Any ideas yourself?"

"It always falls apart."

"The sooner the better."

We disconnected, and I perused the newspaper. The front page contained an article about the World Fairness Bill. We wanted to dictate to other countries what minimum acceptable working conditions and hours should be. Vietnam and Cambodia were objecting, but they carried little political weight. They retained the Chinese, who also opposed the bill, to help plead their case. China presented the delicate task of negotiating with a sovereign power that by virtue of holding massive amounts of our debt was bankrolling the United States. Furthermore, the United States, along with Europe, was secretly lobbying the Chinese to contribute to a bailout fund for the aging continent in which only the Huns had their house in order. Decades of government overspending had finally caught up with the older developed countries, and they contentiously debated in what manner to address their economic stalemate. At least they no longer settled their difference in Waterloo. Flanders. Verdun. Normandy.

My body started to protest from burning too many calories without anything coming in. I vacated the chair, picked up my banana peel, and dropped it in the can.

Sea Breeze restaurant was across the street from the public pier on the bay. Its knotty pine walls, low ceiling, and open windows with thick red geraniums in the flower boxes remained unchanged since radio was the hottest technology. I wouldn't be surprised if Dorothy Harrison had frequented the place, as it was only two blocks from her front door. I took a seat at the counter, and Kathy gave me a refill in my Styrofoam cup before she spoke.

"What'll be, Jake? The usual?" She planted herself on the other side of the varnished bar, one hand on her wide hip, the other holding a coffeepot. Her black hair was tied back tight and her face already glistened with heat. A seasoned restaurant warrior.

"I'll take an order of immortality with dry toast."

"Sorry. Just served our last order. Guy sat in the stool you're in right now. He was faster than you, though. Took a double order of bacon and buttered toast with it." She never hesitated or smiled.

"You're killing me, Kathy, and that's why I need that last order so bad."

She turned without asking me anything else.

A few minutes later, two eggs over easy, crisp bacon, home fries, and a glass of water with two lemon wedges landed in front of me. She placed a small red bowl of sautéed diced onions next to my water glass. I dumped the onions over the home fries and eggs and topped it all with a generous sprinkling of pepper. The golden-brown potatoes that had an incestuous relationship with hot potato chips were the first to go. A guy to my left wore a black Hog's Breath T-shirt. He had french toast. It took everything I am and will ever be to refrain from reaching over and grabbing a slice. I got out my notepad to jot down possible methods to infiltrate and infringe upon the world of Raydel Escobar. Fifteen minutes later I strode out the door with a blank notepad and one idea.

I reached for my phone and called PC.

CHAPTER 6

Escobar

Escobar sipped his bitter Cuban coffee and chased it with a drag from his Montecristo. His swim was over, the sun was out, the music was on, and breakfast was in the wings. It was the perfect sybaritic manner in which to commence a day. Raydel Escobar was a man who enjoyed his senses.

He stood with his back to the Gulf of Mexico, faced his zero edge pool and home, and took another suck on the moist Connecticut-shade wrapper. He smoked two number fours a day, but he counted them as one. Sophia constantly nagged him that even one a day was foolish and insisted on him only smoking half a cigar if he so desperately needed to light up twice.

He did so desperately need to light up twice a day, and so each day he tossed the last half of two Montecristos. But not today. Not yesterday either. Sophia split for two nights and wouldn't return until late in the afternoon. She was scouting for a new dress and Escobar didn't understand why the hell she had to go clear to Naples to buy an evening gown. But she and two friends had taken off, chatting nonstop like chipmunks as they swept out the front door. Had to admit, though, the place was a little less lively when she wasn't around.

He viewed Natalie's flawless glistening back through his exhaled smoke and thought what an enticing painting it would make.

"What time does Henriques get in?" Elvis asked.

"He'll be here in an hour. Where's breakfast?" Escobar asked his bodyguard, valet, and secretary.

It was a simple arrangement. Elvis had been bouncing for him a little under a year when he got caught—not for the first time—with a little weed in his car. Escobar enjoyed playing chess with Elvis and respected the way he dressed for the job. Elvis always showed up early and locked the doors when he left. He treated the club like he'd found his life's mission and never uttered a profane word within its walls. He'd even organized the windowless office and found a box of large yellow envelopes that had belonged to Escobar's father. Escobar kept them and placed them on the shelf next to his father's ancient blue Smith Corona typewriter. Escobar dug Elvis's unswerving loyalty and was also damn tired of hiring new bouncers every six months.

He went to bat for Elvis.

He passed some crisp bills and soft snatch to horny cops who frequented the Welcome In. They, in return, dropped the drug charge, but told him to watch himself; Elvis, aka Terrance Bowles, was still the prime suspect in two unsolved murders. The murder rap didn't bother Escobar. Anyone who changed their name from Terrance to Elvis was good in his book.

Escobar told Elvis to move in and gave him food, use of the cars, and a half-inch of fifties every Friday. In return, Elvis gave him twenty-four hours a day. Every day.

Sophia voiced displeasure, but you can't please everyone.

"Olivia said it'll be out in five," Elvis said. "Why's he coming?"

"We'll find out, won't we?" Escobar grunted and sat down at the round teak table under the red umbrella. "How come Alejo didn't hose down the pool this morning?"

"You ask him, boss. Maybe he just ran out of steam. Why don't you get someone younger?"

"Don't talk like that, Elvis, Alejo's got real Cuba *la sangre.*"

"I'm just sayin—"

"Don't be saying anything," Escobar said.

Olivia paraded out from the house with a tray and plopped it in front of Escobar, making certain it rattled as it hit the table. He snuffed out his cigar and then piled his plate with scrambled eggs and salmon, fresh fruit, and toast. Olivia didn't say anything but turned and walked back toward the house. Escobar noticed that she'd gotten more reclusive the last few times that Sophia was gone and Natalie stayed at the house. Olivia had a good twenty years on Sophia, and he'd recently detected them talking less about housework and more about whatever the fuck women discussed. He didn't think she'd say anything to his wife of five years and wasn't sure he gave a damn if she did. But for added precaution, Escobar recently surprised her with a generous pay raise. She had plenty to lose if she ever crossed him. Still, her attitude was challenging.

"You want her over here?" Elvis asked as he took some eggs for himself after Escobar was finished. There was never enough to take as much as Escobar did, as if Olivia was offering a silent protest for having to cook for more than her paymaster.

"Let her burn."

"Natalie, get over here," Elvis shouted.

Natalie Binelli rolled over on her side, and her large, suntanned breasts spilled over onto the cream white chaise lounge. Her small brown nipples made her breasts seem even that much fuller. She held the pose for a moment to make sure the men knew how lucky they were, and then put on the gold top of her suit. She put on her leather pumps and, like a model on a runway, sashayed over to the table. The easy morning breeze brushed her auburn hair.

"Elvis, pass me those eggs, will you please?" Natalie asked. Escobar had noticed their looks, mostly hers, when Elvis did an hour of weights on the veranda in the late morning after his run, his hair pulled back in a tight ponytail, his shirt discarded on the ground. Natalie took a pitiful amount of eggs, didn't touch the bread, and added some fresh fruit, mostly watermelon, to her own plate.

"You need to eat something, baby, you're going to turn into fuckin' Karen Carpenter," Escobar said.

"Who you talking about?" Natalie asked as she took her hand across her forehead and swept her bangs away.

"You."

"What do I have to do with a carpenter?"

"Jesus H. Never mind. Remember, you've got till noon." She seemed so damned stupid sometimes, almost like she was goading him.

"I know, Raydel. You told me three times yesterday."

"Yeah? I meant to tell you four times."

Natalie's shoulders slumped in an exaggerated fashion, but then she rallied.

"You going to tell me you're looking forward to her coming back, that it hasn't been nice?" Natalie said, going on the offense and sitting up straight. He had sucked them so hard he was surprised they were still there in the morning.

"It's been wonderful, honey. I'm sure we'll do it again."

"I'll take you at noon," Elvis said.

"I got some things to do today. Let's leave at eleven," Natalie said.

Escobar wish she'd at least put a shirt on over her suit when at the table. He was going to say something about her leaving, but decided to grant her dignity and allow her the last line on the subject. Her showing him that she had other things in life besides lying around offering her greased body to the Florida sun.

"When are we getting the rugs in?" Elvis asked.

"Next few days," Escobar said.

"You want me to get Cruz to help, same as last time?"

"Same as last time, we won't know till the day itself."

"You boys and your rugs," Natalie said. "Why do some come by boat and who is Cruz?"

"We just bring the rare rugs in by boat," Elvis said.

Escobar cut Elvis a glance. "Guy show up last night?"

"Sure," Elvis said, "but do we need him? That firm doesn't even send the same guy every night and I got to explain the whole routine."

"That's a problem?"

"No. I just——"

"Doesn't do any good to take extra precaution after we have an issue. I'll tell them to stick to the same guy. If you see Alejo, have him hose down this area, even in the sun. And have him clean the chess pieces so they look good for the party."

"Raydel?" Natalie asked. "Why don't you let me have a rug for my apartment?"

"I told you, baby. I'm just the middleman for the rare ones. I ship them out soon as they come in."

"Why don't you get them delivered to your warehouse like your other rugs?"

"Why don't you eat your eggs?"

He stood up and made a line toward the house leaving Elvis and Natalie in the shade. Let them have their time together.

Natalie had showed up to audition at the Welcome In a little over a month ago and triggered a phone call to Escobar. He had standing instructions to be notified when unusual talent presented itself. She fit the bill. She had the most beautiful chestnut eyes he had ever seen, and she only got better after that.

They screwed in the cabana, the guest room, or his favorite spot, which was on the floor in the middle of his study. Escobar garnered a certain satisfaction as he repeatedly paced over that area of jatoba floor and remembered pounding her soft body into the hard wood. Sophia would come in the next day to place fresh yellow flowers—Christ, that woman was always bringing colored petals into the house—and walk over the very spot. Hell, she deserved it. All her dicking around with that builder Shramos had swelled the price to over $600 per square foot. The broad literally couldn't make up her mind where to put a light fixture. Well, he thought with a smile, two of us can dick around, and I certainly got more than $600 out of those square feet in the middle of the study.

But not last night.

"Just this one time," Natalie had pleaded as she took his hand and backed them into the master bedroom, her flannel shirt hanging unbuttoned on her thin shoulders, her breasts lifting the bottom of the shirt off her waist. No bra. Tight jeans holding those strong ripped thighs that she wrapped around him as if there was no one else in the world. "Just one time, let me believe that it's all for me." Escobar couldn't withstand the effects of a cigar, three Cuban Manhattans, and that damn soft plaid brown-and-white flannel shirt. Afterward she talked of going places with him and spending more time together. She wanted to know if he could run his rug business from some Caribbean outpost. She kept bringing up his business and said she wanted to be more involved in his life. Said she could help him with the books.

Lying in bed with Herb Alpert coming through the speakers, Escobar had thought how smooth it all was: Natalie, Herb's trumpet, and the dark Cuban rum. What did he care if Sophia found out? But if she left, you could kiss away half the dough. Should have signed stuff when they got married, but how do you know that then?

He entered his bedroom and thought of washing the sheets, but that would generate a whole new litany of suspicion. When had he ever washed the sheets? He picked up Sophia's pillows from the floor. At least he'd remembered to use his two pillows and had chucked hers. He made his bed and made certain there was not a trace of Natalie Binelli to be found.

He turned the water on hard and washed her scent off his body.

Paulo Henriques stood under the shade of Escobar's summer kitchen by the pool. He wore pleated summer wool beige pants that nearly touched the still damp pavers behind the heels of his leather loafers. His blue short sleeve silk shirt draped casually over his boney frame like a thin canvas on tent poles. His hair, Escobar noted, was fastidiously arranged to cover as much of his head as possible. Windy day, Escobar chuckled to himself. I bet he unloaded half a can of spray to keep it plastered like that. These East Coast guys, they're all the same.

"It's a heck of a view you got here, Raydel. I'm sure you'd hate to lose it," Henriques said.

"I have no plans to lose anything," Escobar said.

Henriques wiped his hand across his brow but was careful not to touch his hair. "Good lord, it's hotter than the underside of a witch's tit in hell."

"You rather go inside?" Escobar asked, and instantly regretted giving Henriques a choice. He'd make certain it was his last conciliatory gesture.

"No, Raydel, let's be out here where it's open. You got plenty of shade here," he said as he moved out of the sun and took a seat at the large oak table under the high ceiling of the outdoor kitchen.

Sophia's kitchen, Escobar thought. She spent nearly three months planning a $100,000 outdoor kitchen and what do we do? We drop burgers on the grill and pop a few beers with people we call friends.

"Walter wants to know how you're dealing with this tax business," Henriques said. "Seven million to the IRS isn't chicken feed."

"You tell him I got it under control?"

"I think he's looking for something a little more substantial. We can help you out. Arrangements can be made. We can negotiate."

"Help me out? Tell Walter I'm pretty confident I can get it reduced." Escobar thought Henriques and Walter Mendis might like to see his ass behind bars so they could take over his operations. The carpet and rug business proved to be a great cover to launder the cash from his clubs. Escobar assumed that laundering cash was a major challenge for Mendis. Damn Patriot Act. It corralled all-American criminals into the same corner as Arab fruitcakes, and that just wasn't right.

Henriques kept at it. "To what? Seven's a fat nut. What if they knock half, where are you going to get that kind of dough?"

"I'm not going for half; my attorneys tell me I got a good chance of having it all dropped. They said the IRS will work with me, give me time."

Henriques considered Escobar for a moment. "Your attorneys," he said, and let it hang like a crooked picture.

"That's right, Paulo," Escobar said, drawing it out and playing the game, "my at-tor-neys."

Paulo Henriques leaned in across the table. "We've known each other some time now; we do good business together ever since you brought us that first deal. What are you pinning your hopes on, because we both know it sure as fuck has nothing to do with your attorneys. You think the IRS is going to back down to nothing? Just forget the big note you owe them? Feed it to the fish, Raydel. I told you when you set those partnerships up that they were shit. Walter's worried. I'm worried. We can't risk the government sticking their fat finger in our business. You're a scrappy and creative guy, Raydel. What do you want me to tell Mendis?"

Tell him I got an envelope that Washington wants, Escobar thought. And that's my ticket, East Coast boy. That's my ticket.

Raydel Escobar and Walter Mendis had met three times, two times in Palm Beach and once in a desolated field that hadn't received rain in two months. The constant roar of nearby highway traffic sounded like a cash register to their ears. It was in that field where Escobar noticed the stark and unsettling difference between the two men; Henriques was concerned about getting dust on his shoes and Mendis could care less.

At the time of their initial meeting, Escobar had built up several clubs starting with the Welcome In, his home base. A good night there was a few hundred tax-free, cigar, rum, music, and time to advance pawns in a game that dated back 1,500 years.

It had always been thus.

His father owned an old-world joint in Ybor City, and his only son was his constant companion. Young Escobar engaged his father's friends, always in their best guayaberas, in chess matches to kill time in the smoke-filled room populated with laughs, loose hands, and music. His father was first generation and ran a tight ship. You never wanted to be in the room with the man when someone dropped a nickel on the floor. He would enviously point out "real money" when it walked through the door, and that is what Escobar yearned to be someday—real money walking through a door. Escobar knew that owning the bar was not the same as being the coveted subject of muted conversations.

He religiously studied his schoolbooks, chess, and the anatomy of the barmaids who bent over to plant a kiss on his head. By age ten, little Escobar was sitting on his hands, not trusting them when the milky melons landed on either side of his nose. When career day came the counselor suggested engineering.

Escobar just smiled.

From the day he opened his own establishment he set the tone by playing '60s easy listening music that separated him from his competition. His obsession with cleanliness coupled with girls—dancers—a cut above the industry standard, attracted and retained well-heeled libidos and blue-blood discreet money. He insisted his tux-wearing bouncers learn chess so that he could enjoy rotating matches and further add to the atmosphere. The cops, when they came around, were never a serious threat, they just walked out with the few hundred tax-free. Escobar expanded to two more clubs, and the few hundred turned into a grand a night. He fulfilled his boyhood Freudian obligations. He no longer sat on his hands.

He picked up a carpet and rug business, which catered to both retail and commercial clients, for ten cents on the dollar when the housing market collapsed. When the economy recovered, the business took off like a sailboat in a gale.

But he wasn't the man walking through the door. He did the math, and even with a few more clubs and conservative projected growth in the carpets and rugs, it would take years to accumulate serious dough. *Making* money was not the same as *having* money.

He didn't recognize the congressman when he stumbled in one morning around 1:00 a.m. But his bartender did and informed Escobar that he'd seen him a few other Saturdays around the same time. Escobar didn't care; after all, discretion is what he peddled. But then the bartender told him the congressman was gay.

"No way," Escobar had blurted out. "How do you know?"

"We know, trust me," Bernie replied.

"We?"

"Why don't you think I hit on the girls?"

Escobar was a little taken back. How'd he miss that one?

"What's he doing here then?" Escobar asked.

"Haven't a clue. Maybe a ruse to dispel rumors. Happens more than you think."

Then, courtesy of the cops who were twisting his arm, he hatched an idea. He wasn't sure what would come out of the egg, but if three hundred bucks bought Tampa's best, just imagine the possibilities.

"Can you get his tongue down your throat?" he asked Bernie one night.

"Please, baby. Who do you think I am?" Bernie said.

"Next time he's in. Back room at one fifteen."

"And for me?"

"One thousand dollars."

"Two."

"Fifteen hundred or look for another job and I'll put the word on the street that you walk out with bottles." He had surprised himself with his words and tone. Bernie would never steal a drop.

Escobar about dropped his phone when he cracked the back door to take a peek. The congressman's eyes were closed, the music was playing, and Escobar managed to snap a few photos before he felt his insides starting to come out of him. He knew his good part was leaving, and he told himself it would come back, but he knew that was a lie. When he walked away his heart was banging in mad syncopation against the music.

Escobar sat on it for a few weeks while he performed his due diligence on the congressman. At least that is what he told himself. In truth, he wondered if he should just delete the photos. Such an effortless task. Two, three seconds, tops. Get rid of the damn thing and don't go there. Every step he saw himself taking made him retch.

He was watching a new girl perform one day when he casually glanced at the newspaper. The state of Florida was contemplating a new interchange on Interstate 75. His, and Bernie's, political friend chaired the committee. Escobar was too naive to realize what a complicated and competitive process the interchange entailed. Countless power players had jostled behind the scene for years. But few things trump innocent creativity and enthusiasm.

And absolutely nothing trumps a picture of a married, religious right congressman and father of kindergarten twin girls on his knees with another man's cock buried deep in his mouth.

Escobar needed a subtle way to approach the conflicted congressman and knew that while he had the leverage, he needed partners who had maneuvered before within the political arena. Associates introduced him to Paulo, who led him to Walter

Mendis. All three grasped the endless possibilities presented by the picture. Clearly visible in the background of the photograph was a neon YOLO beer sign. "You Only Live Once." Its bright red glow gave the photograph an artistic noir flair. Escobar could hardly bring himself to look at the picture. Walter Mendis could hardly tolerate *not* looking at it. He fondled it in his hands and couldn't stop chuckling, as if it was the damndest thing he'd ever seen. "Unfuckin' believable," he said over and over. Then, "A real cocksucker," and he laughed so hard he choked and coughed up phlegm.

The picture, they agreed, provided mind-boggling possibilities.

Mendis at first dismissed Escobar's freeway play. But it made more sense—and money—than anything else he could come up with on his own. When the interchange's location was announced, they owned the surrounding land as far as one could see with a mounted telescope. The location was a shock to others who had invested time and resources into the project. Several papers noted that the location was not one of the top three—actually not even on the list of FDOT's $250,000 study of where to construct a new interchange. The general populace didn't pay much attention as other headlines bore more weight; the state averaged close to three murders a day in addition to fifteen rapes. Furthermore, the Miami Hurricanes football team was facing NCAA sanctions and yet another dead manatee had washed up on the shores of Captiva. The football scandal received the most press, the rapes—*collectively*—the least, and the dead manatee garnered the most letters to the editor.

Mendis admired Escobar for his balls and patience. An "unusual combination for a novice," Mendis had commented.

Walter Mendis became the congressman's biggest donor. Congressman Michael Kittredge was of no use to him if he lost an election. Escobar was surprised to see a picture behind Mendis's desk of Kittredge and Mendis posing in front of Mendis's pool at a $5,000-a-plate fund-raiser that was kept hush-hush due to Mendis's questionable business interest.

Both men had their arms around each other as if they never wanted to let go.

"Tell him I got it taken care of, Paulo," Escobar said in response to Henriques's question about what to tell Mendis. No damn way was he going to tell them about the letter he possessed. You get a card like that and you hold it tight.

His accountant had structured an elaborate trust and assured Escobar that it was legitimate. He'd taken his portion from the interchange deal and deposited it in several Cayman accounts that the IRS had finally traced. Their opinion of legitimacy differed from his accountant's, and they declared his cut to be ordinary income. He owed taxes plus interest penalties. Ordinary income. What a gas. As if there was anything even remotely "ordinary" about any income he had ever made.

And now Mendis was nervous. Escobar figured Mendis was worried that he would squeal a deal with the IRS to lessen his obligation. He wanted to see if he could make Henriques come clean.

"You know he's worried about the strain—" Henriques said.

"You think I'm cutting a deal?" Escobar whipped into him. "You think I'd sing to the IRS to save my ass and offer you guys up? You think that's me, ratting on my partners? Listen, Paulo, tell Walter to give me one week. At the very least, they're telling me that I can pay over several years. And I got enough put away to pay a chunk up front. Seven days and I should have it all settled."

Henriques leaned back in his chair and waited a few beats. "OK, Raydel, I'll tell him. Seven days. Kittredge can't really get involved, you know. Too visible, too obvious. Knowing what we got on him, you got to think he's being up front. You can talk to him yourself this Saturday. How many people you got coming?"

"Around fifty," Escobar said, thinking, I know damn well I can talk to him. I'm the guy who brought him to you. "We're keeping invitations open; if someone wants to bring cash to the door, they're in."

"Hundred grand, not bad. What's our bit?"

"Ten. Band and food came to twenty. I'll cover incidentals."

"Course, that'd only be twenty people at Walter's house." Henriques flashed a smile and kept it on his face to drive it in.

"Yeah? Well, this ain't Walter's house, and thank God I don't live in Palm Beach. It's nothing but New York City with palm trees."

"I thought you told me you liked New York."

"Not with fucking palm trees."

"Whatever, Raydel. Give the congressman my best."

Escobar was not close with Congressman Michael Kittredge and realized his mistake too late. Mendis had taken over the relationship, the two of them becoming asshole golfing buddies. It never occurred to Escobar that Kittredge would actually embrace his blackmailers. But that was exactly what the congressman had done: keep your friends close and your enemies closer. Unbelievable, Escobar thought. And people think my clubs are a sleazy business.

Escobar thought his partners would give him time to work with the IRS. He also realized that if he were dead, they wouldn't worry about him cutting a deal and taking them down. He didn't think they were those types of guys. But Raydel Escobar knew he was doing a piss-poor job of convincing himself.

"You ready for the next shipment?" Henriques asked.

"What's that?"

"Rugs," Henriques said as he studied Escobar.

"Yeah, we got it. Comes in a few days, same as before. Day before we get a twenty-four-hour call."

"Can Elvis handle it or do you need more help?"

"He's got it down."

"You sure?"

"We got it. But I don't like these. I—"

"We know that. Listen, it's just for a few times, to help Walter out. Where would you be without him?"

"What's a few?"

"Two or three, tops. What the hell we listening to?" Henriques asked and glanced into the air.

"Petula Clark." Escobar noted Henriques's reluctance to discuss exactly how many more shipments were coming by boat to his house. He decided not to push it.

"She's dead, isn't she?"

"I don't think so."

"You and your music. I like it, though."

"It's classic stuff."

"I'm sure it is," Henriques said and stood up. "Sorry I can't make your big dinner. Give my best to Sophia. She always has your place looking tops. She's a good woman, Raydel. You moved up with that one." Henriques let his eyes rest on Escobar for a few seconds. "I can see myself out."

As he walked away, Escobar heard a distinct squeak from Henriques's left shoe every time that foot hit the ground. Escobar couldn't suppress a smile. I know that's just killing him, he thought. He relit his cigar and leaned back in his chair.

The letter, Escobar thought. That's my ticket out of this squeeze.

Escobar didn't think much of Alejo's claim one night when he, Elvis, and Alejo were sitting around the fire pit and draining a bottle of fifteen-year-old Havana Club Gran Reserva rum. The romantic old Cuban, with his surprisingly good English, saying he knew that government secrets were buried within the outside walls of some old church in Pass-a-Grille. Wouldn't say how he knew, just "I heard it's behind the big stone that sticks out on the northwest corner, at least that's what I've been told. Don't know why anybody put it there; bad weather always comes from that way." Elvis poked fun at him until Escobar told Elvis to shut the fuck up and go take a look. I'll be damned, Escobar thought the next morning when Elvis placed an old tackle box next to the eggs on the table under the red umbrella.

He had no idea what was actually in the envelope, but he called the IRS in hopes that it could strengthen his position. He thought it might be good for an extension, or maybe half off. He told them he could just send it to the *New York Times*, but brokering a deal seemed a more capitalistic path. He informed them that he hadn't even bothered to open it, but gave them the date and outside print on the 8½" x 11" envelope: "For eyes only, Allen Dulles to Dean Rusk and Robert McNamara." They'd countered that they needed to confer with other government agencies and to sit on it.

But it wasn't the IRS that called Escobar back. Negotiate with the IRS, the blocked call said. Really, whatever makes you happy. But open that letter and you die. That was over a week ago.

Raydel Escobar didn't necessarily believe the man on the phone, and there was no way for that man to know if he peeked or not until the letter was returned. But if an unopened letter packed all the ammunition he needed, why run the gamut? The envelope remained sealed.

He kept Mendis and Henriques in the dark about the letter. If they thought that picture gave me leverage, they don't know what league I'm in. Hell, maybe I can get more than the IRS off my back, maybe I get years of protection.

This time, Escobar thought, I don't give up control. I run the play.

CHAPTER 7

"You want us to do what?" PC asked me in his machine gun cadence. The guy spit out words faster than Nashville spit out awards ceremonies.

We were standing on a black asphalt parking lot of a beach bar. I didn't know if the sun was in the sky or under my feet. I had called PC when I left the restaurant and told him I had another job for him.

I had tripped over PC and his sidekick, Boyd, when I needed a car trailed that held a pair of Outfit hit men. They delivered and I kept their number. You never know when you may need the service of a pair of scruffy beach bums. I wanted some closeup pictures of the front of Escobar's place, but didn't want to show my face. Not yet. PC and Boyd, with their youthful cockiness, were game for anything.

"Just go up to the door and tell them you're collecting for the NBS, National Bird Society, it doesn't really matter—" I said.

"Look, dude, we got that part. What do you want us to do?"

"Pictures. Lots of pictures, but don't let them see you taking them. Maybe one of you can—" I never finished. With PC and Boyd, I was capable, at best, of only blurting out partial sentences.

"I think we can handle it. What do you think, Boyd?"

"NBS?" Boyd asked.

"I was just suggesting—"

"I like it," Boyd said. His laid-back persona provided a natural counterbalance to PC. "Let's make it the National Bible Society, though, you know, like those Amish that have to take a year off to spread the good word."

"That's the Mormons, man, and it's two years they sojourn without family," PC said.

"Listen, guys, make it the National Banking Society, I could care less. Just don't get caught, it's not worth it. Be careful, they got cameras and—"

"You feeling it, Boyd?" PC asked.

"I'm diggin' this whole Bible thing, man. Let's do a few other houses first, you know, to drop in the roll."

"I'm with you," PC said.

"Want to carry them?" Boyd asked.

"That is *so* good, man."

"Jake, where do we buy Bibles? They even make them anymore?" Boyd asked.

"Don't get caught." I kept it short, which increased my chance of speaking a complete sentence.

"Do they?" Boyd didn't do rhetorical.

"It's a perennial best seller. Check under general fiction," I said.

PC said, "Whatever happened to those guys you had us follow, the hit men, you said, who were crowding your girl?" He nailed his eyes to mine. It was his intensity that had impressed me at our first chance meeting. I had also told him a small lie, and he instantly called me on it.

"You have a bad habit of hesitating when you avoid the truth," he said.

"They are no longer a threat," I said.

He waited and when nothing came said, "They are no longer."

"That is right."

"You're the good guys, right?"

"Straight up with you, buddy."

"Let's roll, Boyd," PC said, picking up the pace. "We'll text you the pictures and call with anything of interest. That's what you said you wanted, wasn't it? See if we noticed anything of interest?"

"Look for details and get pictures," I said.

PC and Boyd got in their '74 black Camaro with chrome wheels, a red flame on the side, and "Endless Summer" plates. PC drove, and he rolled out of the parking lot with the zip of a sleepy turtle, his turn indicator on a good twenty feet before the entrance. PC was a fast talker and a slow driver, and that incongruity struck me.

Kathleen and I decided to have dinner that evening at the Rusty Pelican.

The place was jammed. Whatever happened to the off-season? I slapped a few guys on the back, served up my top smile, and managed to shift a few people to free up two adjacent bar stools. Fine with us. We'd take high barstools over a table any day. Kathleen wore a peach summer dress and draped her white sweater over the stool. The initial reaction from walking into an air-conditioned restaurant from a ninety-plus-degree Florida parking lot was that you'd made a wrong turn and ended up in a South Side Chicago meat locker in January. The number of sweaters you see women in Florida carry in the summer never ceases to amaze me.

My stool was uneven, and whenever I shifted my weight, I rocked. I looked around for an unused stool at the nearby high top tables, but every one had a pair of cheeks planted on it.

Michelle arranged two black napkins with corners facing us to serve as tablecloths. Michelle's hair was the color of lemons. Last time we were in, it was the color of black olives. A 2007 Frog's Leap Cabernet stood proud and erect over my filet mignon and Kathleen's hog snapper. We ate off of each other's plates as if they were one.

"How was your day?" she asked as she took a piece from the middle of my soft pink filet. She didn't eat much beef, but when she did she preferred to kill it slowly with her own teeth.

"I went to the Gulf Beaches Historical Museum. It's right next to the Gulf Beaches Future Museum."

"You did not."

"I did. Furthermore, I guarantee that when and if I ever lie to you, it will be over a much more serious offense."

"You went to a museum?"

"Blows your mind, doesn't it?"

"I've been there. Offer me one thing as proof."

"There's a one-armed docent."

"Every museum has a one-armed docent. Did you talk with Frederick? He's a fascinating person."

"Who's Frederick?"

"The docent."

"Ah, the man with one arm named Frederick. And what was the name of his other arm?"

"Please," she gave me that look, "did you see the man in front of you or did you just see what wasn't there?"

"Did you just see what wasn't there?" I repeated it slowly. "What makes you think I run that deep?"

"Why were you there?"

"It was a pleasant morning on the promenade and——"

"Straight and neat."

I leaned in on the counter and my stool rocked forward. "Someone hacked away on the exterior stone and took a document that has evidently been resting within those stone walls for years. Decades. Your government, Ms. Rowe, would greatly appreciate having that letter back, so if you have it, cough it up because——"

"This is related to Dorothy Harrison, isn't it?"

"Perhaps." By limiting myself to one-word replies I had a sporting chance.

I glanced up at a display of liquor bottles behind the bar. A soft backlight created an amber glow as if the rum itself was generating warmth. There were five rows of bottles arranged from top down: 12, 8, 9, 9, 13.

I checked out Michelle. Two arms. Count them. One. Two.

"How do you know about Dorothy?" I asked.

"Everybody knows about Dorothy. What are you going to do about finding the letter?"

"I worked on it all day. And don't lay that 'everybody knows stuff' on me."

"My question stands."

"Would you like more wine?"

I reached for the bottle of liquid trapped since 2007. It was put into the bottle when the world was right and released after a faceless beast had clenched the financial world—society's blood—in a death roll. The world stopped breathing, and only a faint, dissipating pulse remained when the beast suddenly vanished as quickly and mysteriously as it had appeared. It left a dazed planet wondering what it was and if it would ever return. I refilled Kathleen's glass with the innocent wine.

"We think a guy in your neck of the woods has the letter," I said. I leaned forward, slightly more than I should, and the damn stool tilted with me. I gave everything to her straight.

64

Kathleen knew what Garrett and I did; the run-in with her past and my desire to love——or to at least test my capability to love——one woman in the universe, and for her to be that woman, required a full confession. Miraculously, she never flinched. Never looked away. Still, I harbored reservations about whether I was cut to drop my intensity on one soul and in return have enough room in my life for another person to do likewise. Only a fool whistles down an uncharted path.

"Knock on his door," Kathleen said when I'd finished.

"He'd simply deny everything. I think I'll get a couple of old fishing boats and blow them up outside the house in the middle of the night, cause a serious diversion, then hop the fence and break into the house."

"Well, that can go wrong on so many levels that you need to bring it up just to get it into the shadow of good."

"I like that," I said as I pushed away my plate. I didn't tell her that wasn't my real plan. She might inquire what my intentions were and I was still figuring out how to infiltrate Escobar's life.

"Blowing up boats?"

"Especially that, but I was referring to your 'shadow of good.'"

"I always thought if I could bring something up from bad into the shadow of good, then I had a chance."

"But still not terra firma with good. A purgatory position in which sliding down is easier than climbing up."

"That's right, I suppose. But the chance, the opportunity, is there. And Jake?"

"Yeah?"

"Don't over think this—I was usually referring to color combinations."

I swirled the ruby cabernet around in the glass as her words sloshed around in my head. Kathleen struck up a conversation with a guy next to her wearing a black shirt. I settled the tab, but hesitated just a bit on whether to stay and take on another bottle and to tell black shirt to keep his eyes on his own girl. I stood, gave my stool an unnecessary shove, and walked away like I was vacating a nagging marriage.

The restaurant insisted on using valet parking, and I presented my ticket to the attendant. He retrieved my truck, all of three spots away, and gave me a sheepish grin when I palmed him a five. I retracted the moon roof, lowered the windows, and shut off the air. We rolled down Gulf Boulevard in 5,700 pounds of steel. The warm, heavy, moist night air invaded the truck and arranged the loose ends of her hair so that they danced around her neck and shoulders. I went through three satellite stations and killed the music. That is not something I do lightly.

"How do you know about Dorothy?" I asked again. I was trying to convince myself that I was not enchanted by the lady in the photographs whom I would never know. Yet the lady in the faded red dress towered over my thoughts. Kathleen didn't answer.

"My question stands," I said.

"She had a gorgeous old deuce and a quarter, Jake. Put this truck to shame."

"I like my truck."

"It's not the vehicle, it's the road it travels and the people it carries."

"Can't split those words."

I looked at her. She wasn't smiling, nothing triumphant at all, but sat looking straight through the windshield as if we were driving into the past. Which, I thought, would be a neat thing to do.

We entered through the white gate of the picket fence that had gray dolphins on it and sat in the two chairs on the museum's porch facing the park across the street. Moths danced under the park's lights and farther down under the moths, a group of senior citizens played shuffleboard. A large man must have gotten the puck close to a high-scoring area, for he shouted, "Who-wow!" as if the cavalry had arrived.

"I want to hear your voice," I said.

She didn't say anything for a moment, and then, "I wonder if from this spot all that much has changed in fifty years. I wonder why people don't have front porches anymore."

"What the hell *is* a deuce and a quarter?" Another "Who-wow!" came from the park.

"A Buick Electra 225 with enough steel to get Youngstown rolling again."

"That's a lot of steel."

"It was a long time ago."

"And you know this because?"

Kathleen Rowe did not answer.

"You're anonymous, aren't you?"

"Why, thank you. You create quite an impression yourself," she said and glanced over at me. When she did, the light from the park caught the soft corner of her mouth where her thin lips formed a small smile and gave way to her smooth skin that was just starting to show her age. It was those lines around her lips, crafted by time, which possessed me.

"You support the museum. Top level is twenty-five dollars, and they go undercover after that." Over $25 was a hiccup for her. Life insurance and her deceased husband's business interest left her a cat's hair under eight million. She had no indulgences met by monetary means. Maybe earrings. She had a lot of earrings. And books. A repository of books.

Damndest thing is she had been preparing to divorce Donald Cunningham *before* the Outfit saved her attorney fees and six months of litigious hell. Instead of half, she received all his business interest plus life insurance proceeds. Her delay in filing for divorce, coupled with the Outfit's habit of permanently silencing dissenting opinions, had netted her an additional four.

"They're good people who run this place, but they could be a bit more aggressive in their fund-raising," she said. "They're having their annual fund-raiser next week. I'll drag you to it. Turns out her car sat in a garage for years after her death and now it's the property of the museum. Just in gorgeous condition. Every year at the fund-raiser they park it on the street directly in front of the museum."

"I recall seeing the annual gala announcement when I was there. They never had any children?" At least I didn't recall seeing any such pictures.

"That's correct. Her husband died tragically years before she did."

"She died tragically?"

"You know what I mean."

"An article mentioned that he died in a plane crash. Any other information?"

"Not really. I believe he was on some sort of diplomatic mission. There's just not a lot of information about him."

We were quiet for a moment and I wondered if that was what was in store for me. A diplomatic mission followed by no photographs.

Kathleen said, "It's hard to imagine any problems when sitting on this porch. Tell me, Jake, that all my problems are in my head and that my life is a sun-bathed path unfolding before me."

"Keep your face to the sunshine and you will not see the shadows."

"I forget who that one comes from."

"Helen Keller," I said.

"That's right. Anything else I need to know?"

"It falls apart when the sun goes down."

"Ah, but then we can see ourselves running with the stars," she said.

"'Dwell on the beauty of life. Watch the stars, and see yourself running with them.'"

"Language peaked early with that one. The Romans, I believe."

"Marcus Aurelius. Or maybe a martyr right before a lion gutted him. It was a long time ago."

"Running with the stars." She sang it more than said it, and I imagined the words floating out over the park and joining the moths.

I couldn't shake the lines on the soft corner of her mouth. "Let's take a walk," I said.

I took her hand and we strolled around to the back. It was the dark side of the property, and an untrimmed hibiscus crowded the side of the old church where the discarded stones still lay. I led us up tight against the stone wall and the wild bush and pressed into her. We wrapped our arms around each other's bodies and, on a hot, sultry night so thick you could fold it like clothing and pack it in a suitcase, froze the position. The sea breeze gently touched her hair, and I thought that even when you don't move there are things that move you. I wondered where the wind started its journey and what it brought.

I calmly took off my clothes and laid a bed on the ground beside the bush and under the window. I recalled Frederick telling me that Elissa, the elderly neighbor, discovered the disrupted stones. She must be an early riser as the house behind us was dark.

"I don't want to get too much sand on you," I said.

Kathleen slipped everything off like it was never on and placed her arms back around me. "Oh yes," she said, "I hope I'm brushing it out for days."

I hovered my mouth over the corner of her lips, but did not kiss her. As she exhaled, I breathed in her very breath, her Eden, until my lungs were full and could take no more.

We made love slowly, as if we wanted to be found, to have someone know we were there and to enjoy our time before it, too, was decades gone and then centuries with only the anonymous giving a damn and looking back. Under the window of Dorothy Harrison's bedroom, we enjoyed each other and ran with the stars, while from the park I would occasionally hear, but muted now, "Who-wow! Who-wow!"

CHAPTER 8

The dolphin surfaced four feet from my kayak, tossed me a smile, got a clear look at the naked sky, and then slipped under the surface and back into its world.

Nevis had joined me as soon as I cleared the dock. Morgan had named all the dolphins in our bay after Caribbean islands. Nevis had a slightly shorter nose than the others and her tail was more slender. From a distance, I got them confused, but Morgan could sit on the dock and identify them from a mile out. If he said Nevis was a she, then I was on board. Nevis was the benefactor of fish I caught off the end of my dock that were too small to keep. At first I would toss them to her, but after a while I knelt down and she took them from my hand.

We navigated our way around my island in thirty-two minutes. That was a full three minutes over my personal best, which I wasn't too happy about. But my record time was set in the winter on a calm and cold morning; no way could I match that in the early summer months. The second trip was for leisure as the sun was well into its daily ascent and reflected its blindness off the still waters of the inner canals. It quickly pushed up the pre-dawn temperatures that had never dipped below muggy. Nevis ditched me after the first circumference. Can't blame her.

I hoisted the fourteen-foot kayak over the concrete retaining wall and then pulled myself up. Kathleen and Morgan were on the back porch where she was having coffee and Morgan was sipping his customary morning half beer. Morgan had witnessed the hard stuff ruin too many lives and constructed his own method of dealing with the necessary demon that we all must confront. His morning taste, he claimed, kept him away from it until late in the afternoon.

I bent over and gave Kathleen a kiss on the forehead. "Your hair seems a little sandy."

She smiled. Sort of like Nevis.

"How was the trip?" Morgan asked.

"I think Nevis winked at me."

"She's the most sociable."

"How do you tell them apart?" Kathleen asked.

"How can you not? They are different from each other in so many ways. They just live on the other side of the wall, under the surface, not above," Morgan said.

"But they need both sides," I said.

"Yes. They do need both sides of the water," he said.

I went to the kitchen and grabbed a mug—a silhouette of Mickey, Goofy, and Donald marching up a hill—filled it two-thirds with dark coffee and took a seat next to Kathleen. I was glad Morgan was there. He often showed up early, which got the day off to a good start. I wanted to tell her that last night under the hibiscus was for keeps, and without taking her eyes off Morgan, her hand found mine.

"How do you tell them apart?" she asked again.

Morgan said, "You start by identifying their roles. A calf will have an aunt, another female dolphin that will take care of it while its own mother searches for food. Nevis, I know, was an aunt for Dominica a few years ago when Dominica was raising Little Bart. After a while, you become familiar with their different sizes and proportions as well as habits. Little Bart, for example, will go airborne almost daily, coming out of the water to get a good look around."

"Little Bart?" Kathleen asked.

"Porpoise proportions?" I chirped in. He ignored me and took Kathleen's remark.

"I'll point him out sometime. He's one of the smallest males I've seen."

"Do they really take care of each other like that?" she asked.

Morgan looked at her as if there was no greater topic. "Absolutely. They're joyful creatures that enjoy each other's company. I've seen them mourn a death, just sulk with no playful activities for days. That's when I know that one's been lost. They're very emotional."

"But they are known to engage in infanticide," I reminded him.

"On rare occasions. We have no idea why, assuming there even is a 'why.'"

Morgan took another sip from his beer, placed it behind him, and said he'd catch us later. He had barely drunk the beer that was in the bottle's neck. As he walked across my backyard, a pelican violently dove from forty feet into the water off the end of my dock. My overhead fan starting clicking with each revolution, and for some reason it reminded me of my crooked stool. What is it with the little things?

Kathleen's hand still rested on mine.

I dropped her off at her house and a few hours later PC called.

"You hitting it today?" I asked without salutation when I saw who it was.

"We're done."

"Done?"

73

"You gotta stay with me here, Jake. We tackled it early, God's work is important, man. Let's meet. Boyd printed the pictures. You'll like what we got."

"Same place as yesterday?"

"See you in fifteen."

Fifteen minutes later I walked into the Riptide Bar, an expansive beachside watering hole. The young ladies behind the bars wore bikinis and the beer was ice cold. A sign on the bar by the tip jar said, "For every dollar tip, a Justin Bieber fan dies." PC and Boyd were sitting at a high wood table by the outside bar that had no walls. They wore T-shirts and shorts. Boyd had a cloth hat on, and the back of his T-shirt said "See other side." PC's shirt had a small covered wagon on it and said "I died of dysentery." His sandals were on the ground under his stool.

"You boys spreading the good word looking like that?" I took the stool across from them. At the last second I placed my right hand on the back and made certain it wasn't on a fault line.

"Check this out," Boyd said and shoved his phone in my face. It was a self-portrait of the two of them, dressed in khaki pants and loose fitting long sleeve blue shirts. "This was us this morning and, man, did we rock. Did you know there are Jesus books, Jesus clothes, and Jesus music, and I mean some *seriously* good Jesus rock tunes. We've been totally in it, man. There's a whole Jesus industry. He's bigger than Elvis."

"You guys are a little late to that party. You do know what Jesus and Elvis have in common?"

"Tell us," PC said.

"Both their deaths were brilliant career moves."

PC said, "I see that, man. I see that. What a powerful launching pad a death can be."

A waitress with short brunette hair, two ounces of cloth on her body, and a silver ring in her belly button came by to see if I would like anything. I would like to polish her ring with my tongue, but I doubted that went with the spirit of her inquisition. I ordered an iced tea. PC and Boyd were halfway through their beers.

Boyd spoke. "Your house was to be the fifth we hit. Whole neighborhood is cul-de-sacs. We wanted to get into it, you know, like play acting, then we saw our friend Dan and——"

"That's character acting, Boyd," PC said, "and it's *culs*-de-sac. Here's what we got." He pulled out a dozen pictures from an orange folder and placed them on the table. I started leafing through them and PC kept talking. "I went up by myself and rang the bell at the gate. Some guy's voice booms over the box asking what I wanted. I said——"

"What the hell is this?" I held up a picture of Boyd with a FTD hat and uniform standing inside a grand foyer. "How did you——?"

"Do you ever listen, man?" PC asked. "We ran into Dan the Man on house number two. He delivers flowers and asks about the Bibles, you know?"

"Dan the Man was freaked to see us pushing the good word," Boyd said.

"Who is Dan the——"

"He's a buddy of ours. We laid it out and changed plans," Boyd said. "Made an old hawk decision."

"Boyd, really, man. It's *ad hoc*, Latin, dude." PC leaned in across from me and drilled my eyes. "We connected, Jake, big time. The Man tells us he delivers flowers almost daily to the house, but today he's got a dozen arrangements to drop off."

"They're having some big——" Boyd said.

"I'll get to that," PC said. "So I laid out our plan, Dan's a little hesitant, but we go way back. I bailed his ass out in eighth grade when Fat Scully, the gym teacher, got in his face one too many times for not putting everything he had into push-ups. Dan was never no good at push-ups. Like, really, man, that's education, doing push-ups? Scully called it 'core training.' Don't get me started. Dan just flat out laid Fat Scully down."

"Thing of fuckin' beauty," Boyd said and took a healthy swig of his beer. "Dan unloaded the largest roundhouse in the history of the great state of Florida."

"You got that one right, Boyd. Anyways, Scully's thinking of pressing charges, so I get Jessica, she was my girl—"

"Still is, man, she still is," Boyd said, nodding his head. At this point I wondered if I was stuck in a tour of their formative years.

PC said, "Jessica tells Fat Scully that if he presses charges, she'll have to tell the power that he felt her up. After that, Fat Scully didn't say nothing to nobody."

"He felt her up?" I asked.

"Really, Jake? If you can't hit the pedal, get out of the lane," PC said.

"Tell me what happened today, boys." I took my elbows off the table and leaned back.

PC sat back and took a swig of beer and yelled over to Marlene, evidently the girl with the belly button ring, to bring two more. Boyd whacked a fly on the table and flicked it off.

"So Dan says OK, and we put his outfit on Boyd," PC said.

"This was after we convinced him we weren't really doing the Jesus thing," Boyd added.

"He knows that, Boyd. He wants the skinny. Here we go—I, as bible man, ring the doorbell, they say beat it. Boyd arrives in the van, says he's got flowers. Dan says they always just open the gate for him and let Dan bring them in the house. I tell them I haven't seen my home in two years, preaching the word and all, and next thing you now, we're in the foyer. I'd say Mediterranean with a nod toward Spanish influence and encompassing good use of red and yellow. A drop-dead gorgeous aluminum painting—they're the latest, man. Also some beautiful antique seashell sconces. She asked about Dan, and we said he was sick. She was genuinely concerned. Sweetest person you'll ever meet."

"Big house," Boyd said.

"And I took these pictures."

"Who is she?" I asked.

"Sophia, man. It's her house. You can tell," PC said. "Told us to click away."

"You didn't happen to inquire about a letter while you were in there, did you?" I asked.

"Not picking up what you're putting down," PC said.

"Never mind."

"I asked her why all the blossoms," Boyd said. "They're having a fund-raiser this Saturday night for Congressman Kittredge, whoever the hell he is. Fifty people at two grand a plate. Can't even imagine that. Sophia said she's serving Florida lobster, clams, and roast beef with odd juice."

"Dude," PC said, "it's *au jus*. French. Meaning 'with its own juice.'"

Something clicked in my head about PC, but it would have to wait.

"Give me a minute," I said. I got up and walked toward the beach, cell phone in my hand, Laurel and Hardy at the table. I hit speed dial.

"Good afternoon, Mr. Travis," Mary Evelyn said.

"Mary Evelyn, either you call me Jake or I'm never talking to you again. I'm serious this time. I'm at the top of the Skyway. Don't make me jump. I'm begging you. My blood will be on your hands."

"Now, Mr. Travis, we both know you're bluffing." She had a slight tease in her voice that was new to our relationship. Maybe she was loosening up. Maybe I'd been the stiff one.

I glanced out at the Gulf and saw a boat pulling a parasail. My insides went radioactive.

When I drank at Fort Myers Beach for a year after leaving the army, a parasail harness snapped and two junior high school girls from Wisconsin hit the water from 220 feet. I had tumbled out of a CH-47 Chinook my share of times and knew that my terminal velocity, the maximum speed I would reach falling with a belly to earth pose, was 195 kilometers per hour, or 122 mile per hour. I figured the girls hit the concrete water at around seventy miles per hour.

The man with the light gray beard who pushed the ice cream cart with the white and yellow umbrella on top said he never saw it. He was serving cherry push-ups to two children with his back to the water when he heard screams from the beach. He was a large man and he said his body and cart blocked the small boy and girl from witnessing anything.

He told me he didn't believe in God, but thanked him every day for sending those kids at that time to buy cherry push-ups and for making him so damn fat that they couldn't see around him. Said if he died now, he'd go with the peace of knowing that he'd served his purpose.

I did the imprecise math and derived, for that year, the parasail industry was akin to a dozen Boeing 737 domestic flights crashing every week. No one walks away.

I looked down and away at the sand. A dissipating current shuddered my body.

"Jake?" It was Mary Evelyn's voice.

"Yes."

"I thought I'd lost you. Hold on, he's finishing a call."

I blew out my breath and wondered what the hell had gotten into me—was still in me. I see parasails nearly every day. But sometimes, without warning, everything I am bursts unexpectedly and violently into one direction. The army shrink they sent me to told me I was a man of "extreme passion." Highly unusual for a numbers man, he said while appraising me like a frog in formaldehyde. I asked him if passions could be anything but. He said I needed to develop coping mechanisms. He was still talking when I heard the door shut behind me. I turned my back to the Gulf.

"Talk to me," Garrett said.

"Escobar's holding a fund-raiser for Congressman Michael Kittredge."

"Who the hell is he?"

"My elected representative."

"How did you find out?"

"I'm an informed citizen."

"No, the fund-raiser."

"Thoroughly unconventional means, I can assure you."

"When."

"Tonight. Score me an invitation. I'll take Kathleen."

"How many people?"

"We think about fifty."

"Did he call?"

"We connected a little over an hour ago."

"And?"

"It seems personal this time. I'm not sure he knows that much himself."

"What do you smell?"

Garrett said, "He confirmed the heat's from the State Department. 'Sixty-one. We're coming off Korea and at the edge of Vietnam."

"Not as fun as the edge of seventeen."

"Nothing is."

"Seems more Bay of Pigs time to me. Little early to be worried about 'Nam. But it might not have anything to do with either. Maybe JFK blows altar boys. Listen," I said, "I'm not sure how far I want to go into this with blinders on. The old church used to be inhabited by a lady named Dorothy Harrison."

"I read the dossier."

"Her husband was an early spook. See what we can find on him, his associates. And cleared or not, I open the letter when I get it."

We disconnected, and as I returned to the table I remembered what I had been contemplating before I walked away. Before I suppressed the urge to commandeer a Jet Ski and overtake the parasail boat like a horseman chasing down a runaway stagecoach. *Au jus, ad hoc. Mediterranean with a nod toward Spanish.* Discreetly taking pictures in a strange house. PC, 140 pounds of bones and attitude. And something else.

"PC," I said as I mounted my stool, "how much formal education do you have?"

"Formal education? Really?" PC spit out. "You mean how many push-ups could I do? Fat Scully, man, telling us to do push-ups. When did a push-up ever do anybody any good? Unfuckin'-believable." He leaned in toward me. "Listen, Jakester, I got two things out of school. Mrs. Van Vaulkenberg scrawled

'Life is not fair' on the blackboard the first day of freshman year and never erased it. You complain? She'd point to the sign. And Littlefield—"

"Oh yeah—I remember this," Boyd chimed in.

"—he had over a dozen 'Do Not Chew Gum' signs plastered on the walls of his geography room. One mammoth gum sign was plastered over a map of China like he was trying to suffocate the little red ants. Life's not fair and don't chew gum. Welcome to free formal education."

"You have a bad habit of changing topics when you're uncomfortable," I threw back at him. I was ticked about his observation that I hesitated when I lied. I'd have to work on that.

He eyed me for a moment while Boyd stared at him. "I got kicked out after a prank during my junior year. Didn't matter to me. Milton, the physics teacher, couldn't explain the mathematical relation between the three magnetic fields that surround the moon—and Fat Scully gave me a C in gym. I was out of there."

"You had a physics teacher named Milton?" I asked.

"Really, man. You're too much."

"Any more Latin?"

Boyd took that like a proud parent at a PTO meeting. "He did the school's four-year program in two and they had him taking college-level Latin his junior year."

"French?"

It was Boyd again, "Go on, PC, talk to him in German too."

For a moment we stared at each other and did not speak. Off to my left, Reggie, a broad black man in dreadlocks, was arranging paintings under the small tent. We gave each other a nod. One of his works hung in my study.

"What was the prank?"

Boyd said, "So cool, man. We programmed the county's 911 line so when people called they got a recording, a pleasant lady with an English accent saying, 'Thank you for calling and congratulations, you've been selected to take a brief survey. Please stay on the line after your call.' Then we played Adamo for Strings for a few seconds."

"Adagio," PC said, looking at me and with something new and resigned in his voice like he knew what was coming. I wondered if someone had once stuck him in formaldehyde. "Samuel Barber's 1936 second movement from his String Quartet, Opus Eleven."

"Yeah, that too," Boyd said.

I suppressed a smile over the 911 prank, although I hoped no harm came from it. I held PC's eyes and decided to see how deep he could go.

"Funeral song," I said. "Played at Einstein's."

"Princess Grace's as well."

"And JFK?"

"Loved it. Jackie O had the National Symphony Orchestra play it in an empty hall the Monday after the Outfit nailed him."

"*Platoon?*"

"Made the movie. Dichotomy just shreds you. Are we done here, 'cause I'm not taking any more fuckin' tests."

I imagined he was good for the full fifteen. "You count cards?" I asked. "Play online poker and it all comes easy to you, doesn't it?"

"Whatever, man. We get by."

"I got to go." I stood up and pulled four hundred out of my wallet. "You guys did great. Read the New Testament, it really is great hippie stuff, right out of the sixties." I started to walk away.

"You imagine that, man?" PC called after me. I stopped and turned.

"What?"

"That sound in an empty hall. All that music and no one to hear it."

I held his eyes for a few seconds. "No. No, I got nothing to lay down next to that."

I headed to my truck. The heat radiated up again from the asphalt through the worn soles of my boat shoes. I stepped over a puddle of water left from last night's deluge, called Kathleen, and headed off to get a haircut.

Probably should shave as well—hadn't done that for a few days.

CHAPTER 9

"How do I look?"

They are potentially the most dangerous words to ever float from a woman's lips. And the sooner that any man, regardless of the garment he wears or the continent he walks, realizes there is only an affirmative reply, and that reply needs to be delivered with the utmost of sincerity, the happier his life will be. Fortunately in my case, I had nothing to worry about.

I was sitting in the shade of her veranda watching the charter sunset sailboats chase the sinking sun when her voice again turned me around.

She wore a floor-length ivory dress that dropped under her right shoulder and came up high over her left shoulder. No visible scar tonight. Her hair was pulled back tight and she wore long, straight earrings that sparkled in the reflected rays of the sun. She turned once for me, revealing the low-cut back.

I said, "The tides will pause when you enter a room."

"My, a romantic fool."

"Always a fool for you."

"It's a wise man who knows himself to be a fool," she said.

"That's Bill again, isn't it? Where *do* you get those from?" While we were in the Keys she pulled a dozen quotations out of the air from Cervantes to Flaubert, Shakespeare to Proust. I had to work to keep up with her.

"I did a little more postgraduate work than I initially told you."

"How little much?"

"It doesn't matter. You look very nice in a tux—not sure it's something I ever expected to see. Are you going to be able to transition from a beach bum to a debonair business man?"

"Like Prince Hal, I will transform myself as night turns to day."

"I was *so* hoping we could get into King Henry tonight. And they taught that in the army?"

"Might have picked that up on my own."

"A little night reading?"

"Goes well with night music."

"Do you remember everything that you read?"

"Hardly."

She skipped a beat and then, "Do you remember virtually everything you read?"

"It's meaningless."

"Meaningless is a little harsh, but I get your point. Nice bow tie, by the way. The light purple is sharp. Did an ex pick it out?"

"No."

"You did that?"

"You can't imagine."

I walked up to her and we stood eye to eye. She had never been taller. "And you must have some serious heels under that gown."

"You can't imagine."

"What a waste," I said, "all those quotations in our heads but no imagination."

Kathleen said, "Let's go meet Sophia and Raydel Escobar."

Sophia Escobar stood in the center of the vast foyer and around her everything revolved.

She wore a red dress and had her black hair stacked high on her head. A single yellow flower was pinned to her hair above her left ear. Her bronze cheekbones and cutting figure made her look like a model for a magazine shoot on South American aristocracy. But her laugh revealed her. It circled the room and made her stark colors and intimidating figure go soft. It was warm and rich with no social pretense and matched the sparkle in her eyes and the way she reached out to touch people when she talked with them.

The foyer gave way to a great room the size of Delaware. It contained an eight-piece band emulating the sounds of Herb Alpert and the Tijuana Brass, forty years after they had their run. We approached Sophia, and like an experienced host, she sensed us coming and broke her conversation to meet her newly arrived guests.

I introduced Kathleen and myself. We shook hands and exchanged pleasantries. I had instructed Kathleen to deflect questions about us. It wouldn't be difficult, as most people are eager to hear their own voices. They circle a conversation not with the intent of listening, but with the sole purpose of calculating their next comment and entry point. I complimented Sophia on the band.

"Oh, that's Raydel's doing. He's musically stuck in that decade. His father's music."

"I like his taste," Kathleen said. "And your home is just beautiful, did you decorate it yourself?"

"I did, thank you."

"The antique sconces are particularly attractive and placed just right, it appears, to be seen from every possible angle," I said.

Mary Evelyn's research contained a side bar on the two years it took to construct the house. Sophia had relocated the sconces three times, and each move demanded new wiring and drywall. There was some question as to whether Shramos, the builder, was fleeing Sophia or the IRS when he slipped out of the country,

"Do you think so?" She looked at me intently as if seeking approval. "I did put a lot of time into them. Do me a favor, Mr. Travis?" She touched me lightly on my left shoulder. "Mention that to Raydel, will you?"

"I most certainly will, and it's Jake."

"I like your purple tie, Jake."

"I like your yellow flower, Sophia."

"It's a tradition in my family. My mother always wore a yellow flower."

"My father always wore purple."

"Interesting," Sophia Escobar said with a playful smile. "You might want to fall pretty far from that tree."

"That's my intent."

"Is your mother still living?" Kathleen asked. I thought the question rather blunt.

"No, I'm afraid she is not," Sophia said, appraising her.

"I can't imagine her being more proud of you than right now," Kathleen said.

"That is so kind of you."

I was about to take Kathleen's arm when Sophia inquired where she lived. Kathleen replied that she had a residence on the island but was relocating into a condo downtown after renovations. The two of them vanished into a serious conversation about remodeling and decorating. I slipped away as if I was never there and circulated around the great room. I wanted to find Escobar and Congressman Kittredge. Politics weren't of particular interest to me, but I had read a dossier on Kittredge to know where he, and I, stood. After all, I supposedly laid out two grand to mingle with him.

When we had arrived at the Escobars' home, a legion of Chippendale valets swarmed us and relieved us of Kathleen's Lexus. We thought the Lexus would create a better impression than my truck. I had briefed her on why I was positioning myself to meet Escobar and that I wanted Escobar to be a little uncomfortable, maybe even show his hand. There was dirt in his life—there's dirt in every life—and I wanted to find it. I wasn't counting on luck, but you always wanted to give it a chance. Sort of like peace. Then when the war breaks out, your conscience is clear, or so you'll try to convince yourself as you wipe the blood off your hands. I had impressed upon Kathleen to secure a tour of the house. I wanted to see where the safe room was in the hall leading to the study. I had no reason to believe the letter would be within its double Kevlar-lined walls, but assumed that Escobar was a simple man and would place the letter in the room he designed for maximum security.

A trumpet solo from the song "Rise" rose from the band, and I noticed a large portion of the party had leaked out to the veranda. I migrated outdoors and spotted Escobar and Kittredge holding court by a large outdoor kitchen. Other men were stuck to them like magnets on a refrigerator.

A heavyset young lady in a black uniform and a jungle of blonde hair stood alone behind a teak bar. I couldn't decide if she had spent hours making the mess out of her hair or if that's how she woke up. I asked for Maker's Mark with a splash of Coke on the rocks. It seemed to go with the music. She asked for my name. I said I was spoken for. She said she could share. I told her to dilute my drink but never her feelings. She handed me my drink but didn't let go.

"See, you can share," she said with a smile. I couldn't decide if she was attractive, but she believed she was and that made her so. I like people like that. You can only do so much with your looks, but you have total control over your confidence. I pivoted and refocused on my target.

Four men ringed Escobar and Kittredge, whom I recognized from Mary Evelyn's e-mail. Kittredge wore a Realtor's smile and looked like the type of guy who got his hair cut every Wednesday. Ten a.m. sharp. I have less in common with such men than I do with Elmer Fudd. While the congressman was in his forties, most of his ass-sniffing admirers were considerably older. I wasn't sure how to infiltrate Escobar's group, so I did what I do best.

"Congressman Kittredge, a pleasure to meet you." I barged in with my extended hand leading the charge and dislodged the conversation like a bowling ball smacking pins. "I am thrilled to be able to support your good work."

My improper but enthusiastic entry carried the moment as the circle parted and the voices drifted down. The congressman turned to meet his energetic, if somewhat rude and socially awkward, admirer.

"Why, thank you——"

"Travis. Jake Travis," I said while I vigorously pumped his hand. Escobar was to my left and I caught the corner of his stare. "I especially appreciate your efforts to curb runaway education and health care costs. Your commitment to turn around our troubled country is greatly appreciated, Congressman."

"Thank you, Mr.——"

I didn't let him in. I was the new dog in the circle and I wanted to set the pace. "Furthermore, I'm thrilled to see you standing against the World Fair Business Bill. I have particular interest in that piece of legislation. If American companies are to compete in this global economy, we must be able to seek the lowest labor cost. That has always been the case and must continue to be. We have no right to impose working conditions on others countries."

"Well, Mr. Travis—"

"Please, just Jake."

"I appreciate your support, Jake. As you know, we try to influence those governments, but firmly believe in laissez-faire when it comes to them handling their own business practices. I'm actually catching a government plane later this evening and have a meeting at nine tomorrow on the bill." Kittredge looked at me earnestly, as if he were just recovering from my brash entrance. "Tell me, Jake, what line of work are you into?"

The rest of the circle had little choice but to forfeit their previous line of conversation and relegate themselves to ancillary observers. Escobar was fidgeting with his drink, and my back was partially turned to him. I wanted him to maneuver in order to be part of Kittredge's and my tête-à-tête.

"I'm into imports, Congressman," I said.

"If it's Jake, then it's Michael."

"I wanted to attend a dinner for you last year in Palm Beach, Michael, but was out of the country. I'm sure you raised quite a bit more that evening." Mary Evelyn's information indicated that Walter Mendis's fund-raiser for Kittredge ran five grand a plate.

My faux pas caused a few dogs to shift their weight while others took refuge in whatever drink they carried, no doubt embarrassed for me. Kittredge, however, leaned in a little as he got the scent of a heavy roller.

Escobar shouldered between us. "This is just an informal get-together," he said, "a chance to meet the congressman. I don't believe we've met. I'm Raydel Escobar." I turned slightly and extended my hand.

Escobar was a large-boned man, not muscular or over-weight. He had a medium complexion, Spanish Cuban rather than African descent, and an enviable thick wave of coal black hair. His white tuxedo sported faint gray stripes, with every few stripes a tone darker. His tie and pocket square were black. He carried himself as a man who expected subservience, and his image was aided by his voice—a pleasant bass timbre with soft edges. Some voices don't belong to a particular body, but Escobar's voice perfectly matched the man.

He also reminded me a little of Yogi Bear, except he wasn't a bear, his name wasn't Yogi, and he was real. But outside of that and a few other minor items—I don't believe, for instance, that Yogi wore shoes—he was a dead ringer for Hanna-Barbera's picnic basket snatcher.

"Mr. Escobar. My pleasure, and what a gracious host you are. You have a beautiful home, and I was fortunate enough to meet your even more beautiful wife on the way in." I squeezed his beefy hand hard and pumped it as if I expected to hit a gusher. His grasp was firm, but his fingers were fat and soft.

"The lovely Sophia," Kittredge said as Escobar and I locked eyes. "Raydel was regaling tales…uh…before you joined us, about his two-year venture in building this masterpiece. Sophia has quite the eye for detail."

"Yes, I can see that. The antique sconces are a nice touch, so perfectly placed, don't you think?" I gave him his hand back.

Escobar took a slow sip of his murky drink. "What exactly do you import, Mr. Travis?"

"It's Jake. Pretty much anything I have manufactured for a dime, ship for fifty cents, and sell for ten dollars." That got a hearty men's chuckle from the other dogs in the circle.

"Well," Kittredge laughed, "that's a tried-and-true business model. What are these items?"

"Whatever hot item that little girls need to have. The next big thing," I said.

"And how do you know that," Escobar pressed, "the next big thing, Mr. Travis? Do you have a crystal ball that others do not?"

"Hardly. What I really do, nine times out of ten, is fall flat on my ass. I manufacture something for a dollar, ship it for fifty cents, and write it all off."

"And one out of ten?" Kittredge asked.

"One out of ten, one out of twenty, the second number is irrelevant. What matters is when the iPhone case with an extra battery pack, stuffed monkey with a French name, or in the case of last year, when Asia Annie dolls exploded and every eight- to twelve-year-old girl in the hemisphere needed one more than the air they breathe, that I have the manufacturing, distribution, and cost structure to get in the game. It doesn't matter that it's not my creation, there's a barge load of money in the ancillary items."

I was on a roll and digging my part. "But if those labor costs go up, then you can't sustain the losses while you tread water waiting for the winner. Low cost, Congressman. This country was built on finding low cost. If someone in Cambodia is willing to work for a dollar a day, for as many hours a day as they are physically able, and for as many days as they can, who are we to oppose those choices? Why should we impose our tired, unionized, watered-down version of capitalism upon an emerging country?" The surrounding men resembled bouncing dashboard bobbleheads, as if no finer point had ever been made at an English hunting club.

"Well said, Jake. Tell me, are you on my preferred mailing list?"

"Not until this evening, Michael. Not until this evening."

I pivoted slightly toward Escobar. "What is your game, Mr. Escobar? A man with such an impressive estate must surely owe substantial annual dues to the Internal Revenue Service."

Escobar eyed me for a moment, and I heard the male singer from the band crooning "This Guy's in Love With You." He let it out lazy and slow like hand-churned peach ice cream on a Faulkner Sunday afternoon. I was beginning to think that when the evening concluded, the vehicles retrieved by the Chippendales would be from the late '60s to early '70s—as if the whole night was in a time warp.

"Like you, Mr. Travis, I import and export."

"Mr. Escobar, I never said I exported. Outside of software, entertainment, and dirty money, this country doesn't export much of anything anymore. Do you export or import?"

Our little circle had grown as a few other alpha males joined the perimeter, eager to be near the nucleus. One man, standing behind Escobar and off to his right, was younger, and his shoulders and chest bulged out of his tux. His greased black hair was in a tight ponytail and not a strand was loose. His left ear was pierced and his tuxedo was brown with a lighter shade vest and tie. He was the type of guy I didn't need to look at twice to know I wanted to break his nose. I wanted to break it now. He had appeared when I was talking about the dolls and young girls.

Escobar's public face was his carpet and rug business. I wasn't surprised he didn't mention the strip joints he owned, but I was willing to bet every man in the circle knew about them. Nor did I expect him to mention that he and his partners had profited handsomely when the Department of Transportation put in a new interchange a few years ago. The controversy around the location quickly evaporated as the power brokers moved on to the next big thing. A developer wanted to take 100 waterfront acres south of the Sunshine Skyway off the government's hands in return for 900 acres of brush land. It had the potential to be the biggest development on the west coast, and the dogs were circling and lining up their support. To help pacify the nagging environmentalists, the developers planned on constructing a dolphin safe area, which was just what our bottle-nosed buddies needed with 8,000 square miles of the Gulf of Mexico awaiting them. I wondered if Escobar and Mendis were involved in that as well.

I wanted to squeeze Escobar and see what came out. You don't own three strip clubs and keep your hands clean. You don't put bulletproof glass in unless you anticipate trouble. The more I knew, the more leverage I had. I wanted to use the evening to face off with Escobar and let him know that I was on to him without revealing who I was. I would get enough dirt on him to broker my own deal for the letter.

I could always later announce my intentions and demand that he fork it over. But once I did that, all other options were off the table. He would deny having it. I'd punch him and he would call the cops. The official government stance was that Garrett Demarcus was a lawyer and I an unemployed Florida PI who recovered stolen boats. Both ex-military. Both not on the government's payroll.

"I import carpet and rugs, Mr. Travis," Escobar said, answering my question.

"There must be a lot of money in rugs."

"There must be a lot of money in dolls."

The men facing the house suddenly stepped back as if partitioned by an invisible force. I turned to see Sophia and Kathleen approaching like a sartorial wave, void of swagger yet well aware of the ripples that went out before them. Kathleen, tall in ivory, and Sophia shorter in red. Genghis Kahn could be storming the gates and not a man would have noticed. Kathleen slowed and let Sophia puncture the circle. The men's club, momentarily, was shut down.

"Raydel, you haven't moved all night, and Congressman, your legs have been set in concrete. I'm taking Kathleen on a tour. Anyone care to join us?"

"Michael," I said. I showed my back to Escobar. "Would you be seriously offended if I followed these beautiful ladies? I assume you've had the tour?"

"Actually, I have not. I'd be delighted to join you." He turned to Escobar. "Raydel, I'll meet up with you later."

"Anyone else care to join us?" Sophia asked. No one moved, and I took a few steps toward Sophia to let the dogs pick up the scent that the invitation was already closed.

I could feel the steel cold stare of Raydel Escobar on my back.

CHAPTER 10

Sophia marched us from room to room as I thought ahead to my next encounter with Escobar.

Although I didn't think it was related to his IRS problems, I wanted to know how Escobar and Congressman Kittredge were initially acquainted. I planned to double back, check Escobar's temperature, and push him a little harder. I had nothing to lose by making him uncomfortable.

One thing that became clear as we moved through the rooms was that you could tear the house apart for a month and not find a large envelope. Maybe he stuck it in a bank box. Maybe the letter was in *Chica Bonita,* the Carver's tender. Even in my home, I'd have no problem hiding a letter so that no one could ever find it. And if they accused me of possessing such an item, I'd deny it and tell them to search away while I enjoyed a highball.

Sophia explained how she ripped off the crown molding in one bedroom because it "grated me" as being too large. The next size was too small. She returned to the original eight-inch piece. Each installment necessitated three coats of paint, as "color is instrumental in size perception."

"Indecision may or may not be your problem," I said.

She turned to me. "What? Oh yes, I see. I suppose you're right, although I'm not like that in everything. It's just that you want to get right those things that surround you every day. You become them. Don't you think so?"

I thought of my little house with my outdoor shower. I thought of Morgan's statement that a man should never need anything more than a sailboat could accommodate.

"You're exactly right," Kathleen cut in.

"We build our houses and then they build us," Kittredge said. I was about to correct him on his botched Churchill phrase when Kathleen nudged me, reminding me not to override a congressman. Or did she just feel like giving me a nudge? Either way, to show my eternal gratitude, when Sophia and Kittredge were in front of us, I gave her a hard pinch in the ass. Right cheek. She shook her head without turning.

"And this," Sophia said as we progressed down a long and wide walnut-paneled hallway partitioned with seashell sconces every four feet, "is Raydel's study."

The cavernous room was topped with a twelve-foot coffered ceiling. Ten yards of black glass reflected the night. Escobar's desk occupied one end and rested in front of built-in shelves. A sofa and high-back chairs fronted the desk. A bar and a round poker table with five chairs anchored the other end of the room, where there was also a small table with a chessboard on it. A bursting bouquet of yellow flowers centered a tall table with a marble top that hugged a wall.

"A true man's cave," Kittredge said in appreciation as we entered the chamber.

"Just look at that dentil crown molding," Kathleen gushed.

"Do you like it?" Sophia exclaimed. "It's all handmade. The lumberyards didn't carry the size I wanted. Each piece was cut and measured."

"It must have taken days to measure and cut all those pieces," Kathleen said.

"They did it twice. The first effort just appeared too small for the volume of the room."

Evidently Mrs. Escobar tried on crown molding like she tried on dresses.

"Weren't they glued?" I asked.

"Yes. It took considerable effort, but I had them tear it all down and start over. The size is proportionate now, don't you think?"

"It looks perfect," I said. I was beginning to wonder how Shramos, the builder, kept his sanity despite the crescendo of money he received from his fortuitous crossing of paths with Sophia Escobar.

Kittredge wandered off to the windows and peered out to the pool below and the Gulf beyond. "My goodness, this glass must be over an inch thick," he said.

"Raydel said it was to block the sun," Sophia said.

That, and Uzi machine gun bullets. Apparently she never questioned the thickness of her sunglasses. I wondered what Escobar shared with Sophia. My money was on her being in the dark about much of her husband's affairs, but I would also bet, and bet heavy, that she was willfully ignorant.

We drifted around the circumference of the room, and I slipped behind his desk to view pictures on the shelves. One was of Escobar outside the Welcome In. It was black and white and projected an old-world charm. There were other pictures of him grinning and holding up fish, all taken in a flats boat. Judging by the shades of blue, they were most likely taken in the Keys. No water like that around here. In one photo Escobar held up a good thirty-pound permit with a shark-size bite taken out of its tail.

But the picture that caught my eye wasn't a fishing pose or an artistic black-and-white print. It was one of Escobar, Paulo Henriques, and Walter Mendis standing on undeveloped flat land, each smoking a large cigar with a glass of champagne, or at least champagne glasses, in their other hands. Across the bottom was scrawled "Thanks Bernie." I assumed it was their interchange deal, as it was a scrappy piece of land, but I hadn't a clue who Bernie was. I made a note to see if Mary Evelyn could find a "Bernie" in Escobar's circle. Whoever the hell he was, he made the men in the photograph very happy.

I had a better idea.

"Who's Bernie?"

"Excuse me?" Sophia spun back to me.

"In the photo, the boys are thanking Bernie. I just wondered who Bernie is."

"Raydel and his business associates. I think he's someone who used to work for him, but I really don't know." She waved her left hand in the air as she spoke, as if she could dismiss the whole lot.

Like peace, I thought. I'd given it a shot.

We departed the study and I ran my right hand against the west wall. I hadn't detected any break in the east panels on the way in, and I wanted to know where the safe room was. Six feet from the room and into the hall I felt the break in the wall, and then I discerned the shape of a door.

"What's this?" I asked, and the group stopped and turned. "It's like a crack in the wall."

"Oh, that's the room where we keep the security equipment," Sophia said.

"Ingenious, isn't it, Michael? A door without handles," I said. I wanted to draw him into the conversation so it wouldn't seem as if I, and I alone, had an unhealthy interest in the room. Kittredge came back and ran his hand over the smooth, polished walnut surface.

"Amazing," he said. "I can't detect a handle and there's barely a break in the wood. How does he even get into the room?"

Thank you, Congressman.

Sophia came back to us. "He has a pad, like a garage opener, behind his desk somewhere and it just pops open." She said "pop" like the door would spring off its hinges, which I doubted it would do.

"And if the power's out?" I tried to sound as nonchalant as possible.

"It's battery operated, but even if that fails, he has a key." She moved next to a black-and-white framed picture of a woman's nude body from slightly below her belly button to just under the curvatures of her breasts. Droplets of glistening water rested on her skin like rainwater on a well-waxed car. I wouldn't have been surprised if the floor beneath was wet. "I believe he keeps a key behind the picture that mechanically releases the door's locks."

"Nice picture," I said.

"Raydel just adores that picture. It would be the first thing he'd grab if the house were in flames."

"I'd grab you, Sophia," I said. Kathleen rolled her eyes.

She tilted her head. "You are so sweet."

"But I don't see a keyhole," I said with a casual shrug of my shoulders and hoped I had not overplayed my curiosity.

"It's behind the picture as well." If she questioned our interest for anything more than conversational banter, I could not tell.

"Well, his secret's safe with us," Kittredge said, staring at the picture.

"A woman's body holds the key," I said.

"Yes," Sophia said, "I like that."

"Do you do a lot of entertaining? Your house is so elegant and comfortable," Kathleen asked. She must have sensed that we'd spent enough time on the safe room. I was going to drop it myself, already finding out more than I anticipated.

"Mostly family and Raydel's business associates, but I do one big splash a year. I host an annual Christmas party to raise funds for families in need. This past year we raised $68,000 that we dispersed to local churches. It works so well that way. I mean, we really don't know who warrants the assistance, but the churches do. I want to raise a hundred this year." She turned to Kathleen. "Please tell me you'll come."

"We'd be delighted to."

"Count me in as well," Kittredge said with manufactured enthusiasm and apparently missing the veiled jab at his political dogma. "I wasn't able to make it last year, but I'll try to clear my schedule." Already hedging.

"Are the gifts from the church, or do they just procure and facilitate who gets what?" I asked.

We had stopped at the second-floor foyer overlooking the great room below. The band was on break and I heard Sergio Mendes and Brasil '66's rendition of "The Fool on the Hill" float through the house courtesy, according to our tour guide, of forty-eight Bose speakers strategically installed throughout the rooms and grounds. "He insisted that they be wired with the thickest wires for optimum sound. Outside of his office, it was the only real intense interest Raydel had in the house," she had told us earlier. Sophia rested her hand on the dark wood banister and faced the three of us.

"No, Jake, the gifts are not from the churches. They tell the recipients that the gifts are from anonymous donors. But to say they 'just procure' hardly does their effort justice. The various churches know far better than we do who is the most needy, the most deserving. Their responsibility is to identify the needy and purchase the clothing, food, toys, and, in some cases, disperse direct financial aid."

"Very impressive, Sophia," I said. "I hope you reach your anonymous hundred thousand."

"We will."

"Anyone ever complain about being anonymous?" I asked.

"There is no choice," Sophia Escobar said.

Our foursome dissolved as Sophia excused herself and waltzed away. Kittredge was mobbed by a legion of tuxedos at the bottom of the steps eager to touch his political robe. Kathleen and I indulged ourselves at the buffet of Florida lobster, grilled mahimahi, oysters on the half shell, and crab cakes. A lady in a pale green dress instructed a catering employee in a white uniform where to find matches in the kitchen. Our plates full, we moved our feast to under a vibrant picture, at least three feet by four, of a tropical house with open walls that expanded to water and then took your eyes to a psychedelic burnt orange sunset. The picture seemed to generate its own light. Sophia had explained earlier that the picture was actually pressed onto thin aluminum and she had purchased it at a gallery in Key West. I recalled PC mentioning it and admired his power of observation. And his taste.

I took a bite of lobster. The Florida lobster is also known as spiny lobster or rock lobster. It was fresh, which was interesting as it was out of season. I fumbled for my phone.

"Who do you need to call at this time?" Kathleen asked.

"I'm sending a text to Garrett."

I texted Garrett:

picture of es, Mendis, hen, all thanking bernie, who bernie?

Kathleen said, "Sophia's very nice. She does a lot of good with her Christmas fund-raiser."

"She could do a hell of a lot more if she weren't so damn picky about crown molding."

"That's her choice. She doesn't have to do anything at all, you know."

I did know and I didn't care. I wanted to locate Escobar again. "I'm going to leave you now," I said and stuffed a piece of toasted, buttered Cuban bread smeared with tapenade into my mouth. I followed it with a sip of Maker's Mark and wondered if I had crossed into heaven, but I didn't see a dozen virgins descending the stairs and moaning my name.

"Fine, just drop me. I'm sure I'll find other suitable men to pay attention to me."

"I had no idea that you had an interest in suitable men."

"I might tire of your boorish behavior."

"I might tire of your long legs. Is that boorish enough for you?"

"I'm going to walk into the jungle and mingle some more," she said as she looked at the picture and mocked indifference to me.

"I'm going to kick up the waters. If you meet any suitable men, tell them to get a life. If I see any, I'll send them your way."

I turned and went back outside to the pool where the short, blond-haired bartender was still parked. This time, instead of seeking Escobar, I wanted him to come to me. I received a fresh drink from blondie, who informed me that she was a patient girl. I decided that she was really quite handsome, but maybe a little afraid of that look. I sequestered myself on the far corner of the patio. A five-foot-square chessboard was laid into the paver bricks. Its polished pieces reflected the flickering light of the torches and stood resolute in their spaces waiting for someone to engage them in one of the few games in the world void of luck or chance.

I didn't wait long.

"Did you enjoy the tour, Mr. Travis?"

I rotated slowly as if I didn't give a damn, which on any given day sums up my attitude toward a lot of things.

"Where are the rare rugs?" I asked. It seemed to catch him momentarily off guard.

"Why do you ask?" he said with wariness in his voice.

"I assumed a man who imported rugs would have a great collection himself."

Escobar flashed a relieved smile and nod as if he was finally on board. "You know what they say about a cobbler's son. I'm afraid that it's hard to keep things that I can pass on for such a substantial profit. Tell me, Mr. Travis, do you keep many of your Raggedy Ann dolls?"

"Asia Annie."

"Do you?"

"No, I do not. But decorating one's home with children's items is hardly the same as laying a rare Persian rug on the floor. Nonetheless, I would concur with your business instincts. It would be terribly difficult to pass up the quick profit. Nothing beats making money, real money, over a short spurt of time. The problem is the damn taxes, isn't it? I mean it's one thing to get a strike, but to turn around and forfeit thirty-five percent to Uncle Sam takes the wind right out of the sails."

Escobar didn't say anything, as if he were deciding who I was, what I knew, and where I was headed.

"Mr. Travis, we all must pay our fair share."

"How fast does she go?"

"Excuse me?"

"Your untitled forty-foot Intrepid with four outboards and a cuddy. My guess is north of sixty-five."

The body builder young man with the ponytail and the nose I wanted to eat planted himself next to Escobar.

"Elvis, when are you going to put the letters on her hull?" Escobar asked without taking his eyes off mine.

"Just got the registration back. I'll get it done in the next few days," Elvis said while he looked at me.

"I noticed the pictures in your study, those are some gorgeous fish you caught, but they were all shallow water pictures. One hardly needs 1,400 horsepower for permit. I imagine your boat can outrun about anybody, maybe even the IRS, that's assuming the IRS would be nipping at your tail, wouldn't you agree, Mr. Escobar?" I considered asking about Bernie, but if Bernie was a lead, I didn't want to show my hand. I doubted that my innocent inquiry to Sophia would circle back to him.

We engaged in a good four-second staring match that he lost. He started to shift his weight but caught himself. "You like games, don't you, Mr. Travis? Have you ever played chess?" He nodded at the chess pieces that stood frozen on a hot night.

"I've played a game or two, but I can never keep straight the opening positions of the knight and bishop."

"The knight belongs by his castle, or rook. A schoolboy's simple method of memory."

"I'll have to remember that."

"What's your opening move, Mr. Travis?"

"A knight out, I guess. At least it sounds like a good time."

He eyed me for a moment. "The typical move is pawn to king four."

"Mr. Escobar, have you accomplished anything in your life through typical means?"

He leaned over and pushed the white king pawn two spaces forward to d4. "My father taught me to play. He said every man should be able to hold his own on a chessboard. He always impressed upon me that avoiding mistakes is in itself a brilliant and winning strategy. Why are you here, Mr. Travis?"

I sauntered over to the black side of the battlefield and advanced the knight to Nf6.

"In my experience," I said, "it is the closing moves that matter the most, yet all the attention is paid to the opening. We know the initial positions of thirty-two pieces, and as the game progresses, the possibilities exponentially increase to the point where we cannot see or plan."

"You didn't answer my question," Escobar said.

"What's the boat for?"

"I like speed."

"And I'm here to support Congressman Kittredge," I said.

"You don't impress me as one of the congressman's typical constituents."

"And you don't impress me as someone who takes thrill rides on the water."

"Perhaps I am atypical."

"And I'm not the stereotypic supporter of Michael Kittredge, but his stance on overseas labor laws endears me to his success." I thought of another question I wished I had texted to Garrett and realized I should have thought of it when I first spotted the 1,400 horses on an untitled boat.

"I don't think you have the slightest interest in the World Fair Business Bill," Escobar said.

"Then you are gravely mistaken. I have a great interest in helping Congressman Kittredge pass his bill and keep his seat. After all, Mr. Escobar, what good is an ex-congressman to anyone? I'm disappointed that Walter Mendis couldn't make it."

What if I did tell him I was there to collect the letter? What would his move be? He would deny any knowledge. My move after that? I would have blown my intention. Not that it means that much, but I saw no clear strategic advantage by proclaiming that I was there to collect the letter. I'd save that move for later.

Escobar advanced a pawn to c4. I countered with a pawn to e6 before his hand left his warrior. Speed is everything.

"It's still your move," I said.

"I'll be sure to tell him you came by."

"I understand that you and he owned some land a few years back that became a major interchange."

"It's good to know you read the papers."

"I assume the real story never sees print."

"I wouldn't know about that."

I said, "It's still your move. I suggest g3. I'll follow with d5 and we'll be on our way to Tartakower's Catalan opening that he originated in Barcelona in 1929. I have always admired chess master Savielly Grigorievitch Tartakower."

In my entrance exam for the army, they had me up to thirty-five simultaneous blindfolded matches, some sort of record they were all jacked about. I won them all.

Escobar's face went dead. "I am not familiar with him," he said in a deliberate tone.

"I'm surprised. He and your father had much in common."

"What does Tartakower have in common with my father?"

"He shared your father's aversion to mistakes, Mr. Escobar. Tartakower said 'the winner of the game is the player who makes the next-to-last mistake.'"

Escobar paused and then said, "Elvis, perhaps you would like to continue playing with our new friend. I'm afraid that I've been ignoring my other guests far too long." Escobar's eyes never left me. Elvis, like a chess piece awaiting its orders, had not moved since he joined us. Chess time was over.

"I'd be happy to, Mr. Escobar," Elvis said.

I'd been thinking of my next move, and it wasn't on the chessboard.

"I'm afraid I must be going myself." I turned to Elvis. "Perhaps we can play later."

He laid some silence down before he spoke. "I'd enjoy that."

"Thank you for the evening," I said and walked three steps before I did a Colombo. "What got you involved with Walter Mendis?"

"Pardon me?"

"The photograph behind your desk of you, Henriques, and Mendis smoking cigars. How did you get involved with Mendis?"

Escobar cut me a cold stare. "Goodnight, Mr. Travis. I am sure you can find your way out."

I wanted to tell him that I certainly had no problem getting in, but decided to let him have the last words. I left Escobar and Elvis behind me and placed my drink on the teak bar.

"I'm still here," the blonde said.

"Have a pleasant evening," I said and kept churning.

I called Garrett in the car, provided a capsule review of the evening, and told him that Bernie might have worked for Escobar at one point. I asked him to petition the colonel for satellite photographs of Escobar's place over a period of time, which is what I wished I had thought of doing earlier. I wanted to see if we could detect specific days, or nights, when his Intrepid was gone. I also told him to have Mary Evelyn look into the land deal going down south of the Skyway Bridge and see if Escobar and company had a hand in that as well.

Maybe he did have enough cash to settle his IRS bill and he figured he didn't need to; his quid pro quo being that important to the US government. Auctioning off cheaply secured parcels of land to Cracker Barrel and Exxon with a guy like Walter Mendis in the picture reeked of corruption. There had to be dirt, and if I got enough dirt on Escobar, I would blackmail him into surrendering the letter. Plan A.

Plan B was to grab Escobar, choke him to the edge of death, demand the letter back, and hope he never pressed charges. If I got short of time, I could always fall back on that, but it carried its own drawbacks. Escobar might scream attempted murder. Maximum time in an orange jumpsuit: life.

Not that anyone would find me. But what's the point of that?

I couldn't remember the last time plan A, or B through Z for that matter, was worth a damn. It always came down to who made the next-to-last mistake.

"You're going where?" Kathleen asked when I swung into her driveway.

"A titty joint. Would you care to join me?"

"If only you asked me earlier. What are you looking for?"

"Who."

"Fine, who?"

"Bernie."

"Who?"

"I just told you."

"Oh, that's right. The man you inquired about in Escobar's study."

"You'd like to reconsider?"

"You know, I think I'll call it a night. Bear in mind, though, that in this country you can't legally buy either one."

"What?"

"Tits or joints."

CHAPTER 11

I ripped off my bow tie and stuck it in my inside jacket pocket as I strode through the heavy wood door of the Welcome In. I claimed a burgundy barstool. I didn't think they made them anymore, but this one was in good shape and across from the bartender's sink. A brunette landed beside me before my elbows found the counter.

"I'd like to welcome you in," she said. "I'm April."

"Nice job on the flowers, but I'm waiting for May."

"You've got to go through me first," she said in a rehearsed tone that didn't quite mask her weariness.

"And if I'm looking for December?"

"Then you have a pleasurable and exhausting night ahead of you."

"What do they serve around here besides the Gregorian calendar?" I asked.

"Pretty much whatever you like. Are you heat?"

"No." I laid a fifty on the counter between us. "I'm really just looking for an old friend who might have worked here or passed through. Bernie."

She had green eyes and a low-cut, thin-strapped black blouse with tight dark jeans. Her arms looked like she was only a few days out of Dachau and were in stark contrast to her melon breasts. She had Botox lips, and for some reason all I could think of was what the hell she would look like in thirty

110

years. She wore no jewelry, just skin. She had the cutest little pug nose I'd seen in a long time and I wondered why she just didn't go with that.

"What happened? Did Bernie stand you up at the opera tonight, or do you always tool around town in a tux?"

"It's complicated."

"Let's talk on a couch. I can help you forget Bernie."

"How long've you been here?"

"I've been waiting for you for years."

The bartender, a pumpkin face with a crooked bow tie, appeared on the other side of the counter. "What can I do for you?"

"Stella." I thought it went well with April. I turned back to her. "This music play all the time?" It was the same playlist that was at Escobar's house.

"I know. Can you believe it? Something about what the owner likes. I think they could update it, you know, like every forty years or so. But a lot of guys dig it. How about you?"

"I'm curious whether Bernie worked here once. I'd like to talk to him about a mutual friend."

April hesitated, landed a cold stare, and left me with a beer and a fifty on the counter. I reached for my wallet and laid a Franklin on top of Grant and took my time sipping the cold draft. I was banking on her spreading my interest around and someone seeing the growing pot. The bartender circled back and I asked him how long he had worked there. He replied that he just started and the guy before him lasted only five months. It was looking like a dead end. The land deal was over two years ago, not including lead time.

She slid onto the stool next to me and in one motion cleaned my stash off the counter.

"A man in a tuxedo who wants to know about Bernie," she said.

"You're not May, are you?" I asked.

"May?"

"Or Amy. I talked with April earlier."

"I see. And Amy?"

"Rearranged May."

She gave a small laugh and tossed her blonde hair in a natural and unpretentious manner. "I like that. No, I'm Lisa. Let's go get a cup of coffee, scrabble boy."

"Why?"

"Because if you want to know about Bernie, it'll cost you a cup of coffee."

"What about the bills you just swiped?"

Lisa vacated her stool faster than she had filled it and headed toward the door. I scrambled.

We took a booth in a bright diner two doors down from the Welcome In. Someone had dropped money in a jukebox to hear Lana Del Rey bemoan her sad summer. The linoleum floor was antique yellow and my seat had a strip of gray duct tape, its corners turned up and sticky. The joint needed a facelift.

Not Lisa. She had Grand Canyon dimples and a small, tight mouth. She was a little older than me and coming up on the south side of forty if you stared. I did. Not making forty look good, just good-looking. She was a showroom floor model, and I wondered why the hell no one had driven her home. A waitress wearing glasses and with a blue-and-white-checkered apron around her waist brought her coffee. I shifted my weight to avoid the sticky tape. I told four-eyes that I was fine.

"Why are you tooling around in a tux at night looking for Bernie?"

"I miss him."

"Try again."

"I have some questions for him concerning Raydel Escobar."
I had no idea whether Lisa knew whom she worked for or not.

"You know Raydel?"

"We go way back."

"You tell him that he better start paying more attention to
us, or I'm going to cozy up to his wife."

Guess they knew each other.

"Do you know Bernie?" I asked.

"Do you know pleasure?"

"I do."

"Then why are we here talking business?"

"I followed you."

"You did, didn't you? Now it's your turn to lead. Where to
next?"

"I like it right here."

"Why?"

"One fifty for a business conversation."

"I had no idea it was your money."

"It's not anymore."

"So you think you're entitled?"

"No."

"Then what?"

"I'm just hoping you'll help me out."

She didn't say anything but glanced out the window. Her
hands were placed on the Formica tabletop a foot on either side
of her white coffee mug. They hadn't moved since we sat down.
A red two-door car with a dented rear quarter panel passed
on the other side of the glass and momentarily disrupted our
reflections.

"He worked here a few years ago." She turned back to me.
"He was here when I started and had been around before that.
Nice guy. Not your type."

"My type?"

She leaned in slightly across the table. "What's your name, scrabble boy?"

"Jake. Jake Travis."

"Jake," she played with it as if were her first attempt at a foreign word. "Jake Travis. You have no idea how well I know you. You can't even imagine how many Jakes have looked at me in my life."

"You can't even imagine how lucky those men are, how they may carry that glance of you, your smile, those ridiculous dimples, around in their heads for years. They take it to their graves, baby. And if you think it's all about sex, then you're just another dumb dame."

She started to smile but retreated as her actions caught up with my words. "Thank you. That was nice, I think. Are you always in third gear?"

"Never saw the point of the first two."

"You know you're a member of a highly disturbed gender."

"We're all pretty much cut from the same cloth."

"I'm not so sure about that. Did you ever meet Bernie?"

"No."

"Because if you had, you would know that Bernie never looked at me the way you're looking at me."

"Bernie was gay?"

"Is, unless he met an untimely demise because, honey, they rarely go the other way."

"Where does he work now?"

Lisa didn't answer, but glanced out the window at nothing except her reflection. We sat in silence. She came back.

"Would you like to have lunch tomorrow?" she asked. She tossed it out like a strand of spaghetti to see if it stuck to the wall.

"I can't. I really just need to talk to Bernie." I wished I had hesitated in my answer and at least given her that. "Listen, I'm not some dangerous guy. I don't cause problems. I just need to talk to him." Either Lisa was game or she wasn't. I started to reach for my wallet.

"Stop it. He works at Simeons. Downtown. Probably there right now. They go to four a.m."

"Why did he leave the Welcome In?"

"I don't know, scrabble. Go ask him. That's what you're dying to do."

I got up to leave. "Thank you. I really do just want to talk to him about a mutual friend."

"Perhaps. But like I said, I know men, and I don't believe one bit the lie you just told me."

"What was that?"

"That you're not a dangerous guy."

I left Lisa sitting alone in the booth facing the wall with her back to the door and her hands still quietly resting on the table. BK, Before Kathleen, I'd double back into her life. But no more.

Simeons was thumping to the most obnoxious, obscene beat to ever befall the civilized western world when I hit the door and took the only empty seat at the bar. The lights were dim, the crowd ramped, and I was beat. It had been a long day. It was a new day.

"Maker's Mark, splash of Coke on the rocks," I said to the bartender with a handlebar moustache. I'd decided to return to the night's original partner. "And ice water with a lemon."

"Night starting to catch up with you?" he said.

"More like the years." He smiled as if he cared, but I knew it was just his job. He placed the aged bourbon on the bar. I placed a fifty next to it.

"I was at the Welcome In looking for an old friend, Bernie. He used to tend bar there years ago and I heard he moved over—"

"Bernie!" He yelled at a guy toward the other end. He came down from the other end of the bar, squeezed behind another bartender shaking a drink, and settled in across from me. Bernie wore a black shirt unbuttoned at the top and a cream white tie that had taken one too many spills. "This stud wants to talk to you. Said he knew you at Welcome In."

Bernie said, "I don't recall ever meeting you."

"We haven't had the pleasure," I said. "I need to talk to you about Raydel Escobar and the interchange deal he was involved in years—"

"You a cop?"

"No, I'm just—"

"What the hell do you want with me?"

It was hard to hear and I didn't want to be shouting at him. I was getting more tired by the second and wanted to wrap up whatever Bernie's involvement was. For all I knew he was a dead end, and I was giving up precious time when Kathleen's head could be sleeping on my chest. Pure oxygen. There are not enough nights in the universe to saturate my appetite for that. I leaned in across the bar.

"Bernie, I work for the United States government, and I need to talk to you about your relationship with Raydel Escobar. Right now. Outside." I palmed my Florida PI license and withdrew it just as fast. For all he knew I just found it at the bottom of a Cracker Jack box. I stood up. Bernie hesitated.

"Back room. Follow me," he said and walked away before my feet hit the floor.

Bernie must have assumed that I came in with far more knowledge than I possessed, because he ran his mouth before the door closed behind me. He confessed like a pious schoolboy who got caught spying in the girl's locker room and just knew hell was waiting unless he came clean. He spilled the whole story and insisted that if he knew Escobar would use the picture as blackmail that he never would have consented.

"What picture?" I asked. He went a deeper shade of red, and a thin stream of sweat rolled down his forehead. He realized too late that he'd given me something that I didn't even know to inquire about.

"What picture, Bernie?" I repeated and took a step toward him.

He told me and then rattled some more, trying to extradite himself from the situation, but I wasn't listening. I had leverage on Escobar. I would hold Kittredge hostage and trade his relationship for the letter. I checked my watch—279 minutes to sunrise. Kittredge said he was catching a government plane back to DC and that he had a meeting in his office the following morning, or in about seven hours. I would wait for him in his office. Like a wrecking ball, I would tear it all down until the dust settled and the letter floated free. I checked flights on my phone, secured a "we got one seat left for your late planning, sorry piece of ass, so we're going to charge you the nonrefundable GDP of Kenya to fly with us" ticket, and headed to the airport.

I landed a middle seat between an aisle-seat businessman who pounded his keyboard for life's answers and a fat guy squeezed against the window who made the near fatal mistake of attempting to talk to me while on a plane. Just as I had gone for a run a day ago while Kathleen slept, my random seatmates were showered, energized, dressed for work, and already in tomorrow, while I dragged the previous night like a plow through a dry field.

Fat guy finally sensed my latent hostility and stuck music in his ears, although he kept adjusting his earplugs until I almost shoved them in myself. Sleep batted me around like a mouse in a cat's paws. I finally gave up and jotted on a napkin notes and diagrams on how it all could play out. When the flight attendant came down the aisle for the last time wearing gloves and holding the little white trash bag, I tossed it.

I stashed the peanuts.

CHAPTER 12

Donald Barnsworth sat erect as if an oak tree grew up his spine. I assumed that was his name as the massive desk that he sat behind held a small plaque with those two words on it. Donny had cherry cheeks that would make a seventh-grade girl jealous and a zit high on his forehead that looked like he spent an hour trying to conceal.

For the record, there is a greater chance of me wearing a nametag around my neck than sitting behind a desk with my name on a plaque.

"And you are who?" he asked when my feet were planted firmly in front of the desk. It was 8:39 a.m. and I was standing in Congressman Kittredge's anteroom sipping a Starbuck's dark verona. The ceiling was close to fourteen feet, and large windows gave the space natural light.   I wondered what blue-blooded family tree Donald Barnsworth had dropped from.

"Jake Travis and—"

"You do not have an appointment with the congressman," Barnsworth announced. He hadn't blinked since I entered the room, nor did he glance at a computer screen before his statement.

"That is correct. I do not have an appointment with the congressman, but he has one with me. We chatted at a party last night and he has a meeting this morning at nine regarding the World Fairness Bill. I need to review some items he has concerns with."

"Yes. But the congressman was in Florida until late last evening. You saw him last night?"

"I did. Not even time to change clothes."

"But I don't see, Mr. Travis, how you could beat him back. He took—"

"Donald, right?" I said and leaned over his desk, slipping into his personal space. "Do I—"

"It's Mr. Barnsworth."

"What grade are you in?" Little shit.

Barnsworth shifted in his seat, and his hand was halfway up to his zit before he called it back.

"If you don't have an appointment with the congressman—"

"Do I look like someone who got a good eight hours last night?" You interrupt me, I interrupt you. "The congressman's office?" I asked and nodded toward a tall door before he had the chance to answer.

"Yes, but—"

"I'll take a seat. He'll be glad I'm here. Trust me, Donald."

I sat, stuck the *Post* in front of my face, and hoped that Donny ended up with a girl who was a wildcat in bed. He needed to loosen up. There was an article about a family of seven in the Bronx who were driving to their grandchild's confirmation when their car flipped off a bridge. Grandma had just come up from Puerto Rico for the big event. They died with their best clothes on. I flipped the page and saw that evidently there were still issues to be resolved in the Middle East. Who knew? I sipped my coffee, found the weather page, scanned temperature ranges of foreign cities, and noted the time of sunrise and sunset for the cradle of democracy. Something wasn't right.

Kittredge burst through the door at 8:52. He verbally assaulted my new friend Donny with a litany of questions and abruptly stopped when he spotted me.

"Mr. Travis?" He pronounced each of the four syllables progressively higher like a primitive four-note tetratonic scale.

"Congressman," I said as I stood and extended my hand. He took it out of habit. Politicians. If a raghead wrapped in dynamite stuck out his hand, a politician would take it and ask questions later. His eyes narrowed in confusion.

"What a pleasant surprise. You didn't mention last night that you'd be in Washington, did you?"

"No, I did not. May I have just five minutes of your time before your meeting on the World Fairness Bill?"

"Well, I've got a staff meeting before and——"

"And I've got a plane to catch and need to scoot out of here real fast. Five minutes, Congressman. I think you'll find it well worth your time." I looked at him hard as we stood toe to toe. His office phone rang and Barnsworth picked up the call. Time to bring it home. I touched him lightly on the shoulder. It's a new move I copied from Sophia. I'm always trying to improve my craft. "Let's go to your office and talk about Raydel Escobar, shall we?" He hesitated a second and then showed me his back.

I followed him into his office. Kittredge dropped his briefcase and settled in the black chair behind his desk. On the bookshelf off to his right was a picture of him and his wife and two young girls standing with their backs to water, feet in the sand, and smiling faces attacking the camera. More pictures of golf foursomes. Everybody smiling. A signed football rested on the bookcase behind him. He was home now, in his comfort zone and surrounded by his power.

And in the final minutes of life as it used to be.

"Now, Mr. Travis, what can I do for you and Raydel?"

"I want you to convince Walter Mendis to buy out Escobar's business, whatever that business may be."

Kittredge viewed me with a blank expression. He took the cautious approach and his words came out thick and measured.

"I'm afraid I don't understand."

"Are you aware of Escobar's due notice with the IRS?"

He hesitated and then spit it out rapidly. "I don't know what you are referring to."

"I think you do." I'd been connecting the dots to give myself some direction.

"I'm here to broker a deal: Raydel Escobar has a document that the US government wants back. He gives me the document. Mendis, your big donor, advances him a little cash and takes over his business. The IRS liquidates Escobar's estate and recovers the money he owes. Escobar avoids jail time. Maybe Escobar has the cash, or some combination of the aforementioned. I don't really care." What I omitted was my belief that Mendis, once he felt the heat, might pressure Escobar with any means at his disposal.

I assumed that Walter Mendis had all means at his disposal.

Kittredge took measure of me. "You don't import and export?" It started as a question, but by the time he finished, it was a statement. My silence confirmed his answer.

He leaned across his desk, shoved some papers aside, and said, "Who the hell are you?"

"I represent interested parties. The same fine organization you work for."

"What would possess me to pressure Walter Mendis or Raydel Escobar? I have no desire, no reason, to help you by stepping on my supporters. I don't care who you represent."

I didn't know if it was necessary at that point to take it downtown, but I did. I retrieved my cell phone, brought up the picture, and passed the image over the desk with the same gentle hand I had just touched him with. Kittredge grabbed it without taking his eyes off me.

Bernie had sent me the picture after I promised him that I would keep him out of it. That's not entirely true. I told him he was an accomplice to blackmailing a congressman and that if he shared, I wouldn't press charges. He asked to see my identification again. I told him I would flush his head down the shit bowl if he didn't share.

He didn't take that chance.

Kittredge was tougher than I thought; I'll give him credit for that. He viewed it without expression and calmly handed it back to me. His eyes were cast down at his desk, but when my hand touched the phone he glanced up at me and held my stare with a sadness and contempt that reminded me that this blackmail business was a nasty game. Little late for that. He rose, turned his back to me, and faced the window. The sun had climbed high enough to start its invasion of the room. I let him have some time.

"Who are you?" he asked in a variation of his first pass.

"I'm you, Congressman. The same round table. We are just different layers within layers. My layer doesn't officially exist, but I was the one waiting for you this morning."

"Rules?"

"No, sir. There are none."

"You're fucking despicable."

"If it makes you feel better."

We observed a moment of silence, and then Barnsworth's even voice came over the intercom inquiring if he was ready for the staff meeting and jerked him back to his other world. He replied tartly that he would get back to him and returned to the solace of his window. I could see his pain in his reflection on the windowpane. His face, like his life, was distorted by the white grids that tried to make simple and structured someone who wallowed in complexity. He spoke again while I observed him in the window.

"What do I have to do to keep what you see? How, and why, should I trust you?"

Maybe if he kept his back to me long enough he would turn, and I, like the bad dream I was, would be gone. Maybe yesterday's world was still waiting for him if he just kept his back to me.

"You have no choice but to trust me, and if everyone follows their best interest, we should all be fine. I have no desire to harm you in any manner or disrupt what you have."

His shoulder shuddered. He turned. "You have no desire to harm. Did you really say that? Where do they even get people like you?"

For a moment, neither of us spoke. While on the plane I had calculated the sunrise equation based on how many miles north DC was of my home. When I looked it up in the *Post*, I was off by four minutes. I thought one of those might be due to rounding, but was vexed by my error. I thought that I should be calculating the dilemma I placed Kittredge in, but at that moment, the four-minute miscalculation disturbed me more.

Kittredge continued, "How do you live with yourself? You think I'd be in this squeeze if I had followed my best interest? You think Escobar will go without spilling it all? Everyone's got that picture. What document are you even talking about?"

"That's not your concern."

"The hell it isn't."

I let his anger dissipate from the room and then said, "This is what is going to happen."

I laid out the plan, marched out of his office, and caught a flight back to Florida. I remember the takeoff and landing. In between Santa served me drinks at a Christmas party and herds of ruffian children darted around. They were all mad at me and I had no clue why, and Kathleen kept bouncing off walls and asking who she was. Then I noticed that Santa only had one arm and thought no wonder the jolly guy's so busy. There was someone else with only one arm, but I couldn't recall who or where, and it bothered the hell out of me, and I hoped that whoever he was would forgive me for only remembering what he didn't have.

CHAPTER 13

"Think it will work?" Garrett asked over the phone.

"My other option is to blow up the bay and strangle Escobar until he coughs up the letter."

"That a problem?"

"We'll float this first."

I was on my screened porch nursing a margarita: a shot of Camarena Reposado Tequila, Grand Marnier, and lime juice mixed with freshly squeezed limes to taste. Add three large ice cubes and gently swirl. Drink. Repeat.

It was late afternoon and Kathleen and I planned to swing by her condo before dinner, but I first wanted to cue Garrett in on the plan. A hunter green sailboat towing a white dinghy passed at the end of my dock heading in from the Gulf. I heard the canvas flapping against the wind.

"What makes you think Kittredge will call Mendis?" Garrett asked.

"I was going to impress upon him how Mendis could turn up the heat on Escobar more than anyone else, but it wasn't necessary. Kittredge practically volunteered to call Mendis."

"So Kittredge tells Mendis that Escobar is blackmailing Uncle Sam, and unless he backs down, the government will have a sudden and intense interest in Walter Mendis's finances. Mendis tells Escobar to liquidate, pay Uncle, and cough up the letter. And why does Escobar go along with this?"

"I'm betting that Escobar fears Walter Mendis more than the IRS. Mendis could put a bullet in Escobar."

"We'd still have to find the letter."

"I realize that."

"You think Mendis knows that Escobar owes taxes?" Garrett asked.

"Most likely. But I doubt Escobar divulged the bargaining power that he feels the letter affords him. If Mendis knew Escobar was that desperate he just might eliminate him. Mendis can't afford to have Escobar sing about the interchange deal or threaten his relationship with a powerful congressman. We need Walter Mendis to know that his days as an uncontested man are dependent upon Escobar handing over the letter. We stand aside and let the chips fall."

"When does Kittredge talk to Mendis?"

I glanced at my watch. "About four hours ago."

"And you haven't heard anything yet?"

"No, but it's only——"

"A busted plan," Garrett said. I hate it when he does that.

I crossed the three bridges to Kathleen's house.

I brought along my margarita. Florida has a little-known law that states if you live on an island, you are permitted to have open containers and drinks in your vehicle if you do not travel farther than three miles from any beach. It's the "For God's Sake They Live on an Island" law.

She said to give her five minutes. I waited for her under the covered part of her veranda that overlooked her pool and the channel. My island was to the right and the open waters of the Gulf to the left. It was hell of a spot. I couldn't believe she was chucking it for a downtown condo, but a new name necessitated a new home. I was nervous about her glacier pace of moving, but hadn't mentioned it to her for fear of escalating her anxiety. A man and woman each in their own kayak came by close to the shore. They were battling to make miniscule headway against the running tide and chose the thickest part of the day in which to engage in their struggle. I wondered if they were novices or had embarked on their challenging trip with foreknowledge and intent. I wondered, as I often do, why anyone would desire to exercise during the part of the day that was reserved for margaritas. Twenty-nine minutes later I sensed her behind me.

It had been as fine a use of twenty-nine minutes that one could imagine.

"Stunning. Now I need to buy an expensive cab and sit up straight all night. You know how hard that is for me." I went to her and gave her a light kiss on the lips.

"Thank you. I felt like dressing up tonight. Before dinner, though, I'd like to drop by the condo and show you color samples for my walls."

"Color and I don't get along."

"I know. That's why Sophia and I spent the day together."

"But you're not going to dinner with her."

"You have other attributes that compensate for your lack of color coordination."

"Let's hear the top ten."

"That's a big number."

"Top five?"

"Bring it down, babe."

"Do you have *any* interest in me outside of the physical?" Not that I had an issue with a negative reply.

"Yes."

"And?"

"You're buying me dinner tonight."

"Food and passion—grunt evolutionary needs, is that right?"

"Mainly passion."

"I've been told that mine are extreme."

"Hmm." She let it out as a lyrical tone that would make Handel jealous.

"Don't worry. I'll let reason hold the rein," I said.

"What a shame."

"It is."

"Franklin, right?"

I said, "'If passion drives you, let reason hold the reins.'"

She considered that and said, "If I had to choose, I would run with the stars and surrender to extreme passion instead of holding onto the reins."

I stepped in closer. Kathleen smiled, reached out, and touched me lightly on my left shoulder. Little stars started pinging around in my head.

Member of a highly disturbed gender.

I brought her body up tight to mine and held her, felt her breathing, her ribs, all of her pressed hard against me. I placed my mouth over hers but did not kiss her. Instead as she breathed out, I closed my eyes and breathed in. I pulled away.

"Where would you like to go?" I asked.

"You lead."

I took her hand and we walked out the door.

We stood in her unfurnished condo in downtown St. Pete, twelve floors above Tampa Bay. Our backs were to the water as we appraised her new kitchen and great room that was not great but magnificent.

"Sophia and I spent hours with different combinations of backsplash tiles. What do you think of the finalists?"

Three patterns were taped to the wall behind her granite counter tops and she had just sprayed them with water. If I had heard the name "Sophia" once that night, I had heard it a dozen times.

"The one in the middle."

"Really, because I—oh no, you're not getting away with that. Try. Really look at them. You can do it."

I turned and looked at the water down below and out far. I lived on the water; Kathleen was going to live above the water. They are different ways of experiencing the same vastness. I liked mine better. I could smell it, taste it, bear witness to wildlife's relentless struggle to survive, feel the sea breeze sweep in off the water and experience the vast canopy of stars as they emerge at night to blanket the placid surface. Up there, it was all too distant, too removed. As if none of it really mattered. Perhaps I lived on the water while my mind remained twelve floors up. It hit me as a serious thought. I stockpiled it for another day.

"Jake?"

I turned around to her and transitioned my thoughts. "Where are your books going?"

"Oh, Sophia had a great idea for the shelves in the library. Come look."

I followed her as she glided over the smooth hardwood floor and entered the room she was going to finish as a library. It was vacant. Thick crown molding wrapped the twelve-foot ceiling, and the ten-foot window was partitioned with stained grids. The window faced east. Morning sun. A perfect perch.

Kathleen said, "This was labeled a 'media room.' You know, stuffed cheap chairs facing a blank seventy-inch screen. I just don't get that. I'm putting bookcases on the two sides. I was going to use a ladder, like you see in old libraries, but Sophia insisted they look trite and eat up too much floor space. Instead, she suggested I top the shelves at six feet as that allows for pictures to be hung above them. Isn't that good? I would have placed all sorts of dust-loving mementos on the top or tried to cram every book I own into the room. The pictures will be so much nicer and break it up. I'll rotate the books."

I closed the distance between us.

"What do you think?"

I didn't stop.

"Oh no," she said.

"What happened to 'oh yes'?"

"When was that?"

"The night under the hibiscus."

"What a lovely title."

"Now is different?"

"I've spent an hour getting all made up."

"Twenty-nine minutes, actually."

"I dropped some time on it before you arrived."

"And I've dropped the reins."

"I doubt we'll miss them."

"They are slippery at best, Ms. Rowe."

"Actually, it's doctor."

I hesitated. "Interesting. Literature, right? I thought you were just doing postgraduate work on the side." Our arms were wrapped around each other and our eyes were locked.

"I completed it all and decided to run out of books and into life."

"Nice. Are you running to or from?"

"No talking in the library."

Our tongues shed the cumbersome words and took flight in their own language—slow and moist and warm and searching. We never said another word but lay in the library with her body between the hard floor and me.

The one in the middle. I was right. That is the one I like.

We took a table at a pizza joint two blocks from her condo. Her hair was down, her shoes were tossed, and there was a can of beer in front of her. She had declined a glass. She attacked the pepperoni pie like there was no tomorrow.

A statistical probability for all of us.

We decided to forego the whole "I felt like dressing up" dinner plan when I mentioned pizza and beer. It seemed to fit the mood that the evening had acquired. She talked more about her day with Sophia and that disturbed me. When it was all nailed down, Sophia would likely be without a husband and a home and it would be you-know-whose fault. Maybe she didn't see that coming.

"You realize that Escobar has drawn the attention of the government and that he might lose much of what he has," I said while wondering why we ever eat anything other than pizza.

"He's a bad person?"

"I don't think bad like your ex-Chicago friends, but I wouldn't bet against it either. He owes money to the IRS and is liable to lose his home before it's all done."

She consumed pizza at a frantic pace and then said, "What will happen to Sophia?"

"I don't know."

"Don't care?"

I missed a beat.

"Don't even answer," she said.

"Why ask?"

"OK. Go."

It came out as "Oh-way, whoa" as she had stuffed another piece in her mouth.

I said, "Do you want the version with the disclaimer that I do care? I care for the bird that goes without food and the fish that gets swept into the air, and I certainly care a hell of a lot more about Sophia Escobar. But it's her web and a tenuous one at that—or do you want the one word answer at the end?"

"Spare me the soliloquy."

"No."

She put down her slice of pie and swiped a napkin across her mouth. It had gotten dark outside and two girls in summer dresses were at the counter discussing an app on their phone. Kathleen blew out her breath, made a fist with her right hand, and leaned forward. In a slow motion she brought her fist up under my left eye. When it touched my skin, she pushed in and rotated it back and forth as if she was trying to drill it into my face.

She relaxed into her chair and her fist metamorphosed back into her hand.

"Feel better?" I asked.

"Not bad," she said in a singsong voice. "Maybe you Neanderthals are on to something."

"It's still no."

"Any way you can make it easier for her?" she asked.

"I'll do what I can. Not a word, you know."

"I realize that."

"She'll need you more, later."

She didn't respond to that, and I got the feeling that she resented me telling her what she already knew about supporting a friend. Just a feeling—but I know I'm right. I didn't mention that with a little luck, my plan, once in motion, wouldn't involve me. No need to get her hopes, or mine, up. Things that are up often fall down.

Eventually Sophia would need to know. Kathleen could not carry the weight of my involvement and forever withhold that from her. That was a shadowy foundation for a friendship. I didn't know how deep their relationship would go, but when together, they were two happy girls.

We drove back to her house. As we went over the bridge to her island, I glanced out the side window to view the lights of my house from across the bay. It was in the shadow of the pink hotel that rose behind it against the black sky.

"You OK?" I asked when I pulled into her driveway.

"'OK,' I believe you once said, was for losers." She leaned in and gave me a kiss. "Take care of Sophia. She's a good person."

She was out of the truck before I had a chance to reply.

I looked at the digital clock on my dashboard. Kittredge, according to the plan he and I discussed—meaning he listened and I dictated—should have talked to Mendis long ago. Mendis squeezes Escobar and Escobar supplicates me to relieve him of the letter.

From twelve floors up it all looked nice and neat. But I knew down where the breeze unpredictably changed directions, and life fought to live and killed to see another day, nothing was ever nice and neat.

CHAPTER 14

Escobar

"Who did you go out with today?" Escobar asked Sophia. "Kathleen, the woman we met at Kittredge's bash the other night. She's delightful, and I feel as if I've known her my whole life. You should have a friend like that, Raydel."

"Men don't have friends, they have associates. Who the hell is that guy she was with?"

"Jake?"

"Yeah, him."

"She didn't talk about him much. We spent the day picking out tiles and colors for her condo. Absolutely breathtaking views. She's going to have a real library—it faces east, just incredible feng shui. Oh, and she's going to help me with the Christmas fund-raiser. We'll hit a hundred thousand. I know I can do it with her help." She took a strand of her hair and rolled it in her fingers.

They were enjoying early evening cocktails under the red umbrella, something they rarely did anymore, but Sophia had insisted. Escobar thought of Natalie and wondered how it could only have been two days ago that she was there. He wanted a cigar so bad he could feel spit foaming in his mouth.

"We should have them over some time for dinner," Sophia said and twisted her hair again with her fingers.

"Who?" Escobar took a sip of his Cuban Manhattan. His version was not much more than dark rum, dry vermouth, and ice.

"Try listening, Raydel, it's the latest thing. Kathleen and Jake. They're nice people and they live right here. I'm going to extend an invitation."

"Great idea, Sophia, see if they can do it soon." He wanted to get closer to Travis; the man was clearly threatening him and had knowledge of his IRS issues. He wondered if he was tied to the menacing phone call, almost had to be. What the hell, he thought, if he wants the letter, I'll tell him to bring seven million. Little harder to say "no" in person. Maybe that's what this is all about. Government-style negotiations.

"Really? It's OK? I'll see if tomorrow works."

Her face had brightened like the morning sun after a cloudy day when she replied. He hadn't seen that for a while and wondered if it was because of him. "Sure, tomorrow's fine," he said and tried to sound appreciative of her efforts, but he knew it came out flat.

"I'll give her a call. Let's go out to dinner tonight. I forgot how nice downtown is," Sophia said.

"Not tonight. Henriques and Mendis are coming over. Be here any minute."

"Why didn't you tell me? It's already getting late."

"Last-minute thing."

He saw the disappointment in her eyes, and for the briefest moment Escobar felt bad for his wife, but he had other issues. His headache had been growing all day, ever since Mendis called out of the blue and said he'd be dropping by that evening. No one from the east coast of Florida dropped by the west coast. It was easier to fly to London. Besides, Escobar knew that Walter Mendis didn't make house calls.

"Maybe some other time," he added. And then, because he needed to know what Travis wanted, he continued, "Don't forget about dinner with your new friend. Tomorrow should be fine. You always keep the house looking great, Sophia, let's just have them over here."

Sophia straightened and Escobar recalled when they first met. How he had fantasized about what it would be like to be greeted every day with her energy and positive disposition. Sophia simply never met a day that didn't deserve a smile. As he caught his wife's dark hair shine in the dying sun's rays that snuck under the edge of the umbrella, Raydel Escobar thought he'd take a thousand arrows before he caused her to shed one tear.

"I'll see if they're available. Why is Mendis coming over at this hour? Do you need anything from him?" She shifted her weight.

"He's in town tonight for business. I don't imagine he'll stay long. I told Olivia. I'm sure she'll have something prepared."

Sophia looked as if she was going to talk, but remained silent. Then she said, "She's been quiet the past couple of days. Were there any problems when I was gone?"

"Not that I recall."

"I just wondered. She seems so withdrawn. Elvis didn't say anything to her, did he?"

"He treats her fine. Maybe it's her grandkid. That screw-up's always getting into some sort of trouble."

"Don't talk like that. She's done a great job and it's been a real chore with him."

"I've got enough jobs to worry about," he said and stood up. "I'm going to the study to collect some notes for the meeting." He took three steps before her words stopped him.

"My Midnight Passion was the wrong way." It popped out like a cork finally free of a champagne bottle. She said it staring at the space he used to be in, and the words, with no one claiming them, sat in his empty chair like a teenage daughter who just announced she was pregnant and didn't know who the father was but it didn't really matter because everyone knew things would never go back to how they were.

"What?" He caught himself in time and only partially rotated back to face his wife.

"Lipstick. I always keep the points in the same direction in the tray, but my favorite, Midnight Passion, was facing the wrong direction. I'd never do that." Sophia sat like a rock. Hands on the table. All settled now.

"For Christ sake, Sophia. I don't remember where I put half my stuff two minutes after I drop it." He'd never known three steps to create such a gulf. He quickly walked away from her, but from the corner of his eye he saw her still looking at his vacant seat, at what used to be.

Unbelievable, he thought. Was Natalie trying to screw things up? No more chances. That's the last time she would ever see the bedroom. He had gotten five text messages from her that day and replied only to the first one. She wanted to know what he was doing, where he was going. That broad wanted to be in every corner of his life. Too much shit coming down on me, he thought.

"Paulo, you were right. Raydel, you got one hell of a place here," Walter Mendis said.

Mendis stood at the edge of the pool with no edge. He looked out over the motionless mangroves of the west coast of Florida and to the waters of the Gulf of Mexico where the edge was a sky it never met.

Paulo Henriques stood next to Mendis. Escobar would have sworn they both went to the same damn tailor on the same day. Mendis was shorter and his shaved scalp gave away only to a glimpse of fuzz on both sides of his head. Escobar noted, as he had in previous meetings, that Mendis tilted forward, like a tree pressing the wind. His blue sports coat jacket was draped over his left arm, and Escobar wondered if he slept in the thing. They had flown in from Palm Beach, and Gibbons, Mendis's muscle, drove when they pulled around the circular drive in the black Mercedes S550 sedan. Escobar didn't know how the car got over from Palm Beach or if Mendis was renting it. He wasn't going to ask. He was more concerned about the reason for the sudden visit.

Mendis turned around from the Gulf in a dismissive manner. "How was the fund-raiser for Kittredge?"

"We got fifty-four people," Escobar said. "He's beating the path pretty hard."

"He's not one to circumvent the basics," Mendis said. "He knows you've got to hit these things."

"Well, he's swinging away," Henriques said. "He's spending more time raising money than governing. But he's our man—"

Mendis cut in, "He's our man and his commitment to us makes wedding vows look cheap."

Escobar said, "Let's have a seat. Olivia's going to bring out some fish tacos."

They sat under the red umbrella, once blocking the sun and soon to be blocking the stars. Escobar took a seat that faced the water and then thought that perhaps he should have allowed Mendis to sit first. Screw him, he thought, I'm not sacrificing my view for him.

"Kittredge called me this morning," Mendis said as Olivia placed water with lemon wedges in front of each man. "Said your event was first class. Best music he's heard in years."

"How do you know so much about that stuff?" Henriques asked.

"Not 'how,' but 'why,'" Mendis said. "Don't get me wrong, Raydel, it's classic sound book, but where did you run into it? Shit hasn't been on the radio since the day you were crapping your diapers."

"I played it in the clubs all the time, set the mood, set us apart, you know? After a while I just got to like it. Patrons expected it and I never questioned it much." His father played it in his bar every day, but no way was Escobar sharing that with these threads.

Not with anyone.

"What's gracing us now?" Mendis asked.

"The Association."

"The what?"

"Association. That's the name of the group."

Mendis leaned in across the table. "I like that. Association. That's what we got here. An association. You know, Raydel, bad news has good legs. Kittredge had an interesting visitor in his office, real fast legs, he said, and he's worried that our association is slipping."

Escobar thought of a contentious remark but held back. Olivia placed a plate of fish tacos in front of each man. A stainless steel rack on the plate held three tacos in individual slots. Each taco sported three wedges of tomato atop a crown of lettuce with a palmetto olive between them. How fucking long did she spend on that? He said in a hard voice that surprised him, "Have Elvis make us another round of drinks."

"Yes, sir." She said it with a tone that even the table understood. Mendis let out a chuckle. Olivia left, and for a moment no one spoke.

Mendis consumed a fish taco in three bites. He wiped his mouth with one of the yellow cloth napkins with stitched white egrets that Sophia had just purchased. Escobar recalled how she had sprung the napkins from the shopping bag with unbridled excitement and proudly displayed them to him. Who gets excited over napkins? Now Mendis's drool covered the napkin, and it disturbed the hell out of him. Mendis leaned back in his chair and crossed his legs.

"Why's he worried?" Escobar asked in a nonchalant tone.

"Why is he worried?" Mendis let it out in half time. "Nice of you to be so burdened with our problems. His visitor had the 'YOLO' photo on his phone. His visitor did simple math and figured the photo was worth an interchange. His visitor claimed that you had a letter that Uncle Sam wanted back and that you were—fucking unbelievable as this sounds, Raydel—holding it ransom for IRS forgiveness.

"His visitor, some guy named Travis who Kittredge said made a splash at your fund-raiser, claimed to represent some shadow government association. He politely indicated that if you surrender the letter, the government wouldn't do everything in its power to screw my life." Mendis leaned in across the table. "Now, what am I supposed to do with that? Don't you fuckin' look away from me."

Escobar didn't know that time could freeze on such a warm day. The houses, the air, his thoughts were motionless while he left his body and observed from a distance, unable to formulate action or words. He glanced out to see if he could take some comfort from the water, but it mocked him with indifference. His eyes came back and caught Mendis's dirty napkin that looked like a Hieronymus Bosch print. The stitched white egret already sported drool, spit, and stain. *The shit she doing,* Escobar thought, *buying napkins that look so nice?*

Elvis appeared and placed a drink in front of each man. Henriques picked his up as if he had just come in from the cotton fields. Mendis leaned back in his chair and his eyes locked on Escobar as if no one else in the world existed.

My move, Escobar thought.

"Just tell me, Raydel," Mendis said.

Travis, the guy pressing me at the fund-raiser, fast chess boy, Raydel thought. I'll kill the son of a bitch. No matter how it ends, I'll make the next-to-last mistake.

"Raydel." Mendis said it as a statement, not a question.

"We were having drinks one night when Alejo, my old Cuban gardener, told me a story," Escobar said. He was relieved and surprised that he was going straight into it. He had no choice. He couldn't see, try as he could in his frozen world, the crooked paths that various lies would lead him down.

"You ever see this guy before?" Mendis asked after Escobar was done.

"Who?"

"Travis. Who the fuck you think I'm asking about?"

"No. He was a last-minute entry to the fund-raiser. Showed up with some looker."

"Don't make me earn this, Raydel."

"Nothing, Walter. He poked around, likes games, that's all. Seemed a little suspicious, but nothing to indicate—"

"Why didn't you come to me?"

"It was seven mill. I thought I could figure—"

"Not the fuckin' money. I know about that. The letter."

"Why would I?"

"Say that again."

"Why, when—"

"Why?" Mendis said. "Because you don't know how to handle it, and now you've jeopardized me. I don't like it when other people create difficulties for me."

"Hell, I called the IRS on a whim. I had no idea that envelope was so loaded. How could I? I certainly had no way of knowing it would come back to you."

Raydel liked the apologetic and conciliatory sound of his voice. That's my plan, he thought, stick my tail between my legs and buy time to figure out my next move. He felt order and reason return to his world. No rush. Buy time.

Henriques said, "We know that. We're not accusing you of purposely setting this in motion." Escobar thought that Henriques was talking just to pretend that he had some say in the matter. As if his boney frame carried some weight. It didn't. It was Mendis's show.

Walter Mendis left his drink on the table, stood, and strolled out toward the Gulf. Paulo Henriques turned his tumbler around in his hand, never losing contact with it. Mendis kept his back to them for a few minutes and then reclaimed his seat.

"You're blackmailing the US government," Mendis said. "You—"

"I had no idea that——"

"You interrupt me?"

"No—"

"Don't interrupt me. I'm going to get you out of this, Raydel."

"Can I get you guys another round?" Elvis asked. Escobar hadn't seen him approach. Elvis looked at Escobar. I helped Elvis, Escobar thought, now Mendis will help me. Then he will own me. Maybe that's how these things evolve. Associations.

"Thanks. All around," Escobar said even though the previous ones were still half full.

"Not for me," Mendis said without looking at Elvis. "What's your house worth, Raydel?"

"Eight. Nine."

"This market?"

"Seven."

"Screw your head on."

"Six?"

"Free?"

"All cash."

Mendis said, "I got a banker in Palm Beach, I own him. He'll give you half. I'll float you two, and the bank and I will split the deed on your house. You'll deed over your carpet business, warehouse and retail stores, as well as the strip clubs to me. You tell the IRS you'll pay them full in three years. Kittredge can procure you an extension, and you better thank him. You give the letter back to this guy, Travis."

"I'm two short. Two from you and three from the house. How do I make that up over three years?"

"You got anything saved?"

"Not really. I——"

"Unbelievable. Dump the Carver. I don't care what you paid, write it down and cash out. Fuck you need that for, anyways? Probably haven't even turned the engines in three months. What, half a million, three quarters? That leaves you one point five, tops. Work out a schedule with the IRS, and every penny you make from carpet and clubs goes to them until they forget that you're even alive. We split the business and the clubs around fifty-fifty even after your note is paid off. That's the interest charge on my two mill. The letter goes to the government. You avoid incarceration."

Escobar tried to do the math on what he would make after the IRS was out of the picture. The carpet business was picking up monthly with the housing recovery and the clubs were a cash business. Not many gentlemen wanted to leave a credit card trail. He wondered if Mendis would insist on putting one of his men in each location.

That's it. *Mendis wants his man collecting the cash.*

"By the way, next shipment of rugs is slightly modified. A little higher profit margin."

"At my house again?"

"No time for another point."

"I thought that my house—"

"I thought I had a business partner that put his cards on the table. You just do your job. Don't worry. Just a few more times here. And Raydel?" He stopped talking, making Escobar respond like an admonished schoolboy.

"Yeah."

"Fork over the damn letter. Kittredge will be calling me after his visitor says the heat's off. I'm expecting a calm conversation. Your liability is not going to pressure my life. You understand that?"

Escobar wasn't sure if that was a question that warranted an answer.

"Do you understand that?" Mendis repeated.

"I got it."

"What's it say?"

"What does what say?"

Mendis blew his breath out and took a slow sip. "The letter, Raydel. What on God's green motherfucking earth do you think we're talking about?"

"Never opened it; the envelope had names. Dulles, Rusk, and McNamara. I looked them up. They were big—"

"I know who they were. Those guys left the arena long ago. Dump it, understand?"

"I got it, Walter."

Escobar thought Mendis might want to see the letter, but instead Mendis leaned back.

"Now, where are those cigars Paulo tells me about?" Mendis asked.

Escobar started to get up, but saw Elvis coming with the cigars. Elvis had already cut them, and the men passed around the torch lighter.

"Smooth as a virgin's belly," Mendis said as leaned back and blew smoke into the air. "Who we listening to now?"

"Dusty Springfield," Escobar said, thankful that the conversation had taken a turn.

"Who?" Mendis asked. "Oh yeah. I remember her. Goddamn, I'd storm a beach for a woman with a name like that."

"She was born Mary Isobel Catherine Bernadette O'Brien," Escobar said and instantly regretted his remark, trying to play up to these guys, one who just informed him he would be holding a note on his home and possibly his clubs. Escobar caught that Mendis left the deal with the clubs a little vague and figured his goal was to muscle in on that business. *Around fifty-fifty.*

"You don't say," Mendis said as he leaned in and flicked a glance at Henriques. "You know your stuff, don't you?" He reclined and laughed. "What a world if those record pricks can make Dusty Springfield out of that fucking mess. After a night with that name, I'd have to do a ball check in the morning."

Henriques tossed out a sidekick laugh, then got in on the act. "Hey, Raydel, she dead or alive?"

"The White Queen of Soul," Escobar said and blew smoke into the air, not giving a rat's ass what they thought. What

Travis told him was taking hold. "But she's gone, Paulo, just like the name."

"Just like your boys Dulles, Rusk, and McNamara," Mendis said. "In the end, none of it means shit."

Then why, Escobar thought, is someone trying to tear that letter away from me? And why would I willingly depart with such an object?

CHAPTER 15

Escobar

Escobar and Elvis watched the black Mercedes with tinted glass shielding Mendis and Henriques blend into the night and then reclaimed their spot on the patio. Olivia was clearing the table of the drink glasses, dessert plates, and napkins.

"Get this stuff off of here," Escobar said angrily at her while gesturing toward the table.

She stopped, placed her hands on her hips, and punched him with a hard stare. "What do you think I'm——"

"Get this shit out of here!" Escobar shouted and swiped a dirty napkin at her. Olivia's jaw tightened and she scurried to collect the rest of the debris.

"You heard the plan?" Escobar asked Elvis. He glanced up at Olivia as she practically ran away and caught the tremble of her shoulders.

"I think I got it. He's taking a note on the carpet and clubs."

Escobar mulled the possibility that Mendis was also buying time until he put a contract on him. He wasn't sure who mattered the most to Mendis, he or Kittredge. Mendis ending up with fifty percent of the clubs and carpet business was a game changer. He had no debt on the clubs and thought if he liquidated everything he just might come up with the seven million. Then I'd be penniless and on the streets, he thought. Still, that might be better than working for Walter Mendis.

"And another shipment," Escobar said.

"What did Mendis mean by 'slightly modified'?"

"Haven't a clue. Call Ramon and find out when."

"OK."

"Now. Go."

Elvis extracted his cell from his pocket and headed toward the outdoor kitchen. Escobar tried to think of all the mistakes he could make and realized that if he were good at that, he wouldn't be in his current position.

"Two nights," Elvis said when he returned. "What about Sophia? She can't be here."

"I'll figure it out."

"What about the letter? You going to give it up?"

Escobar assumed that Elvis overheard the conversation. He blew smoke into the air. "I'm still thinking on that."

"We should keep the letter and use it however we can to keep Mendis from moving in on the clubs. They spit out pure cash."

"I said I'm still thinking."

"I've been thinking too. You know I found your father's old typewriter and envelopes—"

"Later. I've had enough for today." Escobar rose and walked away.

Sophia was in bed leaning back on her pillows and reading chick lit when Escobar entered the double doors of their bedroom. She closed her book and delicately placed it on the pale yellow sheet she had drawn up tight around her neck.

"How are the boys?"

"Just business stuff."

"It always is, isn't it?"

"What do you mean?"

"Nothing. After tomorrow I'm going down to Naples to visit my sister for a few days."

"I thought Dwight made you sick. Last time you went you could hardly stand to see her with him and you came back a day early. You're always telling me that she could have done so much better." Not bad timing, though, he thought. She won't be here for the shipment.

"She could have." Sophia placed her book on the bed stand and reached up and turned off the light. "And so could I."

Judas Priest, like I've got time for this, Escobar thought. "Why are you saying that, baby?" He sat on the bed and reached over to kiss her, but she stayed on her side with her back to him. He settled for her cheek.

"I married a strip club owner. I know what I got. But there's decency, you know? Courtesy and feelings that people have for each other, and you need to remember that."

"What are you talking about?" He was going back and forth between the new percentages of the business and what they would look like after the IRS was gone. He wasn't sure he could trust Mendis, but didn't see any choice. And the damn letter. Mendis said a guy would come around for it. Travis again? Maybe I should hang onto it. What's the picture look like if I don't play their tidy little game?

"And if you can't have respect, then you remember that if I leave, half of everything you got goes with me."

"Well, that's just great. I owe the IRS seven million, Soph, so unless I get out of this pile of shit, I don't have a dime. Now, it's been a long day. What are you trying to say?"

She looked at her husband. "What I'm saying is I don't care if you're down to a cigar butt. I'm entitled to half and I'll take it, Raydel, all the way to the ashes in the tray. You need to show respect and have a conscience. I'd never do to you what you've done to me."

"Sophia, I don't have a clue what—"

"It's my lipstick. It's my bed. Don't you *ever* bring her in here again."

She turned her back to him as if she was exhausted by the words, and the implications had stolen something from her.

Fuck a duck, he thought. This just isn't my day. He saw her shoulders shake and thought of Olivia. Well, at least I'm batting a thousand.

"OK. OK, I'm sorry." He felt he should say something else, but didn't know what and suddenly felt small for making her cry. "You're the best thing that ever happened to me, baby." For a few seconds she didn't say anything, and it just hung out there like hope without a home.

"Then how come you don't ever remember that?" Sophia Escobar asked with strength as her anger and frustration trumped her tears.

He got up and padded downstairs to the kitchen to get something to eat, but really to get out of the bedroom. He fixed a sandwich and chased it with 800 milligrams of ibuprofen. He thought of her comment about taking half of his cigar ashes and gave an audible chuckle. She'd do it, too. Toughest sweet girl I ever met. Right there in front of me. I wondered how I missed that one?

Damn letter. Don't know if I'm better off with it or without it. Mendis's going to give me two million and let me pay it off over years while he sneaks in on the clubs. I doubt he's being straight with me. Maybe when this washes out, he thought, I'll unwind it all and get off this high wire. One thing's for certain, this shit with my boat has got to stop. It's just not me. I wonder if that's how he operates—sucks in people like me. But I got to play his game a little longer.

No way, Escobar thought, will I ever be the man with money walking through the door if I take that big step back. What do men with money do? They decide the rules, not someone else.

I've got to hold on to that letter.

He went in the downstairs guest bedroom, but didn't give sleep good odds. He recalled his earlier thought: hold on to the damn letter. It might be the only thing keeping me alive. But it wasn't the letter that kept his mind racing when sleep failed to arrive. It was an image that flashed over and over. It dropped down from the top of his head and bounced off the sides. No matter how much he tossed and turned it rode him hard like a cowboy on a delirious steer and he couldn't shake it.

The image was a yellow and white flag blowing like a hurricane warning on a torrid beach. On the flag, a dirty stitched white egret strained to break free, its wings snapping apart and its raw bones grotesquely protruding out from the frantic effort. It grasped an envelope in its claws and then everything disintegrated.

CHAPTER 16

I landed a final high kick on the smiling pink face that hung down from my garage ceiling.

I had already taken a predawn run that shut me down when my searing porcupine lungs refused to provide any more oxygen to my waterlogged legs. After that beating, I had lowered my canvas punching bag with the grin. The art was courtesy of Tiffany, an ex, and her tube of lipstick. I pummeled it until my arms and legs were limp. Tiffany, when she realized that my boat recovery gig often involved real bullets, ran from me with zest and straight into the arms of Northwest Mutual's Southwest Florida General Agent of the Year. Health, Auto, and Home.

I got dumped in favor of a directionally challenged insurance agent. It was not a good day for my libido.

I settled next to Morgan in my screened porch.

"Have you ever gotten up and approached the day quietly?" he asked. Morgan's ideal morning was posturing himself cross-legged at the end of his pier commencing a half hour before sunrise and lasting forty-five minutes. I joined him once, but it just wasn't right. I never did it again.

We were sitting on my porch as a great blue heron stalked the grassy waters in front of my wall. A great white egret landed too close, and despite their shared ancestry, the heron emitted its primitive guttural call warning its distant cousin to stay clear. It was low tide and the sea grass was laid down like wet noodles.

"You mean?" I asked.

"Not burn a thousand calories before breakfast."

"I've had days like that, but I don't see the point."

"I suppose not. What do you think when you hit it?"

"You assume too much."

"I assume nothing."

"You'd be disappointed. Most of the time, I'm just trying to knock that shit-ass grin off the bag."

"And how's that coming?"

"Not real well, actually." At that moment the heron jabbed at the water and came up with a small fish. "Good morning for the bird."

"Bad morning for the fish," he said. It was our usual commentary when we witnessed life exchanging life in the sea—God's refrigerator for the world. I conducted my usual scan of the paper for sunrise, sunset, and tide schedules.

"I'm going to the hardware store today, pick you up anything?" Morgan asked.

"Toilets, doors, hinges, windows, light fixtures, and sympathy for slow people in check-out lanes that are the root of the world's problems, except for the assholes who wait until after they receive the total from the cashier to start writing out their check—they deserve a slow, tortuous death along with drivers who do only the speed limit in the left interstate lane."

"I was thinking more like light bulbs."

"I'm good."

He left out the side door and walked across the lawn in front of the water and up to his house. A fifty-foot white cruiser with dark tinted windows came by and threw its wake up on my low-tide beach, and the great blue heron was airborne just before the tsunami hit.

Kathleen called a few hours later.

"Pleasure palace. May I have your customer loyalty number please?" I said when I saw it was her.

"You can have my number, but loyalty is a separate package," she said.

"What can I do to secure your loyalty?"

"You assume loyalty can be secured?"

"Someone told me this morning that they assume nothing."

"Mornings with Morgan?"

"I think I read that."

"And what did you learn?" she asked.

"That if you're a fish stay well under the surface of the water."

"And what else?"

"Try as I might, I can't kill myself by running."

"My, our Johnny's having a good day in the classroom."

"It's *Jake*, remember? Why don't you come over and we'll have recess together?"

"Why don't you pick me up at seven? Sophia invited us over to their house for dinner. She said Raydel was eager to meet you again. It's OK, isn't it, seeing Escobar socially again? I told her I'd get back to her after I talked with you."

"Recess. Are there sweeter words to a schoolboy's ears?"

"Shall I tell her we'll be there?"

I thought of my conversation with Kittredge. It appeared everything was proceeding according to plan.

"Tell her we shall be delighted."

"You sure it doesn't complicate your plan?" she asked again.

"My plan is to hear your voice, feel your touch, and lick the ocean's salt off your skin as we walk the solitary beaches of the world."

"Oh dear. You serve that up at ten thirty in the morning?"

"You have no idea."

"Oh, but I do," she said with sincerity, and I realized I wasn't the only one with volcanic passions.

"Seven?"

"Yes, and Jake?"

"Yes, ma'am?"

"Be here at six."

She disconnected.

Zip-a-dee-doo-dah.

I was at her house at 5:30 and let myself in.

"I'm here for recess," I announced.

"Time already?" She stood in her kitchen surrounded with the plastic remnants of a grocery store trip.

"I never was good at that whole time thing."

"Let me guess, you're going to tell me what you're good at."

"Show. Never tell."

My oh my, what a wonderful day.

Afterward, as cartoon bluebirds flirted around the sky, I poured the remains of a bottle of chardonnay into two glasses. She kept hers in the bedroom. I sliced several pieces of hard Parmesan cheese from a block I found in the top tray of her refrigerator, wolfed down a handful of stale salted cashews halves, and ventured into the air so thick that it nearly pushed me back inside. I sat in the partial shade of her covered porch and angled the poolside umbrella to block the fierce, retiring Florida sun that ate up shadows in its quest to catch me. I like Florida in the summer. I like predictable mornings. I like an atmosphere that assaults my senses and is a mixture of salt water and air and creates its own seductive element that is neither liquid nor gas. An atmosphere so dense that it lowers my average miles-per-gallon when my angry V-8 eats it up. If it weren't for the unrelenting hot and muggy summer days, there'd be another ten million people in the state. If God's gifts to the world are the seas, his gift to Florida is summer.

Kathleen joined me without comment, and her essence made the air around me different. Out on the Gulf, heavy air convulsed into a thunderstorm. In the summer, the heat relentlessly rose until it was released by the ecstasy of lightning followed by shuddering thunder and the torrential relief of rain. The earth masturbating daily like an oversexed seventeen-year-old schoolboy. Reload and fire. Reload and fire. The sound traversed the open water like cannons from a distant war.

"I hope it stays out there. Sophia mentioned eating outside this evening," she said.

"It's moving away, about ten miles off the coast now. We'll be fine."

"How can you tell it's ten miles? I can't tell two miles from ten looking over the water."

"Take the seconds between the lightning and the thunder and divide by five. It's a rough estimate of the miles."

"I see." Her interest had waned, but I plowed ahead.

"The formulas are crude calculates of the massive disparity in the speed. The sound of thunder moves at 768 miles per hour, although temperature and humidity will affect that. One mile in five seconds. Light scoots along at 186,282 miles per second. It just hauls ass compared to sound."

"Speed's not everything," she said, apparently finding something in the subject that brought her back. "The thunder might be slow, but what it lacks in zip it makes up with punch. You can feel it rolling the earth and rattling the windows."

She took my last cut of cheese. Really? I wish she hadn't done that. No matter how much I slice, it is never enough.

"I'll concede the feeling, but it's misleading. The thunder is the *sound* of lightning, the rapid expansion of the air surrounding the bolt causing a sonic shock wave. Once the bolt strikes the damage is done, the die is cast. Thunder is a mere messenger, the god Thor, letting us know the heavens have unleashed a 54,000-Fahrenheit-degree bolt of electricity."

"Named 'Thursday' after him, I believe," Kathleen said.

"Your beliefs are right."

"You didn't really say 'rough estimate,' did you?"

"I did. In the future I'll stick to smooth estimates."

"But not in the past?"

"Just testing you. Are we done with English?" I asked.

"Are we done with science?"

"We were never discussing science."

Kathleen said, "No. I suppose we weren't. You could have just said, 'Thunder is good, thunder is impressive, but it is lightning that does the work.'"

"You knew all along," I said with deference.

"I did. But you were rolling."

"The quote?" I asked.

"Twain."

"We haven't spent much time with him."

"Nor he with us."

"His loss. You know, Clemens was a great fisherman."

"You don't say." She had only taken a bite out of the cheese and waved the remainder in her hand like a cruel tease. Typical broad—totally oblivious to her power.

I paused a second, for it was one of my favorites, and then said, "When you fish for love, bait with your heart, not your brain."

She hummed and closed the note with a sip of chardonnay. I thought about what I had just said. Was I over thinking Twain's guidance? Sometimes my brain wanted one life while my heart yearned for another. But I run from heavy thoughts like an antelope being chased by a lioness with hungry cubs.

"I like your dress," I said. It was September red, faded by the summer sun. "You've worn it before, haven't you?"

"No. It's actually new. This is its inaugural voyage."

Where had I seen the color? The portrait of Dorothy Harrison. Why, of all things, did my mind hold onto that?

I informed her on the way to Escobar's that with a little cooperation from him, I would emerge victorious with the letter. We were a fashionable fifteen minutes late when the tires of her bronze Lexus convertible came to a stop on Escobar's driveway. Sophia spilled from the front door like the house couldn't contain her any longer and hugged Kathleen as if the Lexus had delivered life itself.

We followed her into the foyer where she informed me that Raydel was partaking of a drink by the pool. She asked me what would please me. I said realistic public pension assumptions would be nice. Kathleen gave me that look and I told Sophia that I would greet Escobar first and get a libation with him.

He sat on a high stool at his varnished bar. He stood as I approached and we shook hands.

"Mr. Travis," he said, punctuating the syllables.

"Mr. Escobar," I punctuated back.

He walked around behind the bar. "What would you like?"

"A beer would be swell."

"Preference?"

"Cold."

He opened the full-size refrigerator and slid a La Tropical down the bar to me. "I thought Castro shut these guys down right after the revolution," I said, and then took a thankful drink from the green bottle. Great Jehovah above, do I ever love mornings and early evenings. What are you supposed to do with the rest of the day?

"Some guy in Miami got the rights. Supposedly as good as the original," Escobar said.

"Where's your ponytailed friend?"

"His name is Elvis."

"Not Boo-Boo?"

"Pardon me?"

"Nothing. After Graceland's son?"

"Ask him yourself one day."

"I might do that."

"You've caused me considerable difficulties, Mr. Travis."

"How is that?"

"I think we both know. I understand you paid Kittredge an unsolicited visit."

Plan A rounding third and making for the plate. Fans heading for the exit to beat the traffic.

"We conducted a brief conversation," I said.

"I still like my original plan."

"Which was?"

"I hand over the letter and a seven-million-dollar debt goes away. You seem to be a resourceful fellow, why don't you make that happen?"

"I'm just here to see you throw some baby backs on the grill."

"Is it your job to be so annoying?"

"My job is to retrieve the letter. Annoyance is a pro bono sidebar."

"Can you make it happen? It would be well worth your effort."

"I have no negotiating rights."

I didn't care about his IRS dispute, but I wanted to know the contents of the letter. I wanted to discover what Dorothy Harrison and her CIA man were up to. The lady in the portrait mesmerized me, and for some reason I felt I was working for her just as much as I was for the colonel. It was a bullshit thought, but those are the ones you can't ignore. I realized that neither Garrett nor Mary Evelyn had gotten back to me on Jim Harrison's known associates and logged a mental note to bring it up again.

"And if I decide to keep the letter?" Escobar asked.

"My job is to retrieve the letter by whatever means I may wish to employ."

"You're not threatening me, are you?"

"Absolutely."

Escobar walked over to a wood table under an expansive red umbrella. The table held a tray of veggies and fresh fruit. Golf ball-sized strawberries crowded the center of the tray, which was a real shame as I'm allergic to them. Strawberries, not golf balls. He took a seat and torched a cigar. Reposed and confident. Like a silent lightning strike with thunder that came much later. I claimed a seat across from him.

"Lisa gives her best, by the way."

"Lisa?"

"Incredible dimples. Said you need to pay more attention to her or she's going to become real close to your wife."

"You certainly get around. Shall I invite Sophia out here and you can tell her about Lisa? You think that scares me?"

"I think Walter Mendis scares you, and if he doesn't, you're one dumb fucking Cuban."

It was a strong uppercut. It staggered the big bear. He blinked out of rhythm.

"I think I can handle Mendis," he said just before his silence revealed his discomfort.

I leaned across the table. "If you've got to think about it, you can't. Don't try it, Raydel. He plays a different game than you. You can't win this. Give me the letter and save your life."

He let out a nervous laugh. Addressing him by his first name and unexpectedly getting all serious and touchy with him was a good follow-up to the uppercut.

"Why do you presume to know what's best for me?" he asked.

"I haven't a clue what's best for you. But I got a good idea what's bad for you. You're a strip club owner who caught a break. You let it go to your head like a lot of people—lucky to make money and dumb enough to spend it. Mendis is a different breed. He'll take both you and Kittredge down and come clean through as if nothing happened. Guys like him do that for a living."

"I've been working with him for years. I know him a lot better than you do."

"Say it over and over and over. It's weak and you know it." I got up as I saw Kathleen and Sophia approach. "Say it like you mean it and you just might convince yourself. I'm not your enemy. You need a mirror for that." I spilled it quickly to get it out before the ladies arrived.

They were upon us like an incoming tide, bringing smiles and perfumes on a warm night. Kathleen held my eye for a second and then closed the moment with the slightest of smiles. That corner of her mouth, again. Those lines. They just launched me. Extreme passion. The dick-faced army shrink forgot the key word.

Instant extreme passion.

My emotions and obsessions, balanced on a fault line, are always a hair trigger away from exploding upon the world. *Here's all of me, you sons of bitches.*

"Dinner or another cocktail, Jake? What is your pleasure?" Sophia asked.

I'd like to rip off Kathleen's clothes, lay her softly on the edge of the pool so her hair floats in the water, and bury my face deep between her legs until she screams for Almighty God. Anybody got an issue with that?

And I had already blown my pipes. Made a deposit. Docked the boat.

"Dinner would be dandy," I said. Then, to help my thoughts move along, I added, "I was just regaling your husband with how much I admire the property and what a wonderful life he has created here." She smiled from a happier place than where she really was. I suddenly felt sorry for her.

Sophia put her arm around her Escobar. "It is a gorgeous spot, and it looks like we're going to be lucky," she said, giving the sky a glance.

"Luck has a hand in everything." I turned to Raydel. "But your husband has made astute, and correct, decisions. He treats luck with the disdain it deserves. That's what we were discussing, wasn't it? Making astute decisions."

Escobar's eye held mine with a dull indifference. "That is correct. And no one is more qualified than the man who operates his business. But enough shop talk, let's enjoy dinner as the two luckiest men on the west coast of Florida."

"I'll second that."

We raised our drinks to the women in our lives. In the distance was a flash of lightning, but I never heard the thunder. We headed over to the dinner table, but not before I glanced longingly back at the edge of the pool, thinking that Kathleen never knew what might have been.

After dinner, Olivia, who Sophia had introduced us to earlier and I recognized from the fund-raiser, cleared the table of the dessert dishes that held the remnants of key lime tart with a raspberry drizzle.

"Thank you so much for having us over," Kathleen said. "It was all so very good."

"I was afraid we'd have to eat inside," Sophia said. "I much prefer the outside."

"As do we. We rarely eat inside," Kathleen said.

I asked Escobar, "How many outdoor speakers do you have?" It was the second time I'd heard her refer to us as "we" and wondered why it stuck in me.

"I have eight surrounding the pool area."

"Who does this song?" Sophia asked. "I've heard you play it before."

Escobar said, "Brooklyn Bridge. 'The Worst That Could Happen.'"

"Are they still around?" Sophia asked.

"I think so. Johnny Maestro is the singer. Johnny Mastrangelo. Another great New York Italian voice."

I said, "He's a goner. I believe he succumbed a few years ago to the big C. Not far from here, actually." Kathleen kicked me not too gently under the table. What'd I do?

"Really?" Escobar sounded genuinely surprised, even hurt. "What a shame. No one nailed that Jimmy Webb song like he did. He just owned it." He leaned back into his chair, his face relaxed, and wherever that song went that night, Raydel Escobar followed.

"Would you care to join me for a cigar and a Cubano espresso?" Escobar inquired as if we were suddenly old chums.

"A cigar will be fine. I'll pass on the café Cubano."

He stood and walked over to a humidor that sat on the kitchen bar. I had noticed earlier that it had an engraved top, and I wondered if it had belonged to his father or his father before him. He retrieved a cigar, trimmed the end, and handed it to me. He placed a black ashtray on the table. It had "Copacabana" on its side in prominent white letters. I wondered if it was from the original pre-1992 location on Sixtieth Street in New York City.

"That's my ticket to leave. I can't stand the smoke," Sophia said. "We'll be inside."

I sent Kathleen my own half smile. She could take a drag from a cigar that would melt a Hollywood camera.

"Do you understand the conversation I had with Kittredge?" I asked after the womenfolk departed. If he didn't give me the letter, I didn't want it to be because he wasn't aware that his balls were in a vise.

"I know what I need to know."

We sauntered over to the chess game where we had sparred a few nights earlier, but neither of us made a move. "I don't leave here with the letter, then I call Kittredge. He, despite the support Mendis gives him, will tell the FBI to dig deeper, and look harder at Mendis. If Kittredge doesn't turn up the heat, I release the Bernie picture."

"But you won't, and we both know that. You want the letter, and leaking the photo to the press doesn't give you what you want. Kittredge will never turn the heat up on Mendis because Mendis has the picture. Mendis could tell Kittredge that if Kittredge *does* look into him, Mendis will release the picture. Your pathetic scheme would only work if Mendis didn't have anything on Kittredge."

He was partially right, the fat little prick. But not as right as his conceited ass thought he was. I still couldn't see how a guy like Walter Mendis would allow Escobar's tax issue, or any issue, to even remotely threaten his existence. Maybe I should have tried to con Escobar, but it was too late for that.

I started right in, "Mendis doesn't want Kittredge in that vexatious position. Can't take that risk. My bet is that Mendis will do anything to preserve his relationship with the congressman, keep him as comfortable as he can, and make equally certain that the government has as little interest in himself as possible. You're the odd man out here. I'm here to tell you that if you hold the letter, Walter Mendis becomes your enemy. I will make certain of that."

"I'll take my chances," he said.

"You think you got good odds?"

"The next-to-last mistake, I believe you said."

"You're making the last mistake."

"I don't think so."

"That's your call then."

I walked away.

I thought Escobar was trying hard to be someone he was not. I recalled my visit to the Welcome In and visualized Escobar spending his evenings listening to his music, surrounded by the flesh of women, smoking cigars, drinking his dark Cuban rum, and engaging in the bloodless battle of chess where even if you lost, your senses enjoyed the passing moments before you placed the thirty-two pieces neatly back on their squares. Maybe that was as good as life got for him, but he didn't know it and thought he wanted, or needed, more. His passion and hunger would carry him far offshore, but I'm not sure he had a harbor he could return to when the weather turned foul and the angry angels slashed bolts of lightning against his plans.

All the beauty and music gone because of his greed.

Kathleen and Sophia were sitting in the great room. I thanked Sophia and announced we were departing as if the plank was up and the boat was already pulling away. I stood over Kathleen, extended my arm, and in a brusque manner led her out the front door. Within a few minutes we were on Madonna Boulevard and close to her house on Columbus Drive. The warm and soft landscape lights of homes that passed outside the windows were a stark contrast to the chill inside the car.

"What was that all about?" she demanded.

"He didn't turn over the letter."

"That's an excuse for social gaffes?" She spit it out. I didn't need to look at her to know that if her eyes were loaded, I'd be dead.

"There was nothing social about tonight." I was ticked at myself for enjoying a smoke with Escobar.

"Oh, forgive me. Sophia and I aren't real."

"That's not what I said."

Silent homes passed us by.

She wasn't done with me. "You could have been more polite when you told him Maestro died. 'He's a goner'? Really, Jake? That's the sum of your parts?"

She's worried about me hurting Escobar's sensitive feelings? I wanted to jump on that like an osprey shredding apart a fish, but I was done talking that day. I quietly blew out my breath, uttered not another word, and kept my eyes on the road. I hadn't been doing a very good job of that.

When I feel sorry for myself, I do a damn good job.

CHAPTER 17

"We'll head over there the next couple of nights. If he's got business, maybe we'll find out what he's buried in," I said.

"Just because the boat was out thirty days ago doesn't indicate he's on a schedule, but it's all we got," Garrett said.

I had picked Garrett up at the airport. Plan A wasn't dead, despite apparently being thrown out at the plate. While I had no intention to ruin Kittredge's career, let alone his family life—as if people have two distinct separate halves—I couldn't imagine that someone like Walter Mendis would run that risk. My bet was that it just needed more time to unfold. But I don't wait and I like to cover my bets.

We were viewing a satellite photo on the table in my screen porch. An antique Cypress Gardens plate held cheese, crackers, and carrots. Escobar's Intrepid had been gone one night in the last thirty days, and the armed guard was there a few days before it departed, vanished, and then reappeared a few days ago. Kathleen, after we resumed diplomatic relations, confided to me that Sophia planned to visit her sister and would be gone for a few nights.

I planned to still squeeze Escobar even harder until I found out what he was involved in, and then blackmail him into giving me the letter in return for my silence. Depending on how grungy his dirt was, I might or might not renege on my end of the deal. If I couldn't find anything, an outcome I deemed unlikely, I could always put him in a shime-waza, the fatal chokehold that Garrett favored from the beginning. Unfortunately, it carried serious drawbacks, namely the aforementioned orange suit that accompanied prison time if Escobar pressed charges.

The colonel would not risk his network for any one of us. He had made it clear that Kathleen was the only mulligan we would ever receive. I wondered if my desire to retrieve the letter, to not fail him, was amplified by a subconscious yearning, or some primitive urge, to return the favor. Bottom line? I owed him. What had Garrett said? *It seems personal this time.*

I said, "We'll head over around ten and anchor. If he takes it out, she'll leave *Impulse* bobbing in her wake. But at least we can see who takes her and, with luck, what they bring back."

"He never registered the boat?" Garrett asked.

"That's right."

"Drugs?"

"Even money. It's the cash crop of Florida," I said. "I think we can still blackmail him. I'm not contacting Kittredge. Kittredge calls Mendis and Mendis has a persuasive talk with Escobar. It's hard *not* to see that playing out. Perhaps it already has and Escobar is balking at his end. Regardless, the pressure is still on Kittredge and Mendis. In the meantime, we continue to dig and see what else we can use on Escobar."

"You should have run a con. Posed as an IRS agent who needed to verify the authenticity of the document and then never let it out of your hands."

"Thanks. But it's a little late for that," I said. "By the way, what did you ever find on Jim Harrison and his associates?"

Garrett leaned back in the chair, stretched out his legs across the glass table, and stared out at the water where the red blinking channel marker off the end of my dock had started its nightly job. His face, like twilight, was neither day nor night.

Garrett traced his ancestry to his four-time great-grandfather, a Frenchman who first touched US soil as an attaché to the Marquis de La Fayette in 1824 when President Monroe invited La Fayette to tour all twenty-four states. Jacques DeMarcus fell in love with the flatlands of Louisiana as well as a mulatto Creole girl whom he decided he could not live without. The marquis continued without him. Garrett's own mother was Polynesian. Garrett was six feet three inches and looked like a bronze Greek god. When people guessed his heritage the range spanned from Cherokee to African American. No one actually believed anymore that we descended from Greek gods, which in itself is a real shame. He had alopecia totalis since childhood. Apart from eyelashes and eyebrows, not a speck of hair would ever come from his Herculean body. He escaped the Rangers without ever giving in to, or remotely comprehending, the urge to ink.

In the age of ethnicity and body art, Garrett Demarcus is the antithesis.

"Practically nothing," he said.

"Give me the practical part."

"A lot of those first-generation spies started with the OSS, Office of Strategic Services," Garrett said. "The OSS was split up after World War Two between the Departments of State and War. But like a phoenix, it emerged within two years as the CIA. Harrison was an old-timer by Ike's second term."

"I know the history, what did you find?"

Garrett glanced at me and gave me a moment to calm down.

"Not much on James Francis Harrison, but Harrison worked closely with a fellow agent named Theodore Wayne Sullivan, and Sullivan was a man who left a wake. He was a major player in the fifties. A big-time dove that was unappreciated in his time, although his views proved quite accurate."

"Anti-Korea?"

"Pro peace. But that's never been a big seller among men with guns," Garrett said. "Ever since Eisenhower gave his domino speech in 'fifty-four, Sullivan found himself on the opposite side of prevailing doctrine."

I let my mind shift through the clutter until it recalled the era. I popped a slice of Welsh cheddar cheese into my mouth. "The Dulles brothers," I said. "They dominated foreign policy in the fifties. Allen ran the CIA and older brother John was secretary of state, although I believe that John never saw the sixties. But in their day, Allen and John Dulles played with the world like it was a toy left under their Christmas tree."

"About as powerful as two brothers have ever been until the Kennedy boys came, and we know what happened to them," Garrett said. "And you're correct, John died in 'fifty-nine."

"And how is this related to Harrison?" A boat cut across the inside of the channel marker where the sandbar was. It was high tide and it was small boat, so he would be fine. I wondered if he knew that or was lucky.

"As far as we can tell, Harrison's views were lined up with Sullivan's. They found themselves on the outside and they shifted their interest away from Southeast Asia and south toward Cuba. Harrison died in a plane crash, January 5, 1961. A CIA trip that ended up in the Gulf Stream about forty miles off Havana toward Key West. He was, we believe, returning from Cuba."

"So they were a pre-Bay of Pigs team. Were both Harrison and Sullivan in Cuba in 'sixty-one?"

"It appears so. But if they were against US involvement in Southeast Asia, it's very likely that they harbored dovish views on Cuba as well. That would have put them on Allen Dulles's shit list. Bay of Pigs was his bay and his pig."

"And Sullivan? Did he make it to the eighties?"

"No," Garrett said, "Theodore Wayne Sullivan died in a car accident after he left the Occoquan Inn in northern Virginia on the night of November 29, 1961."

"Well, at least he never had to hear disco. The car accident?"

"Sketchy at best. Hit a tree."

"Anything else?"

"Two minor things. First, purely by accident, Mary Evelyn discovered, and pointed out, that Allen Dulles was forced out of office as director of the CIA on November 29, 1961."

I took another piece of cheese and chased it with a salty cracker. I suppose carrots are healthier—and you can have them.

"As I recall," I said, "Dulles took the fall for the Bay of Pigs. Think they simultaneously silenced Sullivan as well to bury the memory, like changing Stalingrad to Volgograd, or do you think Allen Dulles had it in for Sullivan?"

"Sullivan was a vocal opponent and one with credentials and his own power base. My guess was that Sullivan was instrumental in the demise of Allen Dulles," Garrett said.

"And therefore Dulles had Sullivan taken out and on the same day that Sullivan turned in his badge. We'll go with that. What's the second item?"

I took the last slice of cheese. Garrett hadn't touched the cheese or the crackers. He was a carrot man and was burning calories on one as he spoke.

"Second item's even juicier," Garrett said. "According to all known reports, Sullivan was the pilot of Harrison's CIA plane that went down."

"Little hard to die twice."

"That's what I was thinking."

Kathleen rushed through the porch carrying dishes to the outside table on the concrete patio. "Shouldn't Morgan be here by now?" she asked, and a sense of panic accompanied her words.

She was not a woman to panic. When she was kidnapped, her would-be assassin had his arm around her neck and a gun in his hand when she buried her elbow into his stomach and started the sequence of events that saved her life, changed her name, and put a scar on her left shoulder.

But kitchen work? She was a girl in trouble.

"He won't miss dinner," I said.

"He better not. I've got vested time here," she said. She deposited her plate on the table and vanished back into the kitchen.

"You never told me she could cook," Garrett said.

"No. I never did."

"How bad?"

"Thinks the oven's the strangest looking clock in the house."

"Great."

"Hope you saved the munchies from the plane."

Morgan slid through the side door caressing a bottle of cabernet and greeted Garrett. They had developed a quick friendship on Garrett's visits and often spent time together kite surfing at Fort De Soto as well as sailing.

"What's on the agenda?" Morgan asked.

"Kathleen's night," I said.

"Good lord. Remember last time? I'm going to give her a hand."

"We're counting on you."

"What do we know about Mendis?" Garrett asked after Morgan dashed into my house.

"Plays hardball."

"Would he take Escobar out?"

"Maybe. It's difficult to say whether Mendis simply cranks the heat or delivers a bullet to Escobar. The bullet's not our friend—a dead Escobar can't tell us where the letter is."

The colonel could care less if Escobar beat the IRS, ran drugs, or floated up on a pristine Gulf beach in the middle of a sunset wedding. He wanted the letter.

"Maybe we'll find something in the next night that gives us intelligence as to what their current association involves," Garrett said. He took a swig from his bottled water. I doubt he had touched the sauce since our last night in Key West.

The paddle-wheeler churned past the end of my dock. The lower level was a solid window dotted with Playmobil heads. The guests were enjoying a dinner cruise that would culminate at the entrance to the pass just as the sun dipped beneath the water.

Kathleen appeared, her hands buried in thick potholders that caressed a ceramic dish. "Outside, boys," she announced. I checked. No high heels.

We trailed her out to meet our fate, which wasn't nearly as cruel as anticipated. Morgan's late entry to the match no doubt had its intended effect. Our low expectations set us up for a tasteful dinner of bow tie pasta with pesto, black olives, tomatoes, onions, and chunks of salted red snapper. She lit the solitary candle and I poured the wine into Morgan and Kathleen's glasses.

"You're not joining us?" she asked me when I passed over Garrett's glass and mine.

"We're taking the boat out tonight. See if we can see any action at Escobar's."

"Need a pilot?" Morgan asked.

"Only if you're not coming," I said.

He swirled the cabernet in the large glass and stuck his nose deep into the glass. "Tide's in our favor tonight," he said when he came up for air.

"Probably have you anchor farther away. If there's no activity, we'll call it an early night, around two or so. If there is action, Garrett and I will get in the water and get as close as we can. We need to see who and what."

"Why tonight?" Kathleen asked, making motions with her utensils that rarely resulted in one of them finding her mouth. No matter what was placed in front of her, she ate like a bird. Except for pizza. That, she ate like a dog.

Garrett said, "He's had extra cover the past few days, which we've noticed he employs about once a month. Plus, according to our wonderful cook," he raised his water glass at Kathleen, "his wife is out of the house for two days."

"Everything taste OK?" she asked.

"Delicious," Garrett said.

She looked at me, and I was thinking of how to diplomatically tell her to cook the fish in with the sauce in order to absorb the flavor when she said, "You're leaving Sophia out of this, right?"

It was a question, but she threw it down as a warning.

"She's in the middle, and I didn't put her there." The speed of my reply took her by surprise. But like tennis—a fast serve equals a fast return—when you launch a rapid question, you better be prepared for the answers to zing back at equivalent speed. She played again with her utensils and this time actually foul hooked a small piece of fish.

"You'd like her, Morgan," she said, changing tack, but I knew we weren't done. "She's got a heart the size of this bay and plans to raise one hundred thousand dollars for churches to give away next Christmas."

"I believe I've heard of her efforts. Dishes out money to local churches with no strings, right?" Morgan asked.

"That's her. It's as good as anything is, without any pretense or ulterior motives."

"It would be a pleasure to meet her," Morgan said.

"Perhaps when this is over," Kathleen said and gave me a glance. Her message was loud and clear. Sophia Escobar wasn't a concern to me. Kathleen Rowe, however, was the world to me.

I ached for a glass of wine, but kept to water. The sunset charter boat *Magic* glided past the end of my dock with four people on her bow and a few on the aft deck. I heard Barbara's screen door close and knew she had let Francine out for the final trip of the day. I made a note to take over some of Kathleen's dish tomorrow. We had more than we could eat.

Morgan started talking to Kathleen about the moon, just about his favorite topic in the world to discuss. Garrett rose and took an armful of dirty plates into the house.

And I? My eyes were locked on the pulsating red channel marker beacon as if it were trying to send me a signal and answer questions that my brain could not shake. I was stuck on Garrett's and my earlier conversation.

How did Theodore Wayne Sullivan die twice?

CHAPTER 18

We lowered the flag around 3:00 a.m. Nothing had happened except we nearly died of boredom. Welcome to life on the edge. Intense points of waiting.

Not so the next night.

We floated *Impulse* at 10:15, and as with the previous night, Morgan took us to Escobar's, cut the engine, and we poled in close. Garrett and I both wore our wet suits and we brought along the red spinnaker bag. The bag had belonged to Morgan before we commandeered it and christened it our grab bag. It contained satellite phones, extra ammunition, currency, guns, knives, and a first aid kit that was the envy of ER vans. Last time out, it was a lifesaver. Last time out was the night on the beach that Kathleen took a bullet. Garrett, Morgan, and I, that evening, were out fishing at midnight.

That is correct. Kathleen was being kidnapped while I was whistling and casting for gag grouper. Not a day goes by that I don't remind myself of three hard lessons I learned: 1) I am capable of, and will make, stupid decisions, 2) never underestimate your enemy, and 3) I am capable of, and will make, stupid decisions.

It was Garrett who insisted we bring along the red spinnaker bag. When she was abducted, Kathleen managed to sneak out an old EPIRB, emergency position indicating radio beacon, that I had given her as a gag gift. No relation to the fish.

Without the bag, we would have been defending her with light tackle, paddles, fists, and, based on brief conversations that we overheard between her abductors, a superior vocabulary.

Without the bag, there would be nothing fake about the headstone above Lake Michigan.

"Same spot as before?" Morgan asked.

"Same spot," I said.

I spread black paint on my face, put on my Vibrams, and dropped over *Impulse*'s starboard side. Garrett didn't waste time with paint and went off the back by the engine. He positioned himself by the end of the stucco wall at the south side and I camped out in two-and-a- half feet of water by the docks. The house had the same lights on as the previous night.

For an hour I didn't move.

At 12:26 the lights went out and indistinguishable voices floated from the house.

I crept away from the dock and off to the north side by mangroves for a better view. I stumbled upon a large jagged piece of concrete underwater and struggled not to fall down. It was most likely left from when they poured the retaining wall. I froze for a moment after I made my splash to make certain no one heard me, but the conversation seemed uninterrupted. I settled in, partially shielded by the mangroves, and looked through my ATN night binoculars. Elvis and two men with shotguns quickly approached the dock.

"You think he'd give us more notice. He's gotta know when he's getting there," a stout guy with a blue bandana on his head said. I lowered my binoculars.

"I've told you, Cruz, it's all security. Anthony doesn't want to be anywhere too long and he doesn't want anyone to know about his plans any longer than we need to," Elvis said.

"Fuck Anthony," Cruz said and spit onto Sophia's paver bricks. "I don't trust him any further than I can see in the night."

"Than you can spit, dumb-ass."

"I can spit across the Gulf to fuckin' Mexico."

"Corpus Christi, you idiot. Mexico is further south."

"Fine. I can spit to the dead Christ."

"Is that what that place means?" the third man asked. He was the tallest of the three and trailed them as if he were along for a nightly stroll.

"Sure, Victor," Elvis said. "Whatever you want to believe, man."

Victor went straight to the lift box and hit the switch, while Elvis and Cruz stepped into the boat. They had a routine. I was afraid that I would lose their conversation once the engines started and thought of going under the dock so that I would be directly underneath them. Too risky.

Cruz approached the cuddy, unlocked it, and disappeared inside. Elvis was at the wheel, and the third man, Victor, with his gun in both hands, stood on the starboard side looking out into the night. They vanished into the night. I had no idea whether they would be gone for an hour or five. Satellite photos never showed the boat gone during the day, so I had reason to believe they would return that night. I trudged back through the shallow water to *Impulse*, about fifty yards to the south. Morgan had anchored her behind a small mangrove island that provided a natural shield from the house. Garrett was already on board when I pulled myself over the port side.

"Two guys with Elvis, one named Cruz, the other Victor. Heavy guns," I said. "Let's see if we can make out what they haul back. If he's bringing in drugs, and the jail time that drug smuggling brings, he'll crank out the letter in a second."

Garrett said, "Regardless of what comes back in the boat, what I just saw is not what I envisioned from your description of Escobar."

"How's that."

"Whatever he's into makes strip clubs and blackmailing a congressman look like craft time at the old folks' home. The two guns with Elvis weren't from the security firm; they were from the old country. You can see it in their walk. Whether we know what he is into is a moot point. *He* knows what he's into. No way would he press charges and risk scrutiny."

"I agree. Let's see what the old country hauls in from the sea. If it's a bigger rumble than we signed up for, we'll adjust."

A faint smile leaked out of the left corner of his mouth.

Fifty-eight minutes later we heard the throttle down of 1,400 synchronized draft horses slowing over the surface. James Watt wanted a measurement to quantify steam engine production to that of a draft horse. He arrived at a horse exerting 550 pounds per second, or the rough equivalent of 746 watts. One horse=746 W. It's not that simple, but again, nothing ever is.

Garrett and I again slunk over the side. I moved quickly, avoided the submerged concrete, and was in position well before the boat homed in on the lift. I wanted to be in about five feet of water. There wasn't much of me exposed at that level, and if they made me, I could easily submerge and not come up till I was on the far side of the mangroves north of the dock. I had a clear view of the dock and, unless they turned the lights on, was in total blackness. They were out about seventy feet, around twenty-one meters, and closing. Garrett had taken a position in the shallow water to the south under mangrove branches. He had his SASS sniper rifle with him.

The dock lights were off and the boat came in without running lights. They planned to unload, assuming they had picked up their shipment, in total darkness. Even the house lights were still off. Something nibbled at my leg. Back in the food chain. The soft whirl of the lift motor started when they were still thirty feet out. The boat settled into the lift and then heavy footsteps were on the dock above me.

"In the garage," Elvis said.

"Ramon gonna take them all?" Cruz asked.

"We'll see. He's waiting in the garage. These aren't wetbacks paying their own way, and I don't know about those two, especially that one. That's why I called Escobar and he wants to see them. We were told that this shipment was 'modified,' and Escobar went ape shit on the phone."

Six figures got off the boat.

Girls.

An unbridled rage came off the water's floor and took possession of me. All of me again in one direction.

Raydel Escobar smoked Cuban cigars, drank dark rum, and listened to Herb Alpert and the fucking Tijuana Brass. He married a caring and loving wife, who generated as much money for charity as anyone else on the west coast of Florida. He was a respectable blackmailing strip club owner. In America's Wild West capitalistic structure, he was capable of a highly rated TV reality series as long as no one looked in the shadows. For there, in the soft Florida nights, he imported young girls and sold them.

Dirty money and good deeds——the strangest bedfellows to ever emerge from the invention of coinage.

Muffled and confused young voices filled the conversational lapse. I fought the urge to take my knife and drop Elvis and his Oakwood boys and storm the house with Garrett.

Elvis said, "Let's go. Get them around to the garage."

"Move it, *nina chiquitas*," Cruz said.

"What now, Maria?" It was the clear and high voice of a young child. If there really was a God, he was deaf, for the child's voice didn't belong in the same universe with the sound of the men. *You Neanderthals.*

"Stay with me, *poco* Rosa." Slightly older, but still young.

"I am scared, sister. I——"

"Shut up," Elvis said.

I had to get closer to the house. I took a deep breath and silently sunk into the black water until I was flat on the bottom. I moved underwater and used the abrasive concrete I had stumbled upon earlier as a guide to where I was and surfaced next to the mangroves without taking a breath. There were five diminutive dark figures—and a sixth one notably smaller—walking down the long dock silhouetted against the even darker night. Elvis was already on land and Cruz brought up the rear. I had Victor still on the boat and a guy named Ramon in the garage plus the security guard.

Too risky for a shootout. I thought of the concrete below the surface and envisioned my emotions sinking there until I called for them. I slowly blew my breath out.

Visualize an anchor for your emotions, the shrink had instructed, *that way you'll maintain some control, learn to cope, and channel it for a proper time.* What's the purpose if you just harness it, tie it down, I had countered. I had taken his advice, however, on more than one occasion.

The bizarre parade marched around the side of the house, and I lost sight because of the stucco wall. I crawled around the south end of the wall toward the front. I wanted to see if they drove out the front gate with the girls after leaving the garage. I wondered why the hell Escobar was using his house as a drop point. I took a position behind scrub bushes in the vacant lot across the street where I could see through the wrought iron gates. I heard Garrett's low whistle from the other side of the property. I had the better view. We had to wait.

We.

My mind, which I constantly struggle to keep off of shuffle, flashed to the dinner we had at Escobar's. Kathleen referred to us as "we." I wondered what "we" were. I wondered if I truly loved someone, and acted in her best interest, if I wouldn't keep her away from me. If my life was conducive for sharing with someone else, and if not, what choice would I make?

I blew the air out of my lungs in hope that it would take my thoughts with it, but knew it didn't work that way. I focused on Escobar's garage.

CHAPTER 19

Escobar

"What the hell is this?" Escobar demanded of Elvis, the words tumbling out progressively louder.

Escobar stood in his garage with Elvis, Cruz, Victor, Ramon, and Ramon's two men. He looked at the six frightened girls, who stood like frozen lawn ornaments in a single line in the order in which they had entered. He marveled how effortlessly events had spun out of control. There it is, he thought. All your plans turn into a shit show before you know what hit you.

"It's what he gave us. I told him—"

"What? That we take girls? You think they paid for this?"

"He said this is what he was told to bring."

Escobar cut Ramon a glance. "You know it was girls this time?"

Ramon smiled and gave a slight shake of his head. "It don't matter to me whether it's men who end up nailing shingles or *chicas* that someone pays to nail. I just move and unload them. But that one," he nodded his head toward the smallest one, "I'm not taking her," Ramon said. "My guy won't take one that young. Not even as domestic help. She's your problem, Raydel. She can sweep your floor till she's old enough to blow. Then you can pay her to swallow, like an allowance. Extra *paga*."

184

Escobar suppressed a flush of embarrassment from such language in front of young girls. He didn't like Ramon standing on his property. He didn't like Ramon wherever the fuck he stood. He wondered how he ended up in business with such an offensive mouth.

It was only supposed to be one time.

A couple of months ago, Henriques had asked him to do a favor. Sophia, at that time, was staying with her sister for a few days. In retrospect, he wished she were at home. It would have provided him an easy excuse, a negative reply, to Henriques's request. Instead, Escobar had said "sure." After all, they were business partners. Henriques said he had men who wanted to get in the country and were willing to pay a hefty price. Henriques arranged transportation. Henriques had told Escobar that it was high-end service, not some coconut raft operation that ended with a mad dash to touch US soil. Bring them all the way up to Tampa, not the usual South Florida drop points that the Coast Guard suffocated with surveillance. Escobar thought it was a risky business for Mendis to be involved in, but realized he was far enough up the food chain that the only part of the hot operation that Mendis rubbed against was the cold cash.

Escobar had bought the Intrepid at half price—a mortgage broker had fallen behind on payments—and used it a few times to bring in rare, and stolen, Persian rugs. But he was nervous. It wasn't his game, and after a few shipments, he shut it down. The night at Mendis's house, he thought. I ran my mouth on what a great deal I got on the boat and how fast she was. He saw now that Mendis and Henriques had played him.

But young girls? When Elvis had called and told him that instead of grown men, the usual rug shipment was a "half-dozen virgins," Escobar was livid. He realized that Mendis had been building up to this. Mendis's modus operandi, he thought.

Get some idiot like me to take a shipment, and then sneak sex slaves, domestic help, or whatever you want to call them. Ten times the money. The big payday, daddy. And they need a sucker like you.

Escobar had told Elvis to bring them into his garage. He wanted to see them. The garage held four cars, but only Escobar's black 2010 XJL Jaguar was in the bay. Now he wished that he had insisted that Elvis leave them on the boat. He had the strangest sense of relief that his car couldn't talk or judge him, and he pretended that he didn't know why such a ridiculous thought played in his brain like a song he couldn't shake.

Escobar watched a slow smile form over Ramon's face. He knows, Escobar thought. He knows that I'm the last one in this room to figure it out. How much I hate this.

The six girls, with the exception of one, stood with their heads down. They wore simple dresses, and the thinnest of sandals separated their feet from the smooth concrete. The smallest had a lump sticking out from her dress. She was holding the hand of the girl to her left, their bodies touching. It was the girl whose hand she was holding that had her head raised and was scanning the men.

Escobar looked at the girl whose eyes darted from one man to another while she grasped the hand of the younger girl. Defiant. As if clutching the younger girl's hand thrust upon her a confidence and responsibility that she now looked to unleash. But on whom? Her eyes rested on Escobar. She searched no further. Escobar quickly looked away.

"Like hell, Ramon, you know the arrangements," Escobar said.

"I don't take what I can't unload, and no one's handling that one," Ramon said, nodding to the smallest girl. "You need to tie a block around her and drop her off a bridge like a goddamn cat. I'll take the five."

Escobar took appraisal of his surroundings: five men hold-ing guns, and he was sure that Ramon had one as well. Enough ammunition to restock the Alamo.

"I tell you what, Ramon, you want to sink her like a cat, you go do that. But you're taking all six and getting the hell out of my house," Escobar said.

"Put the men and the bigger girl in the van," Ramon said to his men while he held Escobar's eyes.

Elvis raised his gun up slightly and Cruz did the same.

"Elvis, put them back on the boat. We'll tell Henriques that Ramon declined to accept shipment," Escobar said.

"Let's go, *chiquitas*," Elvis said and started to move toward the girls. He never took his eyes off Ramon.

"OK, Raydel," Ramon said with a smile, "everybody just calm down. We'll do what's called a compromise. Ever hear of that, Raydel? I'll take all six. No problem. But I can't have my people thinking that I'm making their lives hard for them, dumping my problems on them, like you're doing to me right now. We all share a little heat and move on to the next ship-ment. Load them up, Carlos. Kill those lights before the door goes up."

He *will* drown her like a cat, Escobar thought. He'd heard stories about Ramon. Not my problem. I got to get them out of here and tell Mendis to get another pool boy. I'm done with this shit.

Escobar had heard stories about smuggling young girls into the states. The supplier told the girls' impoverished families that they would do housework in America and some of their income would be returned to the family. Only young pretty girls were recruited. The supplier would send just enough money back to the family to keep his standing as a recruiter and secure his pipeline. The girls, he remembered being told, usually did housework until their benefactors tired of them. Then they were put out to the streets. He'd even heard that some would keep a girl for only a few days and kick her out. Virgins, with little risk of HIV, commanded top dollar. The families received a little cash and slept with the knowledge that one of them had finally reached America.

Welcome in.

Sex for money. So what, Escobar thought. It's one of my businesses. In some countries and cultures, fourteen was the consensual age, he reasoned. Maybe some were really just used for domestic help. He carried those thoughts like a shield of armor. He glossed over "consensual."

But in his garage. His mind.

Escobar nodded to Elvis, and Elvis flipped two switches, leaving a solitary bulb to disperse light. Ramon's men moved toward the girls.

"Maria!" the smallest girl's voice cried out in panic.

"Hold tight, Rosa," her sister answered, the fear in her voice filling Escobar's garage. But Escobar heard more. There was a challenge in the girl's voice. He wondered where the hell *that* had come from.

"They treat me like a cat?"

"I'll not leave you."

"We pray, Maria?" the younger girl asked rapidly. "We pray like Momma told us." And then even faster, "Jesus loves me this I know, for the Bible tells me so. Little ones to him belong——"

"Shut up, *chicas*," Ramon shouted.

"——they are weak, but he is strong."

Ramon grabbed Rosa and tore her from her sister's grasp. "Get them out of here. This one first, stick her in the van. Now. Move!" His men started toward the girls.

"Maria!" Rosa shrieked again as she reached back for her sister's hand. As she did, a small cloth doll fell from her dress onto the floor.

"Annie!" Rosa said. "I dropped my Annie."

Maria held firm to her hand while Ramon clamped Rosa's right arm.

"Leave her alone," Maria said. Her strength startled Escobar.

Rosa began to whimper. Escobar looked at the ragged doll that lay on its back by her feet and saw that it had only one eye, a sewn-on button. It had a single yellow plastic flower pinned to the side of its head. It lay there worn and dirty, on the clean garage floor of Sophia's bay, staring at him with its solitary eye. He glanced up at Maria and instantly regretted doing so. She pleaded at him with the same searching eyes Natalie used when she asked if they could go places. But this young girl had a raw sense of hope and a frantic energy in her eyes that sent a shudder through Escobar. Something about her earnest plea briefly made him question if Natalie had been playing with him, but he didn't have time for that. Not now.

Ramon gave a final tug and Maria's grasp was broken. Rosa crumpled to the floor and reached out for her doll with her free arm, but Ramon dragged her over the sealed concrete. Maria darted after her and collapsed on her sister.

"Maria, they're taking me!" Rosa screamed.

"Let her go, she is so young," Maria shouted as she lifted her sister off the floor. "We stay here. In this place." She shot a glance over her shoulder at Escobar. She was no longer able to keep the tears from running with her words. "We stay here with you. Whatever you want, but we stay here. Now. With you. Please, with you."

The words sputtered out on nothing but the fumes of desperate hope.

Ramon again broke Maria's grasp and shoved Rosa toward one of his men. "Get them the fuck out of here. In the van, now."

The man slung his gun over his shoulder and reached for Rosa. She let out a high, piercing shriek that would instinctively alarm any living thing. Trapped in the garage, it echoed off the walls. Escobar turned down and away, but the one-eyed doll with the yellow flower in its hair was waiting for him. He looked up.

"Enough!" Escobar shouted. "Leave them both here. I'll take them back. Elvis, contact Anthony, tell him he's taking them back or he'll never see payment from us. We'll never do business with that fat fuck again." He tried to sound indignant, to blame it all on Anthony.

The garage was quiet, like a play between acts, and then Ramon started to laugh, relaxed and slow. "Well, look what we got. Let Raydel have his children. Maybe you want to do this one yourself, Raydel? You like the little black one and you want her on the floor right here after we leave. Is that it? Or are you too afraid to be in this business? Are you a little boy playing a man's game? Which is it? Tell me, Raydel, I want to know. *Cobarde* or saving her for yourself?"

"Get the hell out of my garage," Escobar said calmly.

"Me?" Ramon laughed. "No, Raydel, you're the one who doesn't belong here." He turned to his men. "Grab the four. Let's leave before Raydel tells us it's nap time."

"Cruz, Victor, help them out," Escobar said, forcing his voice to be in command and trying to ignore Elvis's stare. *He knows not to challenge me now,* Escobar thought. The men escorted the four girls out the side door and left Escobar and

Elvis in the garage with Maria and Rosa. Maria gathered the doll and lifted her sister to her feet. Escobar saw no gratitude in Maria's eyes; whatever caused her to break and cry was now buried and controlled.

"What do you want me to do?" Elvis asked.

"I told you, contact Anthony, tell him he's got two coming back."

"We've never done that before."

"We're doing it now."

"We can't do it tonight. Best we can do is a rendezvous tomorrow, but even that might be short notice. What do we do with them?"

"Stick them in the safe room."

"What if they got to use the bathroom?"

"Goddamn it, Elvis, figure it out! Give them food and water, let them piss a few times a day and get them the hell out of this house as soon as you can. You got that?"

"Yeah, I got it."

Escobar thought of Sophia being gone for two more nights. Alejo never came in the house except to the kitchen. Then he thought of Olivia. "Make sure Olivia doesn't see any of this, or extra food leaving the kitchen."

"Sure, boss. I'll take care of it."

Escobar knew by the patronage of his tone that Elvis was fine with Ramon taking all six. Too late now. And food from the kitchen? He was glad Ramon wasn't around to hear that.

"Call Anthony. Call him now."

Escobar wanted to tell Elvis to have Alejo hose down the garage floor in the morning, but he couldn't bring himself to say that.

CHAPTER 20

Five armed men and four girls came out of the side door of the garage.

A sorry-looking white van, no letters or signage, was backed up close to the garage. One of the men opened the back end and partially obstructed my view. A line of four girls, all about the same height, got into the van, and one man followed them into the back while two others got in the front. The gates opened and the van peeled out, its tires screeching as it took the curve too fast. I would have thought they would have planned a quieter exit. It was too dark to get the plates. The remaining two men drove off in a foreign two-door that looked like it had gone through several sets of tires. I wonder what kept them in the garage for so long. I envisioned the girls in the van and felt hopelessness cloak me like it had been biding its time, searching for its victim, and settled on me.

It wasn't my fight. I was in for the letter. But I couldn't walk away from what I'd just witnessed. Some battles we do not seek, they are forced upon us. I thought of Trotsky: "You may not be interested in war, but war is interested in you."

I wondered if anyone else in the neighborhood was thinking of Leon Trotsky that night.

I couldn't fathom any connection with Escobar's clubs. This appeared to be something entirely different. Mendis was too smart to get directly involved in this, but I wondered if he had the source and was using Escobar and Henriques to run the operation and then splitting the proceeds.

But that's not what nagged me. This just didn't *seem* like Escobar's gig. This was a dirty, nasty business. I knew I'd find dirt under his rug, but smuggling girls? I didn't cut him for that.

I made my way back to the boat where Garrett and Morgan were waiting for me.

"Did you see?" I asked Garrett.

"Six girls. One very young."

"Think this has anything to do with the letter?"

"Can't imagine."

"We can't ignore it."

"No. We're going to shut this down."

"Too late for the girls," Garrett said.

"Maybe not."

"How's that?"

"I had a better view than you. Only four girls went into the van. All about the same height."

"You sure?"

"Six off the boat, four in the van."

"We got ourselves a new game," he said with anticipation.

"Yes, we do."

Morgan said, "What are you talking about?"

"We think there are two young girls that were smuggled into the country and they are being held in Escobar's house," I said.

"You've got to get them out," Morgan said. "More than anything, you have got to save them." Morgan was a man who rarely displayed elevated intensity, but when he did, it rose from a fiery core.

"It's not what we thought, but we've got our leverage to get the letter," Garrett said.

"We'll free the girls and trade him the letter for our silence," I said.

"And shut him down?" Morgan asked.

"Absolutely," I said.

CHAPTER 21

Escobar

The deeper Escobar sunk into the abyss, the more he viewed the letter as his salvation.

He rose early, as was his custom. Let the wasted youth sleep away the best part of the day. For a day, he believed, like life itself, was truly sweetest at the beginning when it was well rested, full of energy, and held promise for all that still to come. He had just tapped the edge of the pool for the final time, his wake going out before him and announcing his presence, when he noticed the shadow of Elvis flickering on the water. He lifted himself out and Elvis handed him the phone.

"It's Mendis," Elvis said.

Walter Mendis was talking before the phone found Escobar's ear. "— it was Kittredge. This man Travis never contacted him saying he'd secured the letter from you." Escobar felt his day sinking like a heavy rock in thin water.

"I plan—"

"I talk, you listen. I took care of Kittredge. I told him Travis was bluffing, told him that the first time he called. Did you think I was bluffing when I told you to fork over the letter?"

Escobar had decided that Mendis didn't need to know that he had charted his own course. He would insist that he simply hadn't done it yet. I'm sticking to my plan, he thought. I'll

195

keep shoving Mendis away and hold on to the letter until I get the terms I want.

"We just couldn't find a time that worked before today," Escobar said. The silence that bounced off the cell tower told him what Mendis thought of his excuse. Not that Escobar cared. He anticipated that Mendis would blow a little steam. Besides, he had his own point of contention to bring up with Mendis.

"He's coming over this morning, Walter. It's taken care of."

"Then Kittredge will be calling me."

"I don't know exactly——"

Mendis said. "I understand that you kept two back."

"You had no right——"

"That is not a decision for you to make," Mendis said. "Meanwhile, four more tonight."

"Don't tell me it's not my decision. It's my house. I'm done with this."

"You sealed your involvement when you didn't let those two pass. Send them back out tonight. Bring four in and we'll be done."

"Men or young girls?"

"What, you prejudiced? Girls. You do this one more time and I'll reconsider our loan arrangement to get the IRS off your back."

"I keep my clubs."

"I wouldn't go that——"

"I keep my clubs" Escobar said.

"One more shipment. Then we'll discuss me taking only the carpet business for my lien on your loan."

"You used me. You used my boat. It's a filthy business and I don't want anything to do with it. Men who pay their way is one thing, twelve-year-old girls are something else entirely. I keep control of my clubs, Walter. You can have a lien on the carpet business and house, nothing else."

The line was quiet, and Escobar wondered if he'd crossed another line.

"I didn't know that two would be so young," Mendis said in an even tone that Escobar didn't fall for. "Do the transfer tonight. Take those two back out. You hire a broker yet?"

"What?"

"A boat broker to unload your Carver."

"No."

"Raydel," Mendis said, "move on our plan today and get your ass out of the water, or you'll drown in it."

"I need your word, Walter. Tonight is the last night and I keep the clubs."

They observed a moment of silence and then Mendis said, "Last night. And you keep your clubs."

The air went quiet.

Escobar, his hand shaking, handed the wet phone back to Elvis. "You tell him I was swimming?"

"Why would I do that?"

"Forget it."

He wrapped a white towel around his waist, realized the water on his forehead wasn't from the pool, and sat down to read the morning paper. He placed another white towel on his lap so his drenched suit wouldn't soak through the first towel and ruin the paper. He hated reading the sports page when it was wet. He did everything he could to distance himself from the conversation with Mendis and to pretend that he still held a modicum of control over his life.

"Who's coming over this morning?" Elvis asked.

"Travis. Call him. Tell him to pick up that damn envelope."

"The one I prepared?"

"Yeah. Like we discussed. Everything is negotiable. Travis needs to learn that. Mendis just did."

"The clubs?"

"We keep them, but we got more tonight. Girls."

"So soon?" Elvis asked. He claimed the chair across from Escobar and sat with his elbows on his knees.

"It's the last time for us. Take them around the side and into the van, shut the door and get them the hell out of here."

"The two in the safe room?"

"They go back out tonight."

"That little one keeps praying. I thought that room would be soundproof. Good thing the kitchen's at the opposite end of the house," Elvis said.

"Two layers of Kevlar. Incredible. Keeps out bullets but allows a child's prayer to escape," Escobar said, but then wished he had not.

Escobar noted that Elvis referred to them in different manners, as if he couldn't decide what they were—returns, merchandise, black sticks—he had heard it all over the last twenty-four hours. It didn't matter now. Soon they, and the letter, would be out of his house, and then maybe he'd be able to relax and start working on Mendis's plan to appease the IRS. Olivia came and placed scrambled eggs with salmon, onions, and red bell peppers in the middle of the table and then took a step back.

"Just you two this morning?" she asked Escobar, her hands on her hips. Taking a stand. Escobar wondered if it was impromptu or if she had been summoning her courage for days.

"Yes, Olivia. Unless Sophia's here, it's just us two from now on."

"Because I got other things I can do if you don't respect—"

"I'm sure you got plenty to do," Escobar interrupted her, "I just told you the way it's going to be." Olivia gave him a hard stare, and they were silent for a few seconds.

"You be a good man," she said and turned and strode off before Escobar could respond.

"Why do you put up with that?" Elvis asked.

"Doesn't bother me."

"She's one bad day away from blowing."

"Who's not?"

"You know what I mean."

"She's been with me a long time. Started out as my cleaning lady before I was even married." Escobar thought of sharing with Elvis how Olivia was raising her grandchild, but he stopped short of that admission. Nor would he divulge that he had already funded the kid's college bill.

"Also, I told Natalie I was busy for a few days. I don't want her around here. She's been pestering the hell out of me to come over. Might be one of those nut cases you see in the movies. If I see her again, I'll leave no doubt where she belongs."

"When do you want me to call Travis?"

"Now. Tell him to come over."

"Just like that?"

"No, Elvis, I'm going to meet him at Checkpoint Charlie. What the hell you think?"

"Mendis expects a call from Kittredge. He won't get it."

Escobar picked up the pepper grinder and spread a generous amount over his eggs. He took a mouthful, chewed it deliberately, and sat back in his chair.

"We've been over this. *Everything* is negotiable. I'll take a loan on the carpet business. If I can get the IRS to forego even half, I'm in good shape. Besides, I don't entirely trust Mendis. He'll be pissed. But I got better terms from him today, and I bet I get even better terms tomorrow. Plus, I want to play Travis. He's been goading me since we met and it's time to turn the tables. Everyone negotiates."

Elvis finished a mouthful of eggs and said, "And if you push Mendis too far?"

"He'll appease me just to keep Kittredge in his pocket."

"You'd run that risk with Walter Mendis?"

I don't have a choice, Escobar thought, if I want to be the man walking through the door. But he didn't share that with Elvis. He just said, "Call Travis."

"We run our plan?" Elvis asked.

"Run the plan. He's pompous, conceited, and blows enough gas to float a hot air balloon. After what he did to Kittredge, he deserves this. If he doesn't bite, I'll come clean with him."

"I'll be waiting for him."

CHAPTER 22

Elvis was waiting for me on Escobar's driveway when I brought the front bumper of my truck to within a few inches of his knees. That's not entirely true either. He jumped back a few feet. Then I stopped the truck a few inches from his knees.

He asked me where the little Lexus was and I told him I was saving it to drive up his ass. He wished me good luck with that. I said it was a lot bigger than the green bananas he moaned with. He said it took one to know one. I said the Lexus was a greased primer; the big act was when I ripped him a new exit hole with the truck. He smiled and said there was a good chance he was my father because he rode my mother like a fat cow. It was a pleasant late morning and baby birds were chirping. The driveway was still wet from a hose-down and it glittered in Mr. Bright and Happy Sun.

There's nothing quite like a verbal enema to start your day.

"Mr. Escobar is waiting for you," he said.

"Mr. Escobar isn't handling this the way I would," he said. I was slightly annoyed that Elvis was the one to wind down our potty mouth sophomoric duel. I wanted to be the mature one and quit first.

"Mr. Escobar is keeping you alive."

"Perhaps he's doing the same for you."

"And all these years I've been appreciative of my heart."

Elvis had called and informed me that Escobar required my presence. I said my last trip was a waste. He said he personally didn't care if I showed up or not; he was just doing his job. Regardless of whether I received the letter or not, Garrett and I planned to enter the house at night. PC and Boyd were watching the grounds and reported that they saw no one leave or arrive, nor had the boats moved. We assumed the two young girls were being held pending arrangements to abuse them, move them, or kill them.

Possibly all three.

"He's waiting for you out back," Elvis said and motioned toward the paver walkway that circumvented the house.

"I'd like to go through the house if it's all the same to you. I love experiencing the beauty that dirty money buys." I was hoping to get some sense of where they might hold the girls and was surprised when Elvis told me to come to Escobar's to collect the letter. Then again, he had no reason to suspect that I knew about his human trafficking sidebar.

Elvis remained motionless at the black wrought iron gate and extended his arm. I brushed past him and around the house. Raydel Escobar sat at the table under the red umbrella. He was smoking a cigar and had a coffee cup in front of him. Morning stimulants. I took the seat across from him with my back to the Gulf.

A large and faded envelope rested on the table. It appeared to be sealed. I wondered whose lips had last graced its parchment. I thought of Dorothy Harrison.

"You never read it?" I asked.

"Read what?"

"The letter in that envelope. Did you open and read it?"

"No. Just gave them the address and the names on the envelope."

I glanced at the envelope: 1961, Dulles, Rusk, and McNamara. Dulles, as Garrett and I had discussed, was head of the CIA and leftover from Ike's band. Rusk and McNamara were Johnny's boys. A republican-appointed head of the CIA and the democratic head of State and Defense. I could still feel the hate. I assumed that Dulles considered Rusk and McNamara to be high IQ lightweights. Especially McNamara. Bobby-Mic was one of the whiz kids and his resume for secretary of defense duties highlighted his success with the Ford Falcon. In America, that made him an expert on how many Charlies to incinerate.

"And they knew it came from the old stone church?"

"I don't know what you're referring to."

"Naturally. But they would have figured that out. Must be a smoking howitzer to rattle Uncle Sam. Tell me, Escobar, how did a nice, run-of-the-mill, blackmailing businessman like you end up with an official government document from Sputnik days?" Sputnik was actually 1957, but I didn't expect Escobar to call me on that.

"I found it on the street. I told the IRS what it looked like and where I found it. I hadn't a clue if it was even worth the phone call. Two hours later a blocked number called and told me not to open it. Said he could care less about the IRS."

I granted him a few measures then said, "That's not all he said."

Escobar matched my pause with one of his own. "This country isn't as nice as we think it is."

"Shocking."

"Are you behind the phone call?"

"More like an instrument of the call."

"You seem to want this very badly," he said.

"You seem equally intent on destroying yourself."

"Why do you presume to know so much about me, Mr. Travis?"

"Maybe it's because you know so little about yourself."

"How do I know that you'll deliver the letter to the proper authorities?"

"How do I know that you're not running a meth lab in your house?" Or importing girls and selling them, I wanted to add, but caught my tongue in time. A major achievement for me. I didn't want to do anything to jeopardize the attack plan for tonight and certainly didn't want him to add extra security or be on heightened alert. I had thought of making an anonymous call to the cops, but Morgan convinced me otherwise.

Morgan had plans for the two young girls in the house. He had convinced Garrett and me that hell on earth awaited the two girls in Escobar's house if they were returned to the parents who sold them or turned their heads when they were kidnapped. I didn't question his conviction. He had sailed the Caribbean for over thirty years and I had reason to believe that he had rescued children before. I knew an Italian woman on St. Kitts who ran a one-room restaurant. She also had a hoard of foster children whom Morgan had intimate knowledge of and who greeted him enthusiastically. I was suspicious that he had deposited a few at her doorstep.

"Will the man who advised me not to open the letter call again?" Escobar asked. Something about his tone seemed contrived, but I let it go.

"Raydel." I leaned in across the table. "I know you don't like me, know you don't trust me, and I know you wished I had a fatal accident on the way over this morning, but believe me for one thing and it is this: those people aren't the postman, they don't ring twice."

"All three of your 'knows' are correct. Are we done here? I have other things to attend to."

204

"You haven't offered me anything to eat."

"Nor will I. Your boorish attitude is wearing."

"Boorish?"

"Elvis will show you the way out."

"Boorish? Now, that one hurt. And it's the second time this week. I liked you better when you had a houseful of guests."

"I've never been fond of you."

"That's the first sign of intelligence you've displayed."

"I assume I'll have the pleasure of never seeing you again."

"I have a proposition for you. But you need to throw a little hospitality my way. I'm parched," I said.

Escobar took a moment. Smoke seeped out of his mouth. Garrett had received a call from the colonel whose tone and urgency had strangely dissipated. Apparently the US government does negotiate. Told you. They were willing to work with Escobar on his tax problems if he belted a bar or two about Walter Mendis. It wouldn't work. Escobar couldn't divulge information about Mendis without implicating himself in the skin trade.

"Elvis," he started in cautiously and kept his eyes on mine, "get our friend here a drink."

"See, I knew we could do it," I said.

"Do what?"

"Be friends. Hey, King, a morning beer would be swell," I said, but didn't grant Elvis the courtesy of looking at him while I spoke.

Elvis reached into the refrigerator behind the outside bar and threw me a bottle that I caught with my left hand. I opened it using the side of the table and left a noticeable mark on the unblemished wood surface. The cap fell on the ground. Elvis remained leaning against the bar and to the left behind Escobar.

"What is your proposition?" Escobar asked.

"How's that again?"

"You said you had a proposition," he said with irritation.

"Christ, the stuff I say."

It was just the three of us, which was no match. I could knock Yogi and Boo-Boo's heads together and hand them over to Mr. Ranger and then look for the girls. There was an armed guard at the gate, but I presumed he was the type to run at the first pop of a gun. However, presuming someone's action while they hold a butter knife offers an entirely different set of scenarios than presuming their actions while they are in possession of a loaded rifle and being employed to protect the grounds. I wanted to keep it simple. Get the letter—check that box off. Return under cover of dark, get the girls—there goes another box. I took a long pull from the bottle neck. It was cold and tasted good. I'd have to consider resetting Tinker Bell.

"What do you have to offer me?" Escobar asked. He blew smoke in my face.

"I love the smell of dirty money in the morning. You don't do Wagner, do you?" I asked.

"Who?"

"'Ride of the Valkyries'?"

He stared at me and launched another cloud in my direction. Enough of that. "Here's the deal," I said and leaned over the table invading his space. "We'd like you to tell us about Walter Mendis. You see, the government doesn't really have interest in half-breed scum like you. They're after the men whose big banging brass balls they can hear from a mile away. You serve up Mendis and part of that seven million is forgiven."

Escobar hesitated. "I'm not interested."

"Good move." I leaned back into the chair. I was there to offer the deal, not sell it. "I was going to advise you against it, us being friends and all. You sing on a guy like Mendis and he'll come after you like an alligator that hasn't had a bite in five months. You'll end up buried at sea, which is highly preferable over what will happen to you in the US prison system."

"Elvis will show you the way out," he repeated.

"If it's all the same to you, I have higher aspirations for my final number than suffering a fatal heart attack at two a.m., falling off the head, and landing in a pool of my vomit."

"The hell you talking about?"

"Forget it."

He blew more smoke in my face. I was ready to sign up for a class action lawsuit. Like a knight, Elvis moved three spaces, two, and then one. It put him next to me. Escobar leaned back and put his cigar in the Copacabana ashtray. I wanted it. Not as bad as I wanted the guy's french toast at breakfast a few days ago, but that ashtray would look mighty fine on my table in the screened porch. He took a sip of his coffee.

I stood and said, "It's been a pleasure. Where is Sophia? In the house kneading meatloaf for dinner?"

Escobar placed his coffee mug on the table, rose, and faced me.

"She's out of town until tomorrow. I'll make sure to tell her that you came by and that you are not the charming man you pretend to be."

"I hate to napalm your dreams, but she *will* do a hell of a lot better than you." His eyes narrowed and he looked at me for a moment and neither of us spoke. I picked up the envelope. "I'll see myself out." I walked away with Elvis trailing me.

"Good-bye, Mr. Travis, or whoever you are. I trust I won't see you again. If I do it would be a serious blunder on your part," Escobar said from behind me. I spun around.

"Remember Tartakower?" I asked.

"Who?"

"Our chess friend."

"Ah, yes. The next-to-the-last mistake man."

"He also said, 'The blunders are all on the board, waiting to be made,' and 'chess is a fairy tale of 1001 blunders.' If you're into blunders, and you're the one who brought it up, you should bear those in mind."

I didn't wait for an answer but turned and walked out on the same paver brick sidewalk I had entered on. An old man coiled up a green garden hose at the far end of the pool and I did a double take, but decided I couldn't place him. Elvis shadowed me while Dusty Springfield's "The Windmills of Your Mind" faded slowly behind me. If I spent over a day in his house, I'd think Tricky Dicky was still president.

As the sun pressed into my upper back, I marveled that something so light as the letter could carry such weight. Like a small word, but not even that.

Only a letter.

CHAPTER 23

"Did you read it?" Kathleen asked.

"Not yet." I said.

"Why not?"

"I've got other issues that are more important right now."

"I thought you were dying to open it."

I had swung by her house and we were headed downtown to meet Garrett and Morgan for an early dinner. They had crewed together on a race at the yacht club. I'd left the envelope between my mattress and box spring. I'd told Garrett where it was in case a bolt of lightning took me out.

"I'll open it this evening."

"What other issues?"

"When does Sophia get back?" I asked.

"Tomorrow afternoon. We're tackling bathroom tile next."

"She's going to have some other issues to tackle."

"You keep saying that and you haven't said a thing."

I remained silent and pulled into the valet stand on Beach Drive. We hadn't decided on a restaurant, but the stand was conveniently located in the middle of the strip. I handed my keys to the young man and we ambled over to the hostess stand at South Sea Grill. It was our default location, the place where we ended up when we never reached a decision where to go. Much of what comprises our lives is a default, although not as easily identifiable as a restaurant.

"Outside table for two," I said.

The heavyset yet attractive young lady glanced up at me. Her hair looked like she stuck her finger in a socket and her makeup was one layer too many.

"Certainly," she said.

We recognized each other at the same time. She was the bartender at Escobar's house during the fund-raiser for Kittredge. She glanced at my woman.

"That's the lucky one?"

"Yes. My wife and mother of our eight children," I said.

She smiled at me. "Of course. Do you do threesomes?"

"You just keep coming, don't you?"

"Hmmm...that would be my dream."

I chuckled. She was fun. "Well, I like your attitude, but we were really just thinking of a four top."

"Wow. Not sure I'm even familiar with that. Want to tell me about it?"

"A table with four chairs."

"That's all? There're so many more possibilities with that, you must be joking." She battered her eyes at me.

"I'm serious."

"I'm serious too," she said.

"Strange we have the same name, but I got it first. Just a table, please."

She held my gaze for a moment and then looked down at her seating chart as if it was a Ouija board. "That one will be fine," I said, and pointed to a high top table that backed up to the front of the restaurant. By sitting high, we could see over Straub Park and out to the waters of Tampa Bay.

"Certainly," she said. I wondered if she used that word a lot. She glanced up from her chart. "This way please." We followed her to where I instructed and took our seats on the black wrought iron chairs with blue cushions.

"Serious, I'll be at the hostess stand if you need further assistance." She turned and drifted away, leaving only her back if I cared to reply, which I did not.

"Who's your new friend?" Kathleen asked.

"Someone I ran into at Escobar's. I told her we were married and we adopted autistic children."

"That's not funny."

"You're probably right."

"What other issues, Jake?"

I gazed at the art museum across the street. A horse-drawn carriage with no passengers went by. The woman holding the reins wore a skirt and cowboy boots. She looked sad. Despondent. The horse had a bag attached to its hindquarters and it slowly passed in front of the museum. I wondered if that was art. I glanced back at her and found her bright yet quiet eyes, waiting.

"The girl at the hostess stand—do you think she works on her hair to get that mess, or do you think she has an aversion to brushes?"

She looked at me and said nothing.

"I'd rather not say," I said.

"Why?"

"A light heart lives long."

Our waiter, Brian, uncorked the bottle and offered me a taste. Kathleen had befriended Brian and his partner Steven a few months ago, and they were pumped that she was moving downtown. "Cheers, Brian," I said. "It's never about the bottle, it's the hand that pours it."

"My," he said, "your boorishness might be worth it." He rotated to another table after he filled our glasses.

"Am I wearing that word around my neck?"

"No. That was on his own. Now give it to me straight and neat."

A midnight blue Bentley came down Beach Drive. I wondered if the guy driving it got his money from honest means. You never know. "When Garrett and I staked out Escobar's house the other night," I started in, "we witnessed something that altered the landscape. He's into human trafficking. It appears that he's the middleman using his boat to bring them from offshore and then loading them into a van. We're going back tonight. We're not done with him."

"What do you mean he's into human trafficking? Is he helping people enter illegally?"

"It's not that," I said looking into her hazel-greens. I didn't say anything for a moment and let the silence serve as a meaningful preamble to words.

"This is the part where my heart grows heavy, isn't it?" she asked.

"He's not importing wetbacks to do yard work. We saw six young girls, barely teenagers, get off the boat. But while six got off the boat, only four went in a van that peeled out of his drive. One girl was a small child, and I think she and her sister were held back. I doubt the younger one is a day over ten. I don't know. I know more about Brazilian fire ants than I do about kids. I have the grounds being watched and Garrett and I are going in tonight. If the young girls are still there, we're getting them out."

She didn't say anything and then looked away, down the street and away from what I just said. Away from me. When we first met, I wondered if she could be in my life, and if so, would my shadow world darken her heart? Across the street in the park, a dog tugged on its leash, pulling a lady on the other end. The lady held a small bag. The dog seemed happy. Like all dogs. Fanning the world with its tail. I'd be happy too if someone followed me around and cleaned up my shit.

"How do you know they are sisters?" Not looking at me.

"We overheard them when they first got off the boat."

"Get those girls out, Jake," she said as she suddenly turned back to me. "Shut him down. Hell is empty and they dressed up the devils before they left."

"Nicely put. Beats the original. And Sophia?"

Kathleen took another sip of her wine as if we were at a business dinner and had just learned that we blew the quarterly numbers. A minor setback. "She'll be fine. She'll have me. I'm going to take over her Christmas fund-raiser." She said it quickly, the thoughts turning to words while they were still formulating. "I'll have it in the condo. It will give her, and me, a project with a deadline. I'll let her run it, just use my place." She leaned in across the table. "Are you sure? That doesn't seem to be something he would do."

"Some people you never know."

"Be careful."

"My motto."

"No, that would be smart-aleck, reckless, and arrogant. What are you going to do with the girls?"

Arrogant? I don't really see that. I'd grant her two out of three. "Morgan has a lady on an island that will take them, assuming they don't want to return to their homes, which is a reasonable deduction, considering their parents likely traded them for a few dollars. I might show up at your door."

"I'll wait for you."

"I know."

Morgan and Garrett took the corner and spotted us. Morgan gave Kathleen a peck on her left cheek before sitting down. I poured wine into his glass.

"You're drinking?" Garrett asked and landed a hard stare at the glass. I'm surprised it didn't shatter.

"Apparently," I said. We never mixed firewater with business, but it was too nice a night to pass up, and I planned on only one glass of wine.

"Is Brian waiting on us?" Morgan asked.

"He is," Kathleen said.

"He and Steven can party like it's the last day of the world," Morgan said.

"He has similar deep convictions about you. It's a good motto," I said. "If it does turn out to be the last day of the world, or your last day in the world, you've closed it with style."

We ordered different meals and passed portions around the table. Morgan took on another bottle that he and Kathleen couldn't finish. Every day should end with an unfinished bottle of wine. I stopped after one glass. Garrett didn't say much. He looked at his watch repeatedly and crossed and uncrossed his legs enough times to burn the calories he took in.

"Your guys are good?" Garrett asked.

"Don't worry. They got the place covered."

PC and Boyd took skateboards over and were cruising the neighborhood. Sophia wasn't there, so I didn't worry about them being recognized as the young Mormon missionary and substitute FTD boy that had popped in a few days earlier.

"What time do we sail?" Morgan asked.

"Midnight. Unless my guys note activity." I could sense we were all anxious. "We'll leave soon."

Garrett stood up.

"Or right now," I added.

I settled the bill.

The drawbridge to her island was raised, stalling our forward motion. We sat with the windows down and the moon roof open as a solitary sailboat passed under the bridge. When you live on an island, it doesn't take much to block your path. The bridges used to irritate me as they interfered with my schedule, but I'd grown to appreciate the random interruption of my forward motion. They forced me to enjoy, without vote, the water below, the sky above, and the glow from the pink hotel that softened the underbelly of the night.

And gave more time with the person in my vessel.

"You really haven't read the letter?" she asked. We had been silent, and the sound of her voice made everything else bow down.

"I have not."

"Do you plan to?"

"I do."

"Do you also plan to answer each successive question with fewer words?"

"Yes."

She didn't say anything for a minute. A man on the bridge brought up a fish. He dropped it in a bucket. "It doesn't matter, does it?" she asked.

"Probably not. The letter led me to Escobar. He's blackmailing a congressman and he's selling girls. There's nothing in the contents of the letter that will trump that. But for now it can wait. It's not going anywhere." I was blackmailing a congressman as well, but we'll let that item slide.

She leaned over and gave me a kiss on the cheek.

"What's that for?"

"Having your priorities straight."

"It's a common trait with arrogant people."

I expected a retort, but nothing came. I pulled into her drive and escorted her to the front door. "I'll be seeing you later this evening," I said.

"Be careful," she said for the second time that evening.

I drove away with the same song, Ilo's "Lifeline," playing as when we pulled in. It sounded different without her next to me. It was different. The vacant sound and empty air were as real as everything they displaced. The truck was back to being just a truck.

My garage door went up and Garrett stood in front of the gray steel cabinet with its open doors on either side of him. He held a sniper rifle in his left hand. In his right hand he held the envelope that Escobar had given me. It was open.

"We've got a problem," Garrett said.

CHAPTER 24

Escobar

The guard at the front gate had called Escobar and told him that Natalie Binelli was there and wanted to see him or she would stand outside all night and "scream like a fucking virgin."

"Let her in," Escobar instructed him through the intercom. "Tell her we're out back." Fucking virgin, he thought. There's a cherry you only pop once.

Escobar had thought about taking Travis up on his offer. After all, isn't that what he wanted all along? But sing on Mendis? Escobar didn't even know that much about Mendis's operations. I could spill the conversation about importing young girls, he thought, but that would only serve to implicate myself. With his back against the wall, Mendis would be free to go after me.

But at least it was on the table. Serious negotiations have begun. Now let's see how much I can write off of that seven million bill.

"We got a shipment tonight," Elvis said. "We can't keep Natalie here." They were standing at the bar at the outdoor kitchen.

"I've got a score to settle with her. You may need to calm her down before she leaves."

Escobar had ignored her constant texting and was fine blowing her off now, but it was time to tame this filly. He was eager to straighten out his finances, keep Sophia happy, and rid himself of the increasingly whiny and clinging Ms. Binelli.

She rounded the corner like the heat-seeking tip of a whip screeching toward its target.

"Raydel, you can't treat me like that. I've been calling you and texting and—"

Escobar's right hand was waiting, and with the palm open he brought it in a sweeping arch that caught her flat on her left cheek. Natalie ran straight into it. She started to react but then planted her feet. The force of the blow snapped her head back and she let out a scream and collapsed to her knees. Elvis never moved.

Escobar shouted, "You want to play games? Want to fuck with me? Rearrange my wife's lipstick? Fine. Maybe I'll rearrange your face."

Natalie was bent over like a dog with her hands and knees on the paver bricks. One tan sandal with small red stones was a few feet off to the side, and he wondered how the hell that happened with a face slap. She didn't attempt to get up, and her light blue summer dress heaved in motion with her heavy gasps for air. Did I hit her that hard? Then it hit *him*; I can no longer say that I never struck a woman in my life. For the first time in his life he was thankful that his father was dead.

It was the cruelest thought to just drop in from the middle of nowhere.

Too much pressure. I got to get those girls out of here and get my life back in order. He didn't know whether to reach over and help her or plant a foot in her nose. He wanted to do both. "Get her the hell out of here," he spit out to Elvis.

"Come on, baby," Elvis said, and he gently bent down and put his arm around her. Escobar turned his back.

"Why did you hit me?" Natalie cried from behind him. He heard strength in her voice and thought back to a few days ago when he told her to vacate the house by noon, and she countered that she had things to do and would be leaving earlier. Showing him. "Why did you hit me?" But this time a little farther away and he knew Elvis was doing his job. "I'm sorry I did it, but why did you hit me?" It came through tears, but sounded like she was forcing it, toying with him.

Escobar brought his hands up to the sides of his forehead and massaged his temples. She's like the one in the safe room with her prayers; they just don't shut up.

He fixed himself a Cuban Manhattan and told himself to relax. The banker would be calling in the morning to arrange the loan. Escobar planned to contact the IRS after his call with the starched shirt and start brokering a deal with them. He knew that Travis would be outraged when he opened the envelope, but perhaps now they would bargain with him without the demand that he roll on Mendis.

Why hadn't he heard from Travis? Did he not even open it?

It had been Elvis's idea to create a fake envelope. Elvis remembered the box of envelopes and the blue Smith Corona typewriter in the office of the Welcome In. He went downtown, brought them back, and his third attempt was a dead ringer. Only the font was different, and Escobar realized that if Travis knew what the real deal looked like, he would have balked right away. But he didn't. Nor did he open it. Escobar thought that, at best, the decoy would buy him another twenty-four hours and serve notice to Travis that if they wanted the letter they needed to reduce his bill, and that snitching on Walter Mendis was off the table.

And, Escobar thought, serve notice to Mendis that if Mendis wanted to keep Kittredge happy, he would need to even further soften his terms.

He took a sip from his tumbler and fired up yet another cigar. His body relaxed as the tobacco and amber liquor worked their magic and created a sense of tranquility and control. Tonight, he thought. It all gets back to normal tonight. He took a long drag on his cigar. Hell, I might even do Natalie again. That slap was a stroke of genius. Bet she never screws around with lipstick again. Good God, how the hell did her sandal end up three feet away?

Elvis returned and took a seat next to Escobar. "She calmed down. I told her to fix herself a sandwich in the kitchen. Good thing Olivia's off today."

"You're right. She shouldn't be here," Escobar said.

"I told her to stay in the kitchen. She'll be fine. We won't take any longer than a fly's ass getting them from the boat to the van. Anthony just texted me and knows he's taking two back. He's got four coming in. I texted Ramon and confirmed it's tonight. Cruz and Victor are on the way."

"Anthony knows that you're returning two?"

"Yeah, I just said…"

"I don't care if you told me a dozen times."

"Don't worry. I got it. Those two leave the house tonight."

Escobar took another sip from his rum and noticed that Alejo had the chess pieces shining. Ever since the fund-raiser, Alejo, always neat himself with his shirttail tucked in, had polished the pieces daily, as if he were embarrassed and in some manner had previously come up short in performing his task. Escobar considered the thirty-two motionless and indifferent pieces. They had witnessed him strike Natalie. Like the other night in the garage, he thought, with my car. So much of what makes up our lives are just clueless props. Maybe it's better that way.

Tonight will be the last time that boat ever goes out. I'll rid myself of the prayer sisters. Tomorrow I'll call Travis, if he doesn't contact me first, and get my bill reduced. Then Mendis. I'll teach him to dance to my step.

And I'll be damned if I make another blunder.

CHAPTER 25

"What do you mean, 'We've got a problem'?"
But I knew. I knew like a man who takes a suitcase stuffed with cash and thinks it's cool not to verify its contents.

Arrogance.

I grabbed the envelope from Garrett, who had no intention of answering my question. I pulled out a single sheet of paper.

Mr. Travis,

Despite your prancing, nothing has changed. I possess the letter. In the spirit of cooperation, I suggest that we settle this immediately. I will give you the envelope. The IRS will reduce my bill by 50%. I will pay the balance over four years. This seems, to me, to be a common middle ground. A place where both parties can claim an amicable solution.

I have nothing to say about Walter Mendis other than that he is an outstanding businessman and a pillar of his community.

If you do not comply within 48 hours and grant me assurance that my needs will be met, I am very afraid that the envelope, which again I did not bring upon myself, would be better off in the hands of the New York Times, or perhaps numerous internet sites.

It was unsigned.

Prancing?

"Let's go," I said to Garrett, although I realized he was waiting for me.

"What do you think he gains by slipping you a fake envelope?"

I studied the envelope and allowed myself a twinge of forgiveness. It was faded and I could see the imprint from a manual typewriter. He'd done a good job. Were the names the same on the original? Escobar had no idea whether or not I knew what was on the outside, so I assumed he copied it word for word.

"I offered him the deal we discussed," I said. "He belts a note or two on Mendis, and in return the IRS negotiates. This is his way of negotiating."

"He's letting us know that Mendis is off the table and is buying time for us to work out a deal on his due bill."

"That's correct. But Escobar doesn't know that we know he's harboring immigrants, and possibly kidnapped ones at that."

"Let's close him down."

"Morgan?" I asked.

"Waiting in the boat."

I lowered *Impulse* from her lift and felt the familiar rush of anticipation when the water came up to displace her hull and we settled onto the oldest road in the world. A highway that has remained unchanged since man's first contraption floated upon its surface. Only the vessels and occupants have changed; the road is the same.

PC had texted me that a woman in a blue dress had been let in the front of the house and hadn't emerged. He reported no signs of anyone leaving the home. I asked if he'd secured the supplies for his final scene, and he told me to stop worrying.

"What's the plan?" Garrett asked.

"I'm going straight to the safe room to grab the girls. That leaves Escobar, Elvis, the security guard, or guards, and the woman who they say is in the house. The diversion should draw them out of the house."

"The letter?"

"With any luck the letter will be in the safe room. If not, I'll bring the girls out to Morgan and then I'll confront Escobar. I'll trade my silence for the letter. If he stalls I'll choke the son of a bitch until he sees my point of view. He certainly has no legal recourse no matter what we do."

"What about the riffraff?" Garrett asked.

"With luck I'll be in and out and they'll never know it. If not, preferably tied up and we call the locals."

"I have no preferences outside of walking out alive with the girls."

"I'm just saying."

We reviewed the timetable and fall back options.

"Usual place?" Morgan interjected as we headed into the thirty-foot-deep channel off my dock.

"Behind the mangrove island to the south. What's the tide like?" I asked.

"Rising tide, but not a strong one."

"We'll be fine." I turned to Garrett. "I'll be down soon as I get the girls."

"And if they're not in the safe room?"

"I'll be kicking in doors."

I played a nightmare scenario through my head of having to check every room in the house and how long that would take. As we approached Escobar's, Morgan asked, "How do you plan to empty the house?"

"PC and Boyd requisitioned supplies earlier today for a little fourth of July celebration," I said. "Enough to cause a diversion, but hopefully not too much of one."

"Dark night. It should be a good show," he said. "I hope it doesn't scare Nevis."

"How would it do that?" I asked.

"She just came up off the port bow. Followed us over here."

I didn't bother to look. I placed my serrated knife in the thigh rig and tucked my gun in a shoulder holster under my left arm and inside my lightweight jacket that I wore for its numerous pockets. My Boker folder knife was in the zipped pocket of my cargo shorts. I opted not to wear the short wet suit, as the water would only be about two feet deep. I laced my boat shoes extra tight. Garrett placed his Sig Sauer in his shoulder holster and stashed extra magazine clips in his pocket. His M110 SASS already had its PVS-26 night sight attached to it. Morgan again took *Impulse* in without any lights, cut the engine, and poled us into the black waters under the mangroves.

"Do they go on your signal?" Garrett asked.

"I text PC when we're in position. Within a minute the show begins. He's got yours and Morgan's number, everybody's on group message."

"You're not worried about cops?" Morgan asked.

"I told them not to overdo it. I don't think Escobar will be calling five-oh. That's the last thing he needs with the girls in the house."

"We OK here?" Morgan asked.

"Perfect. But after we leave, turn her around. We may need to exit at a different pace than we came in."

"What are their ages again?" he asked.

"Not sure. Young. Too young."

"Ready?" Garrett said.

I didn't answer, but slipped over the starboard side of my boat and quietly worked my way through the still waters to Raydel Escobar's house. I never heard Garrett behind me, but I heard a dolphin blow from the deeper water. I wondered if it really was Nevis. I was only a few feet onto the shore when I received a group text from PC. Two men with guns had been let in the front gate.

That flushed my plans for a short night and another glass of wine.

CHAPTER 26

Escobar

"Cruz and Victor are here, I'm letting them in," Elvis said as he hurried out of the study and left Escobar alone.

Escobar snatched the remote off the chess table and swelled up the sound of Pink Martini. He admired the group's timeless orchestral sound and unending range of genres. Patrons in his clubs never guessed that they were a modern band. Tomorrow, he thought. I can go back to enjoying the music. Tomorrow.

When Elvis left, he had heard him pound on the safe room door and give the girls a generic "shut the fuck up." He doubted it would do any good as the dozen previous such admonishments had no effect. The little one practically screamed her prayers. The same one she had said in the garage. "We are weak but he is strong." Over and over. He thought he heard them giggling after Elvis's outburst and then one of them yelled that she wanted a brush, and that was followed by more laughs. He should have let Ramon take them.

At first he told himself it was the damn yellow ribbon. How was he supposed to ignore that? But he knew there was more because it kept flashing in his mind even though he tried to stomp it out like a wildfire. It was the way the older girl's eyes locked on his, as if she knew she could turn him and he didn't like the whole mess. He felt disgusted with himself for his weak thoughts and doubts. Money walking through the door, he was certain, never entertained self-doubt. He turned when he heard Elvis enter the room with Cruz and Victor tight behind him. He backed the volume down.

"Anthony's fifteen minutes out. His coordinates are close in this time. We're leaving soon," Elvis said.

"Did you text Ramon?"

"He should be here in ten. He asked if we enjoyed the *nina chiquitas*. I told him they reminded me of his sister, but they smelled a lot better."

Escobar grinned, although he saw not the least bit of humor in the statement. Victor let out a two-syllable laugh, but Cruz gave no expression.

Escobar said, "Why's Anthony so close and early? Hell, it's barely midnight."

"Don't know," Elvis said.

"You see any boats out, just head back. Understand?"

"What if Anthony doesn't take the returns?"

"He will. He's got his orders."

"What he says on the phone doesn't mean much on the water."

"Those two don't come back into this house or onto this property," Escobar said and wondered what he had just implied.

"You won't see them after tonight. I'll wait till the last minute and take them out. You know Natalie's still in the kitchen."

"I thought you were getting her out of here."

"No, what I said was—"

"You sure as hell better make sure she doesn't see this shit. Why didn't you dump her like I told you to?"

Elvis started to go in one direction, but said, "I can't let her out now, she may bump into Ramon coming in. She's OK. I told her to glue her ass in the kitchen and not move."

Escobar rubbed his forehead with his hands, anticipating a thundering headache that hadn't yet found him. All he wanted to do was dig himself out, but he felt himself sinking lower. Being sucked in by something he couldn't feel, yet was as real and as strong as anything he'd ever known.

"Get the girls and——" Escobar said, but was halted by a series of explosions from the front of the house.

"Fireworks?" Elvis asked before Escobar had a chance to finish his thoughts.

"In the front yard?"

Escobar bolted past the men, who followed him down his wide-paneled walnut walls and past the woman with droplets of water on her golden naked stomach. He descended the curved front staircase of his house, passed through the Mediterranean foyer with its nod toward Spanish influence, and flung open the front door. Flashes of red, green, and white exploded in the sky above the vacant lot across the street. Escobar, Elvis, and Cruz looked straight ahead to the far corner of the lot that backed up to scrub land where another eruption of fireworks went searching for the heavens. But Victor watched the streams of bright colors drip down the black sky as if a god had sprinkled cookie glitter on the earth.

"Kids," Elvis said. "We'll clean them out then we've got to hustle out of here so we're not late." He started to move across the drive with Cruz and Victor behind him.

"Wait a second," Escobar said. Elvis stopped and spun and Cruz and Victor piled into him like billiard balls.

"What?"

"You stay here," Escobar said. "Cruz, you and Victor flush them out."

Cruz and Victor sprinted across the drive just as a series of green and white sparkles rained from the sky.

"Pretty solid stuff for some kids," Elvis said.

"That's what I'm thinking," Escobar said, although it wasn't. He just didn't want to greet Ramon by himself if he showed up early. His words ran into the throttle of an engine and the squeal of car tires. A final flash of white erupted in the sky and illuminated a Camaro with a flame-painted side just as it jumped away from the curb about two hundred feet down the road.

Elvis said, "That car was in the neighborhood a few days ago. I saw it while taking my run."

"Think it means anything?"

Elvis didn't answer. He spun and tackled the stairs three at a time.

CHAPTER 27

Sophia had stated the keyhole was behind the picture of the nude female bronze belly with the enticing water droplets that I wanted to lick.

I had entered through the rear door and texted PC from the butler's pantry. During the fund-raiser, I had noticed it was sequestered from the main traffic pattern of the house. Within a minute of texting PC, the fireworks had exploded, followed by heavy feet descending the stairs. I was betting on the fireworks giving me enough time to spring the girls. The addition of two more men to the equation, while not welcoming news, didn't alter my plans. Arrogant people do denial well.

"Come on, baby, be good to me," I whispered as I lifted the picture off its hook and set it on the floor against the wall.

A flat electronic keypad barely broke the surface of the wall where the picture had hung.

There was no place for a manual key.

I picked up the frame. It was heavier than I expected. I ripped off the brown paper backing. No key. No lock for a key. There seemed to be another backing to the frame, but before I ripped the house to shreds, I wanted to make certain they were inside. For all I knew they were surfing videos games in a bedroom. When they spoke the night I saw them, the older girl was called Maria and the little one Rosa. I didn't want to be a one-man band, but I had to know.

I knocked on the door. "Maria? Rosa? Can you hear me? I'm here to help you."

I listened to my heart pounding. Fireworks exploded. And music. Always music. I knocked again. Double Kevlar. Was it soundproof?

"Maria? Rosa?" Louder this time. I leaned in hard and pressed my ear to the walnut wood. Morgan told me he had found Kathleen that night on the beach by channeling all his senses into listening. Some Zen shit. I tried to shut out the music and closed myself to everything except what might come from behind the door. I pounded on it.

"Anybody in there?" I shouted somewhere between loud enough for them to hear over the music and through double Kevlar, but not loud enough for the men standing outside to pick up. I was in no-man's land and knew the mortality rate there was high.

"Maria, Rosa!" I shouted.

"Jesus?" It was the voice of a young girl from inside the room.

"Turn around." It was the voice of Elvis from behind me.

I spun and was met with the extended barrel of a .35-caliber handgun pointing between my eyes from a few feet away.

"Elvis, I thought you left the building."

"Keep your hands out in front of you."

"You don't have the code do you? If so, I can be out of here in no time."

"Who told you to look there?"

"Logical place for a lock."

"We changed to the pad months ago. You're going to turn back around and walk slowly to the study."

"I was thinking more like a beer by the pool, like we did in the old days."

"Move."

"Your choice," I said. "But I want you to know that you can still get out of this alive."

Elvis looked at me and took aim at my forehead. I like my forehead. I turned around and moved toward the study. A young voice from behind the walnut panel shouted for Jesus. Richard Harris's pained voice came through the cranked house speaker. He was lamenting that someone left the cake out in the rain and things could never be the same again.

We've all got problems.

CHAPTER 28

"You packing?" Elvis asked me. We were in the middle of Escobar's study. At least I knew where the girls were. There's a bright side to everything.

"I am. Do you want me to shoot you now or later?"

"I ought to blow your jaw off just to shut you the fuck up."

"It wasn't rhetorical. I was being polite."

Garrett expected me within five minutes and if I didn't come down, he was coming up. I didn't want to be standing there staring at Elvis's .35—that would just be flat out embarrassing. Garrett would blame it on the glass of wine. I didn't need that shit in my life.

"Get it real slow and drop it on the floor."

I reached under my jacket and retrieved my gun. I tossed it on the floor and it slid over to Escobar's desk.

"I said to just drop it."

"Impressive wax job."

"Take your jacket off and place your knife on the floor."

I reached down and unsheathed my knife and let it fall. I took off my jacket and tossed it to the side.

"What do you think the congressman will say about me going AWOL on your property?"

"We're going to the docks and you're going for a midnight swim. You were never here tonight. Hands in pockets and walk in front of me."

"What are you boys up to? Another shipment of prepubescent girls? What do they fetch these days, Elvis, ten, twenty thousand apiece? And then what, out to the street where they decorate their arms with needle marks and finally OD at age sixteen?"

"How'd you know about them?"

"Purely by accident. I was doing laps in front of the house a few nights ago and thinking about how to yank the letter out of your grasp when the shipment came in."

He hesitated a second as if he was going to pursue that line of questioning, but then just said, "Move." He waved his gun toward the steps.

I didn't move.

"You can walk or I can drag you, and I don't give a rat's ass either way," he said. He pointed the gun at my right knee.

I like my right knee. Not with the same affinity I have for my head, but I didn't want it shattered. I considered the probability of him popping me in the knee far greater than a slug to the head. I put my hands in my pockets and approached him at a leisurely pace. He backed up and let me through to the hall. I felt the Boker knife with my right hand and opened it. I didn't know where Escobar and the other men were, but assumed that Garrett had them contained.

Of course, Garrett assumed that I had a girl under each arm and was doing my impersonation of Usain Bolt making a mad dash for the boat.

I strolled down the hall with Elvis, who unfortunately maintained a safe distance behind me. When I got to the paneled door of the safe room I stopped. Elvis did likewise, but not until he took another step and closed the gap. It's all about speed: distance divided by time. I pivoted halfway around to my left and looked him straight in the eye. With my right hand

I slid the Boker knife out of my pocket and held it tight against my right leg.

"I've got friends," I said. "They'll pay for my release. A lot of money for a guy like you." I saw a faint smile on his lips. I wanted him to let his guard down, if not visibly, at least subconsciously. I needed his reaction time to slow down. Distance divided by time.

"Keep walking."

"It could mean some serious money to you." I kept my eyes on him and turned around as if I was going to start walking. "I'm not talking just a few..." I never finished. I crouched low and brought my left hand out of my pocket and swung around fast, reaching out for his right wrist to neutralize his gun. With my right arm I brought the Boker straight into his midsection. Not a sweeping arc, but a direct line. Distance sliced by time.

Elvis coughed out a surprised gasp and his eyes almost came out of their sockets. But a three-inch knife wasn't going to bring him down. I left the knife planted in his stomach and with my right arm reached out to his left fist that was coming in at me. We locked hands and I hooked my left foot behind his right ankle and shoved him backward, falling on top of him. My stomach landed on the handle of the blade and I felt a rush of air blow out of him. Elvis was a street fighter and the surprise and fear in his eyes quickly vanished. His strength came back despite the presence of a steel blade embedded in his upper intestines. We were locked together with me on top and our faces inches apart, our eyes glued together. That is when I seized the opportunity to do what I wanted to do the first time we met.

I opened wide and clamped down fast and hard on his nose, using my jaws as a vise grip.

The cartilage from his nose crackled in my teeth. I whipped my head violently side to side. His warm blood gushed and made everything slippery. I summoned my emotions from the sunken concrete, squeezed my jaws for the sake of humanity, and gave everything I had to trying to tear a hole in his face. His lessened his grip on his gun and I wrestled control of it.

I released my jaw and spit blood, tissue, and bone into his face. His nose rested somewhere below his right eye. I felt the handle of the knife in my stomach, and his warm blood invaded my skin. I brought his gun up tight to his right temple.

"Do you want me to shoot you now or later?"

He spit blood in my face.

"Your eye's next," I said.

His eyes ballooned.

I stood. There was a growing pool of blood on the floor, being fed by the stream from his nose that was leaking blood faster than the knife wound. The new owners would need to get that spot professionally cleaned. His breathing was labored. I reached down and cleanly withdrew the knife from his torso. It hadn't gone in as far as I had thought. "The key or the code to the safe room. Live or die."

"Call me a doctor." His words came out like garbled Springsteen lyrics. With his right hand he hesitantly felt what used to be his face.

I said, "You're a doctor."

"Asshole. Call me a doctor."

"I won't ask again."

He hesitated. "Three-six-*d*."

"That's the best you guys could do?"

"Three-six-*d*. Call me a doctor."

"Sure, Elvis, but first I've got to make sure that three-six-*d* will do the trick."

I yanked a cord out of Escobar's desk lamp of a monkey climbing a palm tree and bound his wrists together. I tied his ankles with an extension cord. I shredded a curtain—it surprised me with its softness—and stuffed it in his mouth. I tightly wrapped another piece of curtain around what used to be his nose to stem the bleeding. His midsection wound didn't look that threatening, but I took his belt off and placed it around his stomach and drew it tight to apply as much pressure as possible.

"Breathe out of your mouth," I said. "Or don't breathe at all. It doesn't matter to me."

I started to walk toward the safe room when his phone indicated that he was receiving a text. I returned and searched his pockets until I located his phone.

there in ten

It was from Ramon, whoever he was. If he was part of the same group that came the other night when there was a shipment, then it would mean three more guys. I texted Garrett and told him we had a party. I texted Ramon and said "ok."

"I'll keep this for you," I said to Elvis as I put his phone in my pocket. I reclaimed my jacket and put my gun in the shoulder holster. I wiped the Boker, closed it, and put it in my right cargo pocket. Elvis's gun went in my left pocket.

I went to the keypad and entered 3-6-d. I heard the lock click and pulled the door toward me.

Two girls. One a little older than the other. Their clothes were dirty and the room had an odor of unclean bodies. The taller girl stood and the little girl was on the floor with a key in her hand. The girl on the floor had mangled hair that doubled the size of her head. The tall one had shorter back hair and a high forehead, as if she could view over the top of the world. It gave her a sense of maturity and I wondered how real it was. A ragged, one-eyed doll with a yellow flower lay on the floor. They looked at me with trepidation. I realized that I still had the blood of Elvis on my face. I brought my shirt up and wiped it over my mouth and face.

I glanced around the room. Paper littered the floor and several drawers were open.

"I'm here to get you out."

"Rosa found the key," the older girl blurted with pride while staring at me. "We searched until we found it."

"Maria decided that we had to get out on our own," Rosa said.

"You didn't see a large envelope, did you?"

"No," Maria said, and confusion masked her face.

"You sure?" I took a step in and started shifting through the mess, but it was mostly security cassettes and an odd assortment of memorabilia. There was a six-inch replica of the Eiffel Tower and a tin button of man's first landing on the moon. It had a picture of the Apollo 11 crew: Armstrong, Collins, and Aldrin. They looked confident.

"Maria didn't think you would come," Rosa said. She stood up, bent her head back, and looked up to my face. "Are you Jesus?" She giggled.

"No. My name is Jacob." I hardly ever use my proper name and wondered what possessed me. Rosa seemed to consider my response as if I had received partial credit. Then she gave me a second chance.

"Are you strong?"

"I am. Let's go, girls."

I wanted to get the girls to Morgan and then return for the letter and make certain that Garrett didn't need help with the two extra men on the premises.

I bent over and scooped up Rosa with my right arm. It was like picking up a pillowcase with sticks in it. I looked at Maria to make certain she would follow and still didn't view me as an apparition. Her eyes were uncommonly—even disturbingly—mature and calm, but there was more. An emanation of hope and relief. My back was to the door and I was facing her with Rosa in my arms.

"Annie," Rosa said.

Maria bent over and picked up the doll, but when she looked back her eyes ran past me and the hope was gone. Her gaze was now mixed with fear and sorrow, and I thought it a most unusual combination for a child. I felt, in some unfathomable fashion, that I had already failed this person whom I did not know. I thought of dropping Rosa and making my move, but I couldn't take the chance with the two girls and such a confined space. Twice in one night.

Maybe it was the wine.

CHAPTER 29

I spun around and faced the six-inch barrel of Raydel Escobar's .357 magnum Smith & Wesson. It was a fine gun and always reminded me of fine wine.

Rotating chamber. Polished wood handle. The beginning of the "magnum" era. Introduced in 1934 at the height of the gangster wars—designed to blow speakeasy doors clean off their hinges—it was an instant classic. The word "magnum," though, is a tad misleading. The Brits coined the term over 150 years ago when they developed an artillery cartridge twice the size of previous ones. The size disparity reminded the Redcoats of the difference between a regular bottle of wine, roughly the size of the standard cartridge, and the double-sized bottle, called a magnum. It's been a marketing misnomer ever since. When I think of Dirty Harry, I think of 1.5 liters of aged liquid Bordeaux. I suspect I'm alone with that.

This particular magnum popped a serious cork and was aimed directly at me.

I had wasted precious time on Elvis. I would not make that mistake again.

"What the hell are you doing here?" Escobar asked.

"I want the letter."

"What happened to your face?"

"I ate Elvis's nose for dinner. What happened to your sense of decency?"

"I never had one. Your misjudgment will cost you dearly."

"So did Elvis's."

"Where is he?"

"The floor of your study, just around the corner, swimming in his blood. I bandaged him up to keep him breathing, but you'll still need a mop." And I needed all the goodwill I could garner.

"How do you know about these girls?"

"I've been over this already with Elvis. I was doing laps a few nights ago off your dock, when he brought——"

"Shut up. They were never supposed to be here. I'm not in this type of business."

"Looks like it to me."

He took a step back from me. Smart move. His gun was level at my eyes. I didn't think Escobar had the guts to pull the trigger. What if he did? I like my eyes. Maria had moved up close behind me and I felt her body next to mine. I wish she hadn't done that. I couldn't maneuver in such a tight spot with two girls attached to me. It would be a fine time for Garrett to make an appearance.

Escobar hesitated and then his conviction came. He took two steps back. "Downstairs. All three of you. You know the way. You try anything funny, I pull the trigger six times and we see what's left. You understand?"

"If I try anything seriously, does that trigger the same response?"

"Start moving."

I didn't budge. "Have you even fired that thing before? It's a beautiful piece, but puts out major noise."

"I can pull the trigger."

"You'd be surprised. That's actually a lot harder to do than you think, and you just can't imagine the nightmares that follow. You can still walk away, you know." I threw it out with all the sincerity I could muster. "You can nail Mendis. The government is far more interested in him than they are in you. You'll get a reduced sentence. More importantly, you'll live. Don't make the last mistake. Think, man. Think where this all leads."

I was giving peace, and Raydel Escobar, every chance I could. His mouth tightened and his jaw clenched. A vein swelled in his thick neck as if his heart was pumping a tide of blood. He seemed, if only for the briefest moment, to see the precipice that his decisions had brought him to. He had choice; a minute decision that would form his life and determine what world awaited him. I felt Maria move closer as if even she understood the delicate situation.

Raydel Escobar couldn't decide who he was, and in the end, that was his most defining characteristic. Like a leaf floating on the water, the currents and winds determined the direction of his life.

"Start walking," he said. His voice was calm and resolved. His hand steady. We are who we are and we discover that at the most unexpected moments.

"Why don't you go check Elvis out?" I preferred to keep the action upstairs and thought I could make a move on him if he went to Elvis's aid.

"Walk."

I turned and started down the hall. Maria moved to my left and I reached down and took her hand. She grabbed it tight as if she had been waiting for it, and I felt bad for not holding it earlier. Like a miniature parade we passed under Sophia's antique seashell sconces. Maria's boney hand was in my left hand and the ridiculous lightness of Rosa sat on my right hip. I took stock of what I had: two guns, two knives, two cell phones, two girls, one doll, and a double bottle of wine packed with gunpowder aimed at my head.

Everything but the letter.

CHAPTER 30

We had just reached the bottom of the stairs when the front door flung open and two men burst through.

"Cruz, haul them to the boat. I got to check on Elvis," Escobar immediately instructed one of the men. Both men had rifles and I recognized them—Cruz's soiled blue bandana looked as if it had never left his head—as the same two that had escorted the girls off the boat the other night.

"Who the hell is he?" Cruz said.

"Just take them to the boat," Escobar insisted.

"Where's Elvis?" Cruz asked without moving.

"This guy jumped him. I got to see if he's OK."

Cruz faced me and cut a look at Escobar. "Tell me what's going on, or Victor and I are gone. We're not sticking our neck out for you."

I started to say something, but remained silent. I wanted to see how this played out. Maria was slightly behind me. Rosa was still on my right hip, clutching her doll with her head tucked under my chin. I was a freakish caricature mutant of Mr. Rogers and Rambo.

Escobar hesitated. "This guy's been trying to muscle in on us and Elvis caught him. Take him out with you on the boat and toss him over, after you put a hole in him."

Cruz looked at me. "That right? You trying to move in on our trade?"

"Actually, I'm scouting for a children's choir," I said.

"You're full of shit, Escobar," Cruz said, but his eyes still held mine. "And you're a lying fuck." He took a step closer to me. "You tell me what's going on, or you're going to watch me take a fat broomstick to one of your little friends."

"Go fuck yourself with it."

His right came in fast and my first reaction was to jerk my head back. But Rosa was on my right and if I ducked I ran the risk of his fist missing me and hitting her. I stuck my face out to meet his punch while I moved my right arm down to lower her away from the incoming missile. It worked. My face stopped his fist, which is the most optimistic spin I can put on the whole sad situation. He rocked me back on my heels, but I stayed up. My head felt as if a thousand tiny needles in unison were fired from the inside through my skull.

I swirled my tongue around my mouth in an exaggerated manner. "You must be a lefty." He started for me again, but Escobar stepped in.

"He's provoking you, you imbecile," Escobar said. "We got to get him out of here. You want to play games, do it on the boat. Now take him out. I'm going to get Elvis."

"He won't be joining you tonight," I said. I had a piece of Elvis's nose cartilage that had been stuck between my upper left cuspid and lateral incisor and it finally broke free courtesy of Cruz's right hook. I spit it out at Escobar. "That's part of his nose. See if you can put it back on for him."

Escobar looked at the piece on his polished wood floor and then glanced at me like he was seeing me for the first time. But Cruz never took his eyes off me. He smiled. He smiled like he knew what he was dealing with and was back home on familiar ground. It was not what I wanted to see.

"Let's go," Cruz said in a calm voice. He drew a small pistol from his jacket and pointed it at Maria. "And if you say one more thing, one word, I shoot the little cunt that's hiding behind you. I shoot her as she holds your hand, and you will still be holding her hand when her life leaves her. You will be holding her hand when you drag her bloody body over the floor. If you understand me, shake your head up and down."

I nodded my head up and down.

Maria grabbed my hand and moved in close until she was pressed hard against Elvis's gun. Rosa started to cry. A soft whimper, and then from the whimper, words of desperation as if they were no longer to be believed but they were all she had.

"Jesus loves me, this I know, for the Bible tells me so. Little ones to him——"

"Shut her up," Cruz said.

I remained silent.

"——belong, they are weak, but he is strong."

"Move!" Cruz shouted and pointed his gun in my face. I turned around and started for the back door when I heard the sound of rapid gunfire popping from the front of the house and down the street. I was beginning to think Garrett called in sick.

I pivoted and saw Escobar and Victor looking toward the front door, but Cruz never took his eyes off me or his gun off Maria. "My promise holds, *comprende?*" he said. I nodded my head up and down.

We heard the staccato retort of more gunfire. "What the hell," Escobar said, staring at his front door as if he'd never seen it before. "Think that's Ramon? Cruz, keep a gun on our friend. Victor, see what's going on."

Cruz said, "Maybe our friend here brought company, and Ramon's having target practice with him. You ever meet Ramon?" He smiled at me. "He would have eaten that piece of nose. Escobar, you check on Elvis, Victor, watch this guy and shoot the girl if he moves. I'm going out front to see what's going down."

Escobar hesitated. I wondered how he would take the change of command. "I need to know what's happening," he said and followed Cruz out the front door. Elvis deserved better. That left Victor standing in front of me with a gun. The house was now strangely quiet except for the music, which I was beginning to think was part of the air that Escobar breathed.

"Jacob?" I was startled to hear my name coming from Rosa. "Yes?"

Victor didn't shoot me.

"Was that really part of a nose?"

"No. I made that up."

"Can we leave now?" Rosa asked.

"What do you think, Victor?" I said, looking at him. "My assault team is outside shredding Ramon into noodles, Elvis is disfigured for life, and your two friends are next. Time to look out for yourself. Why don't you ride the boat to freedom? Go, before I change my mind."

He looked at me for a few bars and then said, "Shut up." He had a pronounced scar that ran under his right eye and wore a turtleneck sweater the color of dirty snow. In Florida. In the summer. I couldn't place his accent and wondered where he was from.

"The clock is ticking on your life. It's your decision whether or not you see another day."

"I said shut the fuck up."

"You actually added 'I said the fuck' the second time around." His jaw tightened and he cocked his head like a dog. There was hesitation in his eyes. I brought it home. "If you want to live, you need to leave." This time he didn't answer me, but kept his gun level with my eyes. I'd really had enough of that for one evening, but was carrying too much weight to do much about it.

"Jacob?" Maria this time.

"Yes?" She stepped out from behind me and took one pace toward Victor, which placed her between him and me.

"I need to use the bathroom." Maria still held my hand and squeezed it several times in rhythm.

"What do you think, Victor?"

"She can pee in her pants."

"Then she'll smell like you."

"Just shut—" He never finished as spitting small arms gunfire shattered our conversation. He gave the front door a quick look and shifted his weight. He glanced at me and back to the door. His gun was still pointed in the general vicinity of my head, although he lowered the angle as if considering my offer.

Maria continued, "I really need to use the bathroom. And Rosa should too if we are to go on a boat ride."

I didn't say anything. Maria squeezed my hand as if she were trying to tell me something. Maybe she sensed that my options were limited. Maybe she just needed to pee. The pain in my head increased exponentially with each beat of my heart.

She released my hand and took two solid steps toward Victor. "Please, sir, I really need to go."

She was now directly in front of him and partially blocked his view. It was the gustiest move I'd seen all night. Maybe in years. How old was this girl? In a relaxed pose, I slipped my left hand into my pants pocket and felt the handle of Elvis's gun. Two more shots echoed from out front. Escobar's house was at the end of a deserted street and the nearest house was empty. Still, between the fireworks and guns, it wasn't hard to imagine the police soon responding to someone's curiosity. Besides, although I doubted it, Garrett might be in trouble.

It was time to close down romper room, clamp my wise-ass mouth, and get the job done.

"Victor, let her pee and let us go," I said. I shifted Rosa so she was sitting higher on my right hip. She held her head up straight and clutched her doll in her right arm. I stood relaxed with my left hand in my pocket holding Elvis's gun.

Victor looked at me. My own gun was under my left shoulder. He knew I couldn't reach it without dropping Rosa.

"Go," he said with a tone of resignation and didn't take his eyes off of me. Was he telling me to leave with the girls, or letting Maria know it was OK to use the bathroom?

"Where is it?" she asked.

Victor took his eyes off me for a split second and glanced around the room. I chose not to question his last word. I had already screwed up by burning time to bandage Elvis. Victor was about a foot taller than Maria, but it hit me that no one stood taller than her in Raydel Escobar's great room. I brought my right arm up, hooked Rosa's head, and turned her into my body while I simultaneously kept my eyes on Victor's gun. I quickly raised Elvis's gun and squeezed the trigger twice. At the last instant I looked past his gun and into his eyes, and I wish to hell I hadn't done that. He met my gaze with surprise and then he went down.

We are who we are and we discover that at the most unexpected moments.

Maria stood over the fallen body and then calmly turned and looked at me. There was no expression on her face, and that rocked me more than Cruz's right.

"You shot him?" Rosa asked. She sat erect on my hip and looked down at the body as she might peer at a fish in a pond.

"He was a bad man. I'm putting you back into the security room."

"But Maria needs to use the bathroom," Rosa said.

"No I don't."

"Let's go," I said and stepped toward the stairs. I wanted to get them out of there.

"No," Maria said from behind me. I turned and looked at her. She stood with her feet apart and her arms at her sides. Victor's body was on the floor behind her, but now the once white sweater was turning crimson as if invaded by a creeping medieval plague. "Not there. Anywhere but there."

"Fine. I'll put you in the kitchen." I hurried down the long hall and Maria followed.

"Why did you say you had to use the bathroom, Maria?" Rosa asked. Maria didn't answer.

"Stay here until I come back for you," I said as we reached the doors. I was anxious to get outside, help Garrett, and get the hell out of Dodge before the men in blue arrived. I pushed through the door and took two steps into a large and well-lit kitchen. Across the room was an enormous center island with an assortment of pots and pans hanging on hooks.

I heard a woman's voice from behind me. "FBI. One move and you're pushing up daisies."

"Oh for Christ sake," I said, staring at a brass frying pan and wondering who the hell really used brass frying pans, "is there anybody who's *not* in this house tonight?"

CHAPTER 31

I spun around to face my assailant *du jour*. But it wasn't her gun that locked my gaze.

Her left cheek looked like a rotten grapefruit, swollen and yellow and red. It was hard to ignore, which was a real shame as the rest of her was a considerable improvement.

Her milk chocolate hair swept over half her forehead, and her low-cut, light blue dress struggled to restrain her left breast. She held a standard issue Glock .22 with both hands in a posture that was right out of the agency's training manual. Her figure and bedroom eyes were straight out of a Victoria's Secret catalog. With a body like that, I felt sorry for her brain.

"Do you people really say that?"

"Back up," she said.

"Take it easy."

"Back it up, buster."

"Buster? Where'd they recruit you from, Yale?" I took two steps back—no need to make her ask three times while she had a gun pointed at my pulsating head. Nothing new about that, although it was getting tiresome. Maria stood behind me and clutched my hand while Rosa sat straight and proud on my hip.

"Who are you? Where did you get those girls?"

"Slow down there, Annie Oakley. Let's do one at a time."

"Where did you get them from?"

"Found them in safe room upstairs."

"Outside Escobar's study?"

"You know about the study?"

"We have blueprints. What were you doing there?"

"Unbelievable. I was looking for Easter baskets and—"

"Don't be smart with me."

"Lady, I'd be hard pressed to produce any evidence that I'm even a distant cousin of smart."

"What do you mean unbeliev—?"

"We'll dance later. There are bad men with guns still loose on the property. I don't like bad men with guns."

She hesitated. She had certainly heard the shots when I dropped Victor, and I assumed she was waiting in the kitchen for someone, or something. In all likelihood she had heard the shots from outside as well. If there was more of her coming, I had to get Garrett, Morgan, and myself out of there.

"Back to the big theme. Who are you?" she asked, but this time slower with more curiosity and less demand in her voice.

"I'm one of the good guys," I said.

"He's Jacob," Rosa said proudly. "He bit off the man with the ponytail's nose." She followed it with her nervous giggle. Maria stepped out from behind me, as if to protect me and challenge the lady in blue.

Maria said, "He shot a bad man with a gun."

"From the mouth of babes," I said. "I'm Jacob the good guy, who shoots bad people unless I'm hungry, and then I eat their nose. Now identify yourself, agent in blue."

She relaxed her pose, but not the gun. "I'm Natalie Binelli, special agent, FBI. I've been working under cover as Escobar's mistress, investigating Walter Mendis and Paulo Henriques. Mendis uses associates to smuggle illegal aliens into the country, and we believe that he may be using Escobar. We also believe that, on occasion, he smuggles in young girls. Some for sex and others for domestic help. Some have been kidnapped and others traded for loose change. We got word that four to six units might be coming in tonight, so I came back to the house. My job is to make the call when and if the boat comes in."

"Why didn't you go directly after Mendis?"

"I did. That fish didn't bite."

"You're not afraid he won't recognize you?"

"I make sure I don't run into him. Besides, the bait was a blonde with glasses."

I tried to picture her like that, but needed to focus on a greater issue. What if there were more feds in the neighborhood and her backup team heard the outside gunfire and decided to close in without her signal?

My job was to retrieve a letter for an agency that didn't recognize me. I had no right to be in Escobar's house. Then Rosa shifted her weight and my perspective. Returning them to their home was not an option, and I was positive that is exactly what the FBI would do. I was risking too much for my two young friends, and Morgan had laid out a nice life awaiting them. Freeing them from the house was no longer the sole objective. It would only serve as a moral victory.

"Moral victories do not count." Tartakower.

"Your turn," she said to me.

"I'm Jacob Travis, DEA. What's unbelievable, to address your earlier concern, is that Uncle's got two agencies here. We believed that Escobar was bringing in drugs. I heard these children through the wall and got them out. Is your backup team approaching due to the gunfire outside the property, or was that gunfire the result of your team?" If she wanted DEA identification she was flat fucking out of luck.

She lowered her gun. "It wasn't us. My team isn't even in the neighborhood. We weren't certain anything would occur tonight, but on a hunch I dropped in on my own. They can be here within twenty minutes when they hear from me. We need the units on US soil to make an arrest. My team storming the house kills it for us. Without the units, our night's a bust.

"But I don't think we need the new units whether they arrive tonight or not. With those," she waved the gun at my girls like they were hanging pots, "and the story they can tell, even if Escobar calls it off tonight, I'm going to call in and shut him down. We'll offer him a generous reduction of his charges if he implicates Mendis and Henriques. Why didn't DEA notify us that you were here?"

"Why didn't the FBI give us a courtesy call?"

"Not my concern."

"Will you return them to their home?" I asked.

"We have no facilities. Our arrangement is that the units are returned to their home country as soon as possible."

I didn't think Special Agent Natalie Binelli was a bad person, but it would be a cold day in hell before the FBI got their hands on my little "units."

"Do you know what the outside shots were about?" she asked.

"Escobar's trigger-happy men scared away kids," I lied. I assumed that Garrett was the noisemaker as his job was to cover the front. He must've run into the men who I saw in the white van the other night who drove away with the four girls.

"The shots I just heard in the house?"

"Guy called Victor. Know him?"

"No."

"It's too late now."

She looked at my two girls as if she coveted them and said, "I need to contact my team and let them know you're here. I assume you need to do the same."

"Of course," I said. I put Rosa down on the wood floor. "Girls, go sit at the table. Ms. Binelli and I need to make some calls."

Maria took Rosa's hand and led her to a large wood table surrounded with high chairs. I casually walked over to Binelli. She held her gun low on her right side. She was a few feet away from the wall behind the door where she had positioned herself before we entered the kitchen. The FBI could have Escobar, nothing else. I was four feet away from her.

"Call your team first," I said, "then I'll..."

I lurched forward and took both her arms with my hands and spread them back wide out to her sides. I lifted her off the ground, took one large step back against the wall and—politely, and I'd like to think with a sense of aristocratic courtesy—slammed my body into hers. The move caught her off guard and she tried to bring a leg up to kick me in my groin, but there was no room between us. I saw surprise and anger in her eyes, but the anger seemed to stem more from self-disgust. Her breath blasted out on my face from the impact of my body. It was accompanied with a low grunt. I moved my left hand out to her right hand and pinned it, and her gun, on the wall. It was the Elvis move, but she was a hell of a lot prettier. Her eyes were level with mine as I suspended her a foot above the floor and flat against the wall. I felt her breasts on my chest and her breath in my face. Her eyelashes were thicker than thirty-pound fish line and her soft brown eyes gave no hint of panic. She gave a final grunt as she tried to break free her right arm. I felt her relax. I didn't. I leaned my weight into her.

"Drop the gun, Natalie," I said.

"No."

"The last time I was in this position, I ate the guy's nose. Now drop the gun."

Natalie Binelli leaned her face even closer. Her body went limp and soft. She slowly blew her air, and the heat of her breath warmed my face. "Go ahead, cowboy," she said in a husky voice, "take a bite."

Good lord. She didn't get that from the training manual.

I squeezed my left hand hard around her wrist and slowly bent it sideways. Binelli never took her eyes off me and showed no pain until a final wince of her face as she dropped the gun just before I broke her wrist, which I really didn't want to do.

"You signed up for fuck pad duty for God and country?" I asked. Our faces were still inches apart.

"Whatever it takes. You've got dried blood on your face," she shot back at me.

"Whatever it takes. I'm going to put you down now."

"I'm going to kick your balls to Cancun." She leaned in and kissed me hard. I had no doubt that her intention was to bite my tongue off. I broke away from her and dropped her to the floor. I spun her around and shoved her, gently, face first against the wall.

"Maria," I said, "bring me Ms. Binelli's purse. It's on the counter behind you." I heard Maria's feet paddle on the wood floor and then she stood beside me holding the small black purse.

"Turn it upside down," I said. Maria emptied the contents onto the floor and a cell phone tumbled out. I stepped on it and heard a heavy crack. I turned Binelli back around and leaned in on her body. Our faces again were only inches apart.

"Ms. Binelli, I don't want to leave you tied and gagged for your male chauvinistic pig fellow agents to find. But if necessary, I will. We know what the next page of your career will look like. Do yourself a favor and relax. I'll be out of here in a few minutes and Escobar, and whatever he brings in tonight, is all yours. But not these children. They are not going back to the parents who sold them. They will have a life worth the effort, and the risk, both you and I have put in stopping Escobar and Mendis. Their names are Maria and Rosa, Natalie. And don't ever call them 'units' again. Do we understand each other?"

She didn't say anything for a brief moment and then asked, as if we were chatting at a dinner party, "What happened to the side of your face?"

"It stopped Ramon's fist."

"Ramon Sanchez?"

"We were never formally introduced."

"He's wanted for murder in three states."

"Nice to think the other forty-seven are so involved. What happened to *your* face?"

"Escobar. I started to defend myself, but couldn't without giving myself away."

"He attacked you?"

"And you didn't?"

That one landed, but I didn't have time to debate.

"You're all in," I said with admiration.

"The only way."

I reached under her dress and felt up her legs. Even though her left arm was free, she didn't budge. I found a small revolver strapped high on her left thigh just below her panties and added it to my gun collection. It was a Smith & Wesson Bodyguard 380. Nongovernment issued. The FBI sanctioned only the Glock .27 as a secondary smaller weapon. She never took her eyes off me.

"This is about those girls?" she asked. Maria still stood next to me.

"Maria and Rosa."

"Why?" she asked.

"You didn't just ask that question, did you?"

She hesitated and broke eye contact for the first time. She came back at me. "I left her, Sophia, a signal. And if Maria and Rosa have to go back to their homes to save hundreds of others from being sold, I have no problem with that, cowboy. We believe that if we return girls, that we put a stop to it. All parties will know that it's not going to work anymore. I wish it weren't that way for them, but we do what we can. It's not within my responsibilities."

More gunfire. I was wasting time. Either I could trust her or I needed to tie and gag her, which would take even a few more precious minutes. The Elvis mistake. I had to commit to one path or the other. I had just taken her guns, and I now realized I was going to give them back. Probably screwed up smashing her phone too.

"It's within mine," I said. "I need you to watch these girls while I make sure my buddy's OK. Then I'll pick them up and be out of your life. Give me ten minutes and the rest of the night is yours. You can have the girls that come in on the boat tonight."

"Where's your buddy?"

"Not sure."

"What if they call it off?"

"They won't. Too much money and we won't create any more issues for them. If they do, we'll work something out."

"Do I have a choice?" she asked, and I doubted that she believed the crap I just threw out about them not calling it off.

"We all do."

I was already on thin ice with her, but I wanted to ask her about the letter, just in case she knew something. I picked up her Glock.

"Listen, have you seen an old letter, or overheard Escobar discussing a document that he came to possess?"

"What are you talking about?"

"Nothing."

"Jacob Travis. DEA, right."

"My name is Jacob." That was twice in one night. "You might need these. Take care of my girls." I took her small revolver from my pocket and tossed it to her. She caught it and I placed her Glock on the table.

She pointed her small revolver at me and for a moment I wondered if I had misjudged her. We stared at each other as a few seconds of measurable time ticked away forever. What was she thinking?

"Fuck Yale," she said.

"Excuse me?"

"I'm from Vassar." She lowered her gun. "Theater major."

You never know what you're going to find in the kitchen.

CHAPTER 32

Ileft Vassar with guns and girls. I bet she could play off the grid. The way her unflinching eyes, partially hidden behind the ends of her bangs, locked on mine when I felt up her thigh, groping for her nongovernment-issued gun is what bought me.

I exited the side kitchen door and nearly tripped over the bound and gagged security guard. His wide eyes pleaded with mine, but I kept going. I moved around to the front corner of the house and stood flat against the wall. I sent Garrett a text telling him that the girls were in the kitchen, two men down in the house, and no letter. I heard voices from around the corner on the driveway.

It was Cruz. "What the hell happened, Ramon?"

"We drove into an ambush, but I think it's just a guy unloading on us. Carlo's minus a leg and Orlando half his head. Where's your other guy?" Ramon's voice was new to me.

"He's covering some gringo that broke in the house and tried to break out the two you left behind," Cruz said.

"You kept them in your house?" It was Ramon's voice. "You are some sorry piece of shit, Escobar. Where's Elvis?"

"Upstairs without his nose," Cruz said. "Gringo ate it."

I thought of slipping around the corner, but I didn't know if their guns were drawn or not. The apron of the driveway was a good forty feet square, and once I revealed myself, there would be no place to hide. I texted Garrett and asked his position.

"Who shot us?" Ramon asked.

"I haven't a clue," Escobar answered. His voice was shaky. He was done.

"You don't have a clue?" It was Ramon's voice. "Someone was camped out like a Mexican bandit waiting to unload on me, and you don't have a motherfuckin' clue? Fuck you, Escobar. I'm not standing out here under these lights, and I can't move the van before I change the tire."

"What about Anthony and the shipment?" Escobar asked. He pushed the words out like he was trying to re-establish his ground.

"You don't get it, do you, man?" Ramon said. "Something's seriously wrong here. I'm getting out of here alive. You're on your own."

"Anybody tell Anthony?" Escobar again. "He'll be waiting with the shipment."

"Let's take the boat," Cruz said.

"Damn straight. You got the key?" Ramon asked.

"In the ignition," Cruz said.

"Are you going to meet Anthony?" Escobar asked, and even I felt sorry for him. He was probably standing within a few feet of the others, but wasn't even in the same universe anymore.

Cruz said, "You just don't get it, man. It's done. Let's go."

I had my gun drawn and hoped they came my way, but they must have gone in the house because I heard footsteps and then nothing. If they wanted a bullet omelet before their trip, Binelli was serving.

With the transfer off, my goal was to gather my girls, beat the letter out of Escobar, rendezvous with Garrett, and sneak out to *Impulse*. Binelli would be stuck with nothing, but I didn't see any other play. I had to think that she at least entertained that possibility. *What if they call it off?* She certainly had to strongly believe that they would call it off. What would be her angle? Maybe she was planning to double-cross me and at first opportunity would herd Maria and Rosa into a government van.

I raced around to the backside of the house to be in position when the men came out, and felt my phone vibrate. But it wasn't my phone. I reached in my pocket and took out Elvis's phone.

position in ten, four rugs, where are you

It was from Anthony, and he had coordinates with the message. Plan Q, or maybe it was "Double B," I'd lost track, burst into focus. I wasn't sure I wanted to go there, but I wanted to keep all my options open. I texted back:

delayed a little be there soon

I sent a text to Morgan. I was crouched low in the bushes at the rear southeast corner when I spun around with my gun drawn. Garrett settled in next to me.

"Who's watching the girls?" he asked.

"Natalie."

"Who's Natalie?"

"Cute little FBI agent I ran into in the kitchen. Top shelf at a toga party. She's sitting the two girls. Feds' already on Escobar for trafficking and she was undercover. They picked tonight for the sting because they got word of another shipment, waiting offshore as we speak."

"Escobar's got two government nets on him at once," Garrett said, almost with a note of condolence.

"Makes you feel sorry for the guy. What the hell did you run into out front?"

"Guys in a white van. Two down but one got through. What happened to your face?"

"I ate Elvis's nose and stopped Ramon's fist."

"About time you contributed."

"No problem. She's from Vassar, you believe that?"

"Who?" Garrett asked.

"Toga babe."

"That's in Poughkeepsie, isn't it?"

"I believe you're right."

"Her plan was to send the girls back to their homes where they would more than likely be placed back into the blender."

"Not our two."

"She came around to that. But she wants, and I promised, what's coming ashore. Except it's been called off at this end, which I suspect she knows. But I confiscated Elvis's phone and I've got the drop-off coordinates."

Garrett gave me a small smile, the left side of his lip curling up. "Using both sides of your head tonight."

"New territory for me."

"What are you thinking?"

"We get the four off the boat and Vassar has what she needs to trap Mendis and less incentive to take our two away."

"Our job is to secure the letter," Garrett said.

"I know, but we can't walk away from this. Why haven't they come out of the house yet?"

"How do you know about their plan?"

"I overheard Ramon and Cruz, the only two left standing," I said. "Ramon's the guy you let through. They plan to hijack the boat and adios to Graceland."

"I stopped two out of three."

"Just saying, that's all."

"I suppose a new face was part of your plan?"

"We're even. Theater major, believe that?"

"Who?"

"Vassar."

"She's in the right place then."

"How so?"

Garrett said, "Our plan turned into a choreographed riot, one level up from smeared shit. Escobar?"

"I doubt he'll leave; besides, I promised him to Vassar. But before I turn him over, I need the letter. That's the new flight plan. Meanwhile we can't let these guys surface and ruin someone else's day. You want the front or back?" I asked. "They should have been out by now."

"Let's both hit the back."

Two gunshots popped from inside the house.

Binelli and the girls.

"I'm going in the kitchen," I said. "You take the back door and we enter the house on the count of ten. With me."

"Ten's the count. Three, two, one," Garrett said, accelerating the pace of the words.

He darted around to the back of the house. I sprinted to the side kitchen door, fighting the visions exploding in my mind. *One thousand, two thousand, three thousand.* I opened the door with my gun drawn and saw Natalie Binelli with hers arms extended straight and her Glock pointed at the door leading to the house. Maria and Rosa were under the table. Binelli spun when I entered.

Four thousand, five thousand, six thousand.

"What happened?" I asked.

"Ramon—I think it was him—stuck his head in. I got off a few rounds, missed. I need to call backup."

"No."

Seven thousand, eight thousand, nine thousand.

"I missed. He knows we're in here. We just can't—"

I burst through the door into the large foyer just as Garrett flung himself through the back door. Cruz was to my right. I was to Garrett's right, so I took the right side as he would cover the left. I shot Cruz twice in the torso and heard Garrett's gun go off, but realized he also shot Cruz. Four bullets. There are guys on death row that won't be that fortunate. His blue bandana shredded with brain matter. I wondered why Garrett went for the head instead of the body, but he was always a better shot than me. But if Garrett went after Cruz, that meant Ramon wasn't to be seen. Or Escobar. The house screamed with an eerie silence except for the soaring, closing chords of "MacArthur Park," which now held center stage. Forty-eight Bose speakers reigning over the smeared shit, choreographed riot. A seven-minute, thirty-second song. Too long for radio, they said. It had been seven minutes since I put Elvis down and then I knew where Escobar was. The big bear had finally gotten it right and followed his heart.

"I'm going to the study," I told Garrett. "Escobar's there. Guy called Ramon's loose."

I took the steps three at a time and, halfway up, looked out through the wall of glass just in time to see Ramon sprinting in a line toward the docks. He pumped his arms like he was on the last lap of a track meet.

"He's heading to the water," I shouted down to Garrett. He spun and ran toward the back door. I ate the rest of the steps and slowed at the end of the hall leading to Escobar's study. I drew my gun and cautiously entered the room. Escobar was bent over Elvis with his back to me. Elvis's eyes went wide when he saw me. I quickly closed the distance.

"Travis," Elvis said, but his voice was different.

Escobar spun around while fiddling with a gun in his hand. I kicked it away.

"I want the letter."

CHAPTER 33

"I can't stop the bleeding," Escobar said.

The curtain I had stuffed and tied in Elvis's mouth was off to the side. His hands were loosened but still tied, as if Escobar had started in on them but then switched his attention to Elvis's midsection. A swamp of crusted dried blood rested on his stomach, and Escobar had a damp towel that he was using to clean the wound. There wasn't that much more blood on the floor than when I'd left.

"Did you hear me?" I asked.

"Help me out here."

"I want the letter."

"For God's sake, man, he's dying."

"Who's not? He's just got the inside lane."

"I'm taking him to a hospital."

I grabbed a high-back chair that faced Escobar's desk and spun it around so that it fronted Escobar and Elvis. I sat and crossed my legs.

Escobar glanced up at me. I didn't think Elvis was in imminent danger. I wanted to get the letter, take the boat out to intercept the other girls they were smuggling, and then get out with Maria, Rosa, and the letter. It was a tall order, and it seemed that the longer I stayed in the house, the more jobs I picked up. But I figured I was halfway there.

It was time to end my time with Escobar.

"Fork over the letter, Raydel," I said. "And when the human smuggling charge, maybe kidnapping as well, hits the fan, we can put in a good word for you. You can push it up to Mendis, and the feds will show you some leniency."

"I had nothing to do to with this." His attention was now focused on me. His eyes pleading.

"With what?"

"Those girls. They were—"

"Spare me. I found them in your safe room."

"Listen to me." He stood and glared at me. "That's not me. Mendis used me. He knew I had a fast boat. A month ago he asked a favor. Said..."

"Said what? You want to kidnap a twelve-year-old? What do you play me for?"

"It wasn't that. He brought in guys who paid, paid a lot, to come into the country. No girls. Working men. I wasn't comfortable with it, but he said it was for one time. Then he did it again. When I got in trouble with the IRS, he brokered a deal between us, but insisted on one more shipment, said it would be 'modified.' I had no idea until Elvis called me from the boat."

"Let me guess, you're such a swell guy that you couldn't send Maria and Rosa out into the cruel world, so you held them back."

"That's right," Elvis said. His voice was thick like when you're out in the cold for too long and your jaw freezes up. "I called him. He had me take them to the garage. Kept two smallest back."

"Touching." I stood and faced Escobar. "I want the letter." Elvis was prone on the floor between us.

"You can't negotiate, or you would have. You have no authority to drop charges," Escobar said.

"I'll do what I can."

Escobar broke eye contact. What was he thinking? Did he really think that holding the letter at this point would give him greater assurance of avoiding incarceration? He looked past me at the bookshelves beyond the desk and back to me.

"I keep it until I talk to my lawyer. I'll let him negotiate with the authorities."

I blew out my breath. I took a step closer. We now stood face to face with Elvis on the floor between us. "I'll choke it out of you."

"If I'm dead, or unconscious, you'll never get it. Not even Elvis knows where it is. Why do you want it so bad? I told you. I'll have my lawyer handle it."

I didn't believe the Elvis quip, but if the colonel wanted a private practice attorney to be in possession of the letter and use it as a bargaining tool, he never would have called me. But I couldn't get that through to Escobar. I couldn't think of anything he wanted to trade for the letter.

"Give me the letter."

"I'm calling my lawyer."

Elvis coughed.

We locked eyes like we had the night I called him one dumb fuckin' Cuban. I was wrong. Escobar was one emotional Cuban. Without dropping his eyes, I moved my right foot and put my toe into Elvis's midsection. He screamed.

"What are you doing?" Escobar shot Elvis a glance then back up at me.

"I want the letter." I twisted my toe. Elvis curled up and moaned.

"What the hell, man. You'll re-open the wound."

"I want the letter."

Escobar's face contorted like a topographical map. He lurched forward, but I slapped him hard across his cheek. He started to come at me again.

"Don't," I said.

He hesitated and then dropped to his knees and put his right arm under Elvis and started to move him away from me. I put my left foot on Escobar's shoulder and pushed. He fell backward and scrambled to his feet.

"Why do you hold onto it?" I asked, and was surprised at the strain in my voice. I could see where I was going, but I was too far in to turn back. All my scheming, all the effort with Kittredge, and the only thing I brought to the party was brute force. *Neanderthal.*

Escobar glanced around his study as if he were trying to answer my question. As if he held some crumb of hope that he could save it all. Perhaps he saw Sophia coming through the door with a bouquet of fresh yellow flowers and inquiring how his day was. Maybe another party played in his mind like a silent film where men in tuxedos and women in evening dresses sipped liquid dreams and pretended, if only for the moment, that everything was fine in their lives. And perhaps for that moment it was, and looking back now, he saw too late what he let get away.

"I can't give it to you," he said. The sadness and disappointment in his voice broke me for just a moment.

I put my toe back into Elvis before I had a chance to question my action. I would get the letter. Like a horror show, the letter had exploded into grotesque proportions, as if it was calling me and my whole life lay within its contents. I didn't know what the rest of the night would bring, but I knew I was going home with the damn thing.

"I want the letter, Raydel." I twisted and Elvis screamed and rolled to his side, but I kept my foot on him and prevented him from turning fully away.

"You wouldn't," Escobar said.

I pushed my foot. A low grunt came from Elvis.

"He'll bleed," I said. "He'll die on the floor while you protect your precious letter."

I felt my foot slide as the fresh blood seeped from the wound, but kept my eyes on Escobar. Escobar glanced down at Elvis and then cut me a look.

"I'm calling the cops."

"He'll be dead. I'll be gone." I put more weight on my foot. Elvis howled. "I want the letter."

"I'm calling the police." He moved toward his desk.

I dug my foot in again and this time left the pressure on. Elvis tried to roll away.

"I want the letter."

"No. The cops and my attorney."

"Give me the letter, Raydel." I pushed.

Elvis shrieked.

"You're insane."

"I want the letter."

"Stop, I'll—"

"The letter. Now."

"OK. Stop. Stop it."

"Bring me the letter."

"Please, it's down the hall. Just go get it."

"Do I look like I prance? Is that what you called it? Prancing? Let's see you prance, big bear. Bring me the letter."

I shifted my weight.

Elvis again.

"You're a madman. It's just—"

"The fucking letter." I extended my open palm.

"OK, but—"

"Now."

"It's just—"

My foot.

Elvis.

"Move, man! Move! Move!"

Escobar sprinted out the study door and stopped in front of the picture of the nude lady with water droplets on her stomach. The picture rested on the floor where I had left it after I took it off its hook and tore off the brown paper on the back as I searched for the key. He paused for just a second, as if considering his actions. He kicked his right foot through the picture. Then his left and then his right again as if the picture was to blame. An 8½" x 11" envelope fell out of the back, but Escobar kept kicking, and his sobs and breath drowned out the music that played on like the band on the *Titanic*. He hurried back, his face twisted, tears sliding down his flushed face as if the droplets of water from the painting had leapt over to him and found themselves a new home, a new body to tease. He pulled up a few feet from me.

"Here." He shoved the envelope into my outstretched hand. "And you can burn in hell."

He fell to his knees and tended Elvis with the towel he had when I had first walked in. I wiped my bloody right foot on the wool rug in front of his desk and marched out of the study with the letter in my hand.

I'd paid my debt.

CHAPTER 34

I met Binelli halfway down the hall. Her gun was at her side.

"What was going on in there?" she asked in a tone that held a thousand words.

"Escobar had something I needed to retrieve, but we're square now."

"What now?" She made no move to shoulder her piece.

I had the letter. I could grab Maria and Rosa and be home in ten minutes and Binelli would come up empty. She knew the transfer was off. After all, she had likely tripped over Cruz's body on the way up the stairs. Tough break for her, but we do all have problems. Nor did she know that I had the coordinates.

It was decision time.

I tried to pretend that I wanted to shut Mendis down. Maybe that was part of it. Certainly the girls out in the Gulf would fare better in the hands of the FBI, even if they did return them to their broken homes. That was getting close to it. But in the core, I couldn't let Binelli down. I'd wandered into a war and she was in my foxhole. There is no greater cause.

"Transfer's still on. I've got the coordinates and I'm going out to bring the girls back for you. You negotiate with Escobar to get Mendis. I leave with Maria and Rosa."

"Right," she said, but her voice was low and guarded. My delay in answering her question cost me credibility points with her. "What's that?" She waved her gun at the envelope. Her eyes never left mine.

"A document that our government wants returned."

"Anything to do with the girls?"

"No."

Neither of us spoke for several seconds and then Binelli said, "I can go either way here. You realize that, don't you?"

"I know. Stick with me, Vassar. I've got to make the rendez-vous so I can get your 'units.'"

"Don't toy with me."

"Withdrawn. Give me an hour and we all get what we want. I suggest you re-introduce yourself to Escobar and cuff him. Don't let him call the cops."

"You're really not fond of the law, are you?"

"That's about the size of it. Where are the girls?"

"I left them in the kitchen." She paused a few ticks. "You got forty-five minutes."

She strode off, toward Escobar and Elvis, her gun at her side. I folded the envelope and stuffed it in my inside jacket pocket.

"What happens if we're not back within that time?" Garrett asked me.

I stood in the Intrepid viewing Ramon's tangled body in the chain link fence in the shallow waters. I recalled first spotting the fence when Morgan and I scouted the house, and at the time I didn't know what purpose it served. I do now. *Collects dead bodies.*

"We're not going to find out. But she knows we could have split with our two and not committed to the transfer. Likewise, I thanked her for not taking Maria and Rosa when she had that opportunity."

"The letter?"

"My inside jacket pocket."

"Nice. How'd you get it?"

"I threatened to kill Elvis."

"That's the only thing that would turn Escobar?"

"Yup."

"If he wasn't into trafficking girls, I might like this guy."

"He claims he was railroaded into the girls and had no idea that they were being brought in on his boat."

"Believe him?"

"No."

"Why not?"

"Because I don't want to."

"What are the coordinates?" Morgan asked and saved me from agreeing with Garrett.

I had texted Morgan earlier and told him to meet us at the Intrepid. I wasn't worried about his safety as I planned to stuff him into the cuddy when we approached Anthony's boat. I gave him the coordinates and lowered the lift with the remote. A sense of familiarity and relief came when her hull floated on the water, and I wondered if there was something deep in my genetic code that made me so comfortable with water. Maybe it's because all living things evolved from water—The Grand Womb. I don't question it. Morgan idled until we cleared the mangroves. He unleashed the 1,400 horses. These weren't beefy draft horses, but three-year-old thoroughbreds. We skimmed the crest of black waves on liquid wings. Garrett and I sat in the center seats and held fast to the white-powdered aluminum railing that circled the seat. Morgan flipped on the Garmin, took a glance at the screen, and then killed it.

"Ten minutes," he shouted above the roar of the engines.

"Think the signal Escobar gave you is correct?" Garrett shouted, even though he was next to me, our sides touching.

"Not even sure he knows it, but I didn't have time to beat it out of Elvis. But his reaction to my question told me what I wanted to know. There's a signal."

"Using what he gave you?"

"Not a chance."

Ten minutes later, Morgan throttled back, and the speed and roar diminished in unison, bringing back the still and quiet night that had never left us. A light blinked several times at ten o'clock off our port side.

"That's our signal," Garrett said. "Let's go in dark."

"Down below you go, Morgan," I said and put my hand on the wheel.

"I'm fine. I'm going straight in. It gives them less to shoot at or see as we approach. I'll leave us a path out."

"Go below. This isn't your battle."

"You didn't just say that, did you?"

I was going to serve up a pointed retort, but recalled asking Binelli the same question and saved my breath. I got out Elvis's cell phone and texted Anthony a message:

signal battery dead, returning two back to you

I didn't know if Anthony would receive it in time, let alone believe a dead battery, but I hoped that by mentioning the two we were returning, he would relax his guard when we came in without the designated signal. No other beacon came from the dark, and Morgan kept the Intrepid on a steady course in the direction of where we had last seen the light.

"See it?" Morgan asked. No. I swear the guy's got owl eyes.

"Hundred feet at ten o'clock. I can't make out any figures yet," Garrett said. He was on his knees along the port side with his Sig Sauer in his right hand. His SASS, M110 Semi-Automatic Sniper System, laid on the deck. The SASS, although equipped with night vision, wouldn't be his choice at close range.

Morgan took the night binoculars out of the radio box and peered through them. "Looks like two guys plus the captain. Open bow. I see a small head. More heads. They're exposed."

"Positions?" I asked and finally saw the shape of a boat emerge from the black.

Morgan kept the Night Owls glued to his face and said in a quiet voice, "One guy behind the wheel, another off their starboard side with a gun."

"The third?"

"Directly behind the captain."

Garrett ducked beneath the gunwale. "What's the cue?" he asked.

"Let's go with 'stand up, Elvis.'"

"How you plan to get that in?"

"Closing fast. Your guy will be between nine and ten o'clock." I said.

Morgan eased the throttle in and out of gear to keep the boat at the slowest controllable motion. The engines operated seamlessly as one. I told him in a low voice to keep her running in case we needed to hightail it out of there, although as I spoke I realized he inherently knew all that. His intuition to leave an exit route indicated that not only was he with me, but he'd been here before.

I'd have to conduct a serious talk with him someday.

He positioned the Intrepid with a controlled drift until the other boat was clearly visible. We approached port to port. No other flashes of light came from her, but that didn't tell me anything. I stood slightly behind Garrett and was fully exposed above the Intrepid's low gunwale. It was not an ideal position, but I wanted to appear as nonthreatening as possible. My right hand was tucked behind me, holding my gun. Elvis's gun was in my pocket along with the Boker knife. My five-inch serrated knife was strapped to my thigh. Escobar's double-barrel rested on the deck. The distance between the boats was cut in half. It was long and narrow like the Intrepid, and then it was upon us.

"I've got two I'm supposed to return to you," I shouted.

A man with a rifle held across his body shouted back at me. "Who the fuck are you? Where's Elvis?"

Another man stood at his side and forward. He appeared to be unarmed, but then I saw a shotgun in his hand as well. The captain had one hand on the wheel and I couldn't see his other hand, but I presumed it was on the throttle. Morgan had our boat in idle and we were drifting slightly away from the approaching boat. If he needed to whip the horses, he had nothing but water in front of him. Several bobbleheads were now clearly visible in the bow. But this was no dinner cruise. I had no intention to answer his first question.

"Too much tequila," I said.

"Elvis don't drink tequila," the man shouted as he raised his gun and pointed it at me.

"No shit. That's why he's on the floor. Stand up, Elvis."

Garrett stayed on his knees but sprung his body up, both hands on his Sauer. He fired two rounds into the man with the gun, who got a shot off while I jerked my gun up and fired into his companion just as he too launched an errant shot. I felt a sting on my left arm just below my shoulder. Garrett's target fell backward and then lurched forward into the water while the man I hit collapsed straight down. The high, piercing sound of shrieking girls filled the night. I took aim at the captain.

The man behind the wheel crouched low and hit the throttles. The boat's bow shot out of the water as he cut his wheel hard to the starboard. The force from the five props pushed the

Intrepid sideways and threw a wave of saltwater over her deck. I shot two rounds and missed. I lowered my gun. An errant shot now would go directly into the bow and its human cargo.

"Go! Go! Go!" I shouted to Morgan. He jammed the throttles down and banked hard to port and flipped on the running lights.

"Five engines," Garrett said.

"We can't catch it," Morgan said. The quiet night had again erupted into angry outboards spinning their stainless steel props over 6,000 times a minute. "She's probably not that much faster, depending on the props, but she got too much of a head start."

Garrett started to reach down for his SASS, looked at my upper left arm, stopped, and said, "How bad?"

"I'm fine. Get it."

He reached down and came up with his SASS. He brought it to his eyes. "Hold me," he said.

"Move a step forward," I countered. I placed myself behind him and with my right arm reached up and held the white aluminum rail that supported the T-top. I put my left arm around his waist and hugged him tight.

"Do you have a clean shot?" I said.

"We're losing them," Morgan said.

"Take it!" I shouted and felt the quiet recoil of the sniper rifle as it reverberated through Garrett's body.

"He's hit," Garrett said. The lead boat swerved hard to port and started to make a circle and come back toward us.

"It's slowing down," Morgan said. "He must have fallen on the throttles."

"Can you get next to it?" I asked.

He looked at me and we both understood. If we got too close, the boats could collide and if we didn't catch them, the girls on board were lost. If we followed it, both boats could run for hours and eventually sputter out of gas a thousand miles offshore. Or we might watch them crash and die on the rocks of Egmont Key. Either way, their probability of survival was a little less than hitting the Powerball. Morgan cut through the circumference in an attempt to intercept the runaway vessel.

"I'll try to match its arch and get in as close as I can," Morgan said. "She's coming down, not much over twenty." The uniformed growl of four engines diminished as their rpms noticeably decreased.

"Three or four feet is good," I said.

"That's too close."

"Seven or eight, tops."

He nodded, and we gained on the boat as it continued a lazy and noncommittal circle back toward the direction we had come from. Morgan guided the Intrepid slightly behind the boat and throttled back even more. Garrett stood next to Morgan with one hand on the white aluminum T-top rail and the other holding his Sig Sauer. The low white aluminum grab rail that started just under the T-top ran around the front of the bow. I crawled up on the bow with my left hand on the rail for support. My upper left arm was already numb. As we closed in on the runaway, I made out figures in the bow, but didn't see any sign of the two men still on board.

Morgan maneuvered the Intrepid to within twenty feet. The runaway kept bouncing away as the waves on the Gulf's choppy surface jerked it wildly from side to side. I realized it was going to be more difficult than I had imagined. Morgan couldn't bring the Intrepid in too close for fear of a collision. I glanced back over my shoulder and saw Garrett standing with his gun aimed at the boat.

"How fast?" I shouted to Morgan. I wanted to calculate my jump. He glanced at the instrument panel.

"Twenty. Twenty-two."

"Close as you can."

"Jump when a wave gives you a few feet."

Garrett's arm was suddenly around me and he reached inside my jacket. He pulled the letter out. I'd forgotten about it.

I felt the gentle and powerful surge of her engines, and Morgan brought the bow of the Intrepid up to about ten feet off the starboard side of the runaway. Huddled figures were in the open bow and I made out the shape of a man on the deck. I crouched about a foot off the edge of the Intrepid's bow. I wanted to jump when a wave from either boat closed the distance and granted a few precious feet in my favor.

The runaway suddenly swerved in our direction. I sprang forward with everything my legs could give, cleared the bow rail, and stretched for the cockpit of the runaway boat.

My hands made it. Not much else.

Just as my feet left the bow, the Intrepid fell into the swell of a wave and diminished my spring. I was in trouble. I managed to grab the aluminum side rail of the runaway with my hands. My left arm screamed in protest. The boat dragged me through the water and the waves smashed my body into the hard fiberglass side. My body settled into a quick and unfortunate rhythm of bouncing between the water and the side of the boat like a loose rubber fender that was left tied to a boat cleat.

My mind flared to the girls in Fort Myers Beach who fell from the sky in the parasailing accident and I knew that they hit the water a lot faster and harder than I was. This, I could do.

I tried to swing my legs up over the side, but had little control over them. Letting go was not an option. By the time

Morgan and Garrett fished me out, the boat would be lost in the night. Besides, maybe this jump was the best I could do.

The boat veered away from me, and for a moment it was all I could do just to hang on, let alone try to climb over the side. I steadied and managed to pull myself halfway up the side before a wave caused separation between my body and the boat. I slammed again into the side. Suddenly something solid was under my left foot, and I was able push off and hoist myself over the side. I landed on a body.

"He's dead, but I ain't."

I looked toward the voice in the aft of the boat and saw a man leaning against the transom with a gun pointed at me. He had a crooked smile, as if he didn't have the energy left for a straight one. His shirt was crimson and there was blood on the deck, and then his head split in two. He was still reclined against the transom, but now his head was like a boat, with port and starboard sides. But both red.

Garrett's bullets had to have passed within inches of my own head. I made sure the man I landed on wasn't going to surprise me. I went to the helm and slowly eased the throttled down to neutral. Morgan pulled the Intrepid up next to me and Garrett grabbed the rail.

Everything that had been so loud was now quiet except my body, which bellowed with pain.

"Six inches?" I said to Garrett.

"Closer to a foot. I had a good angle."

"How good?" He didn't answer me, and I knew there was no damn way he had a foot clearance. Garrett held the boats together and Morgan jumped on board with me.

"Ready to move them?" he asked. In the bow were four huddled girls. Staring at me. No talking. No space between them. Huddled masses yearning to breathe free. I think each one had soiled her dress.

"Let's get them back to Escobar's," I said. "They belong to a woman in blue."

We moved the girls to the Intrepid, put several rounds in the other boat's transom, and left it sinking behind us. Morgan got out the first aid kit and I taped a gauze bandage high on my left arm.

After a few minutes, I took the bloody thing off, recycled it in the Gulf, and applied another one.

CHAPTER 35

"Who's he?" Binelli's words were aimed at me, but her eyes drilled Garrett.

Garrett stood in the corner of the kitchen with his SASS over his shoulder. The overhead can lights illuminated his polished copper head like it was a low wattage streetlamp. He had not spoken since we entered the house. Garrett had returned the letter to me, and it was back in my inside pocket. I had checked in the boat and it had the exact same address that the fake one had. I didn't open it. I didn't think that Escobar would hide a fake. Besides, I'm arrogant.

"Tonto. He's with me," I said as I looked at Binelli looking at Garrett.

"That's your team?" she asked, turning her attention to me. "Team" came out a few notes higher than the previous words.

"Budget cutbacks." Escobar sat in a chair and Elvis lay on the floor with a pillow under his head and feet. Both were handcuffed.

She glanced down at them. She had applied new bandages to Elvis and stemmed the bleeding. "Elvis needs a doctor," she said. "I'm calling an ambulance as well as my team as soon as you two clear the premises." Her eyes came back to me. "What happened to you, cowboy, lose a heavyweight fight?"

"I used my body to punch out a boat."

"And the bandage on your left arm? Needs to be changed, by the way."

"Wrong end of luck."

"Do you charge up every hill you see?"

"Pretty much."

"You work with Tonto every time?" She eyed Garrett again.

"Pretty much."

"The u…girls at sea?"

"In the garage." Morgan had taken them there and then planned to bring *Impulse* around to the dock.

Maria and Rosa sat on chairs by the table. They were cleaned up since I last saw them. Neither had spoken when I came in. Natalie Binelli had her house in order.

"Is your story ready?" I asked.

"Pretty much." She let that stand by itself for a moment and then said, "What did you leave at sea?"

"Nothing."

She started to say something, but stopped. She was better off not knowing.

Binelli asked, "What about Victor and Cruz? They'll do a ballistics test on the bullets."

"The ones in Victor came from Elvis's gun."

"Nice. You that good or did you get lucky?"

I didn't answer.

"Hey, Elvis," Binelli said and looked down at him, "they may pin a murder charge on you as well. But don't worry, you can plead self-defense." She glanced back up toward me. "And Ramon?"

"Caught in the chain link fence."

"Not so good."

"Untraceable bullets. Same as Cruz. Tell them you don't have a clue."

"And you and Tonto?"

"Were never here."

"You hear that, boys?" Binelli said and eyed her collection of gagged and tied men. "Any shit from either of you, and Elvis, I'll tell them you plugged Victor in cold blood. You can kiss away your self-defense plea." She got on her knees and looked into Escobar's eyes. Escobar looked calm, like a fish that was still breathing but had given up the fight and lay on a dock resigned to an incomprehensible fate.

"Raydel," Binelli started in, "in exchange for your cooperation, I'll put in a good word with the attorneys. Remember what we discussed: the more you talk about Mendis, the less time 'Folsom Prison Blues' is the only song you ever hear again."

I'd been thinking about Escobar on the trip back in and what he told me in the study. Not so much what he said, but how he said it. His voice. His tone.

I took a step toward Binelli and said, "Why don't you tell them that while you were still under cover, Escobar, overcome with guilt, informed you that Mendis switched from smuggling paying men to kidnapped virgins without clueing him in. Escobar contacted you in hopes that you might be able to place the two girls he held back. Tell them that you had spun some tale about a cousin in Appalachia that took in wayward children and he remembered that."

It was quiet for the first time in forever. Someone had finally killed the music. I wondered who would play it again, and knew that whatever they would play, it wouldn't be the distinctive chords of Raydel Escobar.

"Well, I'll be. I never made you for Mr. Magnanimity, cowboy. And why would I do that?" Binelli asked.

"It will help establish him as a credible witness against Mendis."

"I see." She paused and said, "You think they'd go for that?"

"I think you can sell shit to a farmer."

She turned to Escobar and bent over. "You got that, Raydel? We'll have a few minutes after these Rangers leave to go over our story. But I like you, Raydel. Your stiff dick has no conscience, and lord knows Sophia bent way over when she picked you out of the bottom of the barrel, but somewhere, in your more important organs, you're not half bad."

Binelli came back to me.

"You got a chance?" I asked.

She hesitated before she answered. Her skipped beat told me more than her words. "I got it. They gave me the pension team. They're not too much into questions."

Her false sense of bravado clunked when it hit the floor. She was a tough woman and made the right decision, but we both knew she had a tall tale to tell her superiors. But she had Elvis and Escobar hog tied, four young girls safe and sound in the garage, and two dead henchmen—one who was wanted in *three* states. She had enough hero attributes to carry her out of here with her career intact, perhaps even enhanced. There were holes in her story, but she was a wrecking ball, and they couldn't deny that.

"Thank you for indulging us," I said. "You weren't bound to help in any matter. You made the right decision, Natalie, you—"

"Leave," she said.

I strolled over to Maria and Rosa.

"Let's go, girls." Rosa stood on her chair and I put my arm out. She stepped forward onto my right hip. Home position. Maria didn't move or take her eyes off me.

"Where are we going, Jacob?" she asked.

"Do you want to go back to your home?"

"No. Our parents sold us. That is what happened, is it not?"

She wasn't going to hear that from me. "I know a place for you and Rosa. A place where you can go to school, a place where you can live, and a lady who will love you and take care of you."

"Is it here in America?"

"No. You cannot stay here. They will send you home. It's an island, but a better island than where you came from. I go there often and like the place very much."

Maria looked at me as if considering whether to believe me or not. I wondered if she would appraise people like that for the rest of her life. I couldn't blame her, but it seemed a heavy burden for someone so young. She reached out and took my left hand in her right hand. The feel of her hand flashed my mind back to when I struggled to get into the runaway boat and I had found sound footing. What would be protruding out the side of a boat?

I started to leave, but heard Binelli from behind me.

"Cowboy," she said. I twisted back around. She held my eyes and waited a measure. "If you moral crusaders ever need any help, call me. Leave a message at the Hoover building."

"We just might do that. One question."

"Shoot."

"How long were you standing in the hall outside Escobar's study?"

"Long enough to see what you did."

"Why did you come up?"

"Didn't believe for one second that crap you shoveled about them not canceling the hand-off. The gunfire and Cruz's brain matter splattered on the sunset of the aluminum picture confirmed my suspicion. Figured if we were to have a chance to save the girls on the water, it would be on the coattails of some idiotic hotshot like you."

She looked like the same woman I met an hour earlier, but you never know.

"Here, in the kitchen before we knew the transfer was on," I said, "why did you trust me?"

"You said one question."

"Indulge me."

"That's easy, slim. You gave me my six-shooter back."

Lord, could this girl ever rumble. And I bet her parents thought she'd never get a job with a major in theater.

She staged a smile that would buckle any man's knees, and I knew then that Raydel Escobar was screwed beyond his imagination the day Natalie Binelli waltzed into the Welcome In. Somewhere in his life, between the music and Sophia, Raydel Escobar got a glimpse of the shadow of good, but it eluded him, running one step ahead, as he stumbled in the dense.

I remembered it just as I was about to depart the kitchen. The collateral damage of war. I turned one last time to face Escobar. "Look at me, Escobar," I said. He glanced up. "Delete the picture. Keep Kittredge out of it. You understand?" He nodded.

"I got one for you," Binelli said. "What's with that envelope?"

"It's my job."

"That's not what I saw."

"I owed someone."

I walked out with Rosa on my hip, Maria holding my hand, and the letter rubbing against my sore rib.

CHAPTER 36

I stuffed the letter into the radio box.

"As we planned?" Morgan asked when we boarded *Impulse*. He had taken Rosa from me and placed her in the bow where she clutched her Annie doll even tighter, which I would have thought to be impossible. I don't think she trusted boats. Maria sat next to her.

"Straight to Kathleen's. Give her a couple of days to clean them up, buy clothes, and requisition whatever's needed for the journey."

We idled out of the shallow and dark waters of Raydel Escobar's front yard for the final time. I heard a dolphin blow a few feet off the starboard bow.

"Nevis," Morgan said. "Amazing that she followed us in the Intrepid. She's not familiar with that boat, which shows her loyalty is to us. Like a dog, she wanted to come on our journey."

"They can't exceed much over twenty miles per hour for a short burst," Garrett added. "She must have kept at it even though she had to be way behind. When we circled back toward shore chasing the runaway, she picked us up again. Never would've believed it unless I saw it."

"Pretty incredible," I said. I went to the bow and got on my knees so my face was level with both girls. I suddenly realized how ill-equipped I was to relate to their world, to their reality. *Let me tell you about Brazilian fire ants.*

"I'm taking you to my friend's house. Her name is Kathleen and——"

"That's a pretty name," Rosa said.

"Yes, it is. It is a very pretty name and she is a very pretty lady. She's going to give you some food and a nice place to sleep for a couple of nights."

"Will you be there?" Maria asked.

"I live close by. I will see you tomorrow. The day after tomorrow you will start your journey to your new home. It's——"

"Stay with us," Rosa said.

I hesitated. "I'll stay with you tonight. You'll like your new home. A wonderful woman will take care of you——"

"No, she won't," Maria said with anger, and her change of tone startled me. "No one will take care of us. No one cares or even knows what is happening to us. We were left in a room all alone." Her lip started to quiver and for the first time she seemed to break.

I was tired. Every bone in my body hurt. My left arm was somewhere between numb and hell. I was pretty certain I had a mammoth headache, but it just couldn't hold its own against the other neurons shrieking for my attention. A couple of teeth, thanks to Cruz's right hand, coupled with my inability to control my tongue, were barely hanging in there. My hips were starting to freeze up; they weren't designed to be boat fenders. I put my arms around Maria and gave her a hug, and a long breath left her.

I pulled away and looked into her moist eyes. I had no idea where I was. "You'll be fine, Maria. I promise you." It sounded like total shit, but I didn't know what else to say. I got up and walked back to the helm where Morgan and Garrett sat.

"She's following us back," Morgan said.

"Who?" I asked. The irritability of my voice surprised me.

"Nevis. She's off the bow."

"Fucking dolphin, Morgan." I spit it out with disgust. The night had landed more punches than I thought.

"Saved the day," he said in an even voice, not letting my mood infect him.

"How so?"

"How do you think you got in that boat?"

I thought back to the struggle to get my legs over the side of the runaway boat. My foot had found something solid and that allowed me to push off and get over the side. I thought it might be a boat strake, but knew it was too wide. I couldn't imagine anything else.

"No way," I said.

"She was positioning herself the whole time you were trying to get on board and she finally got under you."

"I don't believe it. Garrett, you see any of that?"

But Garrett Demarcus didn't answer me. He wasn't going to waste his time if I didn't believe Morgan. He looked at me like I was the sorriest thing he's seen that night. I knew then how little I know about anything worth knowing.

I looked out at the black and tried to clear my mind. But the only thing I saw were Victor's surprised and innocent eyes staring back at me in disbelief. I wondered what he meant when he said "go," but his final gaze conveyed everything that my mind fought to deny. I feared I was as flippant with someone's life as I was with my tongue. Piss on him. He wore a turtleneck. For all I know he was East Slavic mob trash that had killed before, but never would again. Still, his eyes would be added to my luggage. It was already over the weight limit, and there's a price to pay for that.

CHAPTER 37

Morgan settled *Impulse* silently alongside Kathleen's dock. To the east the drawbridge was rising. I wondered for what other reasons anyone else would be on the water at that time. The air felt as if someone had draped a moist, woolen blanket over the ground. But as we trudged up from the dock, the lights from her house beckoned us like an inviting cabin in a Colorado winter night.

The back door swung open when we were ten feet away.

"We've got company for you," Morgan said as he brushed past Kathleen and carried Rosa into the house.

"Jake?" Kathleen asked when I stopped in front of her. I held Maria's hand. "Are you OK?"

"Business is brutal." I gave her a light kiss on the lips and neither of us closed our eyes.

"You're arm's bleeding."

"It's nothing."

"Your face looks like it got in a fight with a spiked telephone pole, and don't tell me I should see the pole."

"Where the devil are my slippers?"

No smile. Maybe even a frown masking a hint of frustration. Disappointment. She started to say something but changed direction.

"Who's your new friend?"

"This is Maria. Maria, this is Kathleen."

She took Maria's hand from me. "Let's go inside. Are you hungry, Maria?"

"Jacob, you are going to stay here, right?" Maria asked. Her feet were planted apart, as in Escobar's room. But this time there was no dead body behind her convulsing on the floor and fighting for a life it no longer possessed. That was why I had tried to rush the girls up the stairs and, when Maria refused re-entry to the safe room, eventually into the kitchen. Victor dying was not a pretty sight.

"Yes. I'm going to sleep on the couch. You and Rosa will sleep in a bed tonight."

Maria looked back at Kathleen. "Yes, I am very hungry."

"Outdoor shower, Jake," Kathleen said. I had a change of clothes in her house as well as a spare set I kept on *Impulse*. I started for the door and heard her from behind me. I stopped but I did not turn around.

"I thought you'd be back sooner. It was hard. It was hard waiting and not knowing. And you're hurt. And to look—to look like that."

I remained silent.

"Did you get the letter?"

"Yes." My back was still toward her.

"I hope it was worth it."

I walked away.

It had been a cluster fuck of a night and I just had to get it behind me. I had stared down the barrels of more guns in one night than in the last two lifetimes. I stripped down and turned the water on cold, which in summertime Florida is a lesser degree of warm. I scrubbed myself with the soap and shampoo that she kept on a small white plastic table that was missing one of its legs. I stood there a long time until everything was washed off, although I knew it wasn't. I went to my boat and applied a double bandage and put on a long sleeve shirt to cover it all. It was only a graze. Just the high left arm. Little left of the heart.

When I went inside, Morgan had placed a midnight cruise smorgasbord of eggs, toast, potatoes, and bacon on the table. Garrett was in from the dock and Kathleen had showered Maria and Rosa. Rosa wore a long T-shirt that stopped between her knees and her ankles, and Maria was in a coral summer dress that fit her well. I wondered where Kathleen got it. Both girls had wet hair and Rosa brushed her locks over and over again.

Kathleen hadn't made eye contact with me since I'd come in from the shower.

Garrett reached for the eggs when Rosa said, "Don't we pray first?"

"That's a very good idea. Why don't you say a prayer for us, Rosa?" Kathleen said.

And while she did my mind drifted to Escobar and Binelli. I'd have to give her a call someday and see what they got on Mendis, if anything at all.

"Jake." It was Kathleen. "I said would you please pass the juice." She had to look at me now, and when she did I saw a small smile form on her lips, but it was only for the others. Like a clown's smile, letting everyone see what they expected to see. The lines around her mouth that I had breathed in the night under the hibiscus seemed deeper. Or was it just the angle of light?

I retrieved the letter, and Morgan and Garrett ran the boat back to my dock. I crashed on the couch and slept like a plank until the sun came through the windows looking for me and no doubt wondering why I was so late.

Kathleen told Maria that she'd be back in few minutes, and then drove me the short island-hopping trip over three bridges to my house on the other island across from hers.

"Do you still like me?" I asked as we went over the first drawbridge. The top and windows were down and the air conditioning was on low—our preferred method of traveling side streets. The aggressive heat was starting to build, and it mixed with the cold air coming out of the car's vents. The air was like water faucets, either hot or cold. No middle ground.

"No." Her hair flew around her face. She usually tied it back, but not this morning. I realized how much I liked it, how different she seemed, when her hair was free.

"I bet I can win you back."

"You probably can." Neither of us spoke for a minute.

"It's hard," she started in. "And when you came in with a black eye, dried blood in your hair, a bloodied bandage on your arm, covered with salt from the Gulf, and sporting your omniscient frivolous glib, then I know. I know that you are risking it all. And don't get me wrong, the cause is great. But is it always? You chased down a letter and freed two girls, and yes, their lives will be better, so much better for it, but is it always so clear that you risk everything we have for something, or someone, who is new? Who you don't know? Because I don't see priorities so clear, so black and white. I don't get that."

"Get what?"

"Get what? Really, Jake? You flirt with death. The big Game Over. And you don't get it?"

"I do it for you and the kids." She didn't seem that ticked last night, meaning earlier this morning, although we didn't have that much time together. She'd obviously been percolating overnight.

She shook her head. "I don't know why I even try. Does it occur to you that you're sacrificing *us*? Or are you in it just for the thrills?"

"You can always go back to your books."

The split second that cast left my lips, I wished I could bring it back. What the hell is my problem?

She cut me a look I'd never seen and pray to never see again. "Did you just say that?" It came out in an alien tone, as if we had crossed into new territory and were now different people with a strange new language.

"No. No, that would have been someone else." I had to scramble to keep the situation from escalating. But it was like jumping on a hand grenade after it had already gone off. "I'm sorry for that. Pretend I never said it. Can we do those things?" She shook her head slightly, which was hard to detect with her hair flying in random directions. We pulled up to the red light and stopped. She looked straight ahead.

"I can't believe you said that." Still looking straight ahead.

"I'll cease it today. Walk away as the luckiest man in the world and never look back."

Straight ahead. I wasn't even there.

I kept at it. "Right here, right now. Say the word. Don't tell me you'd fear bitterness or resentment from me. There would be none. I'd bag groceries every day to walk with you."

That earned a glance. "Stop it. Just hug me next time. Not some little peck on the lips and some lame movie tag line. Stop pretending. Is that too much to ask, Jake, or do you really want me to go back to my books?"

"I think I'd rather have died than have said that."

"No, it's you'd rather die than love anyone other than me." No smile, just straight up. The light flicked green, the car jumped, and my head jerked back. Kathleen never did more than ten over and she never wasted a second in getting there. There is no law limiting the rate of acceleration.

"I didn't think he knew anything about love," I said louder to overcome the howl of the air and rumble of the road. *Omnis-*

cient glib. I was going to remind her that her "spiked pole" comment was not exactly the depth of seriousness, but part of my brain was telling the rest of it to shut the fuck up.

"Once in his life," she said without looking at me. I wanted to know like hell if she could look me hard in the eye and lay that same line down about her. And if she did, what would I do to protect her light heart?

I had lied. We both knew it. I wouldn't last a day with the grocery gig. Maybe we had run as far as we could. What was I supposed to do, put a name around my neck and sit behind a desk? Do that until I stopped showing up in photographs and call it a life?

The Florida air tousled her hair like it was trying to rip it off her head. She kept her eyes straight ahead as if there was oncoming traffic that commanded her attention, except there wasn't. We crossed the final bridge to my island and neither of us spoke another word.

How strange that my quest to get the letter was partially driven by my indebtedness to the man who helped me secure Kathleen's life. And how that very quest may have inadvertently caused a gulf between us that no bridge could span. I'd known this woman less than a year, and we both bore scars on the left side. Not far from the heart.

Walk away. For her sake, walk away.

We pulled into my driveway, and I desperately wanted to say something, but nothing came, and as I was thinking, I got out of her car. Before I knew it I was in my house, and I hadn't said a damn thing.

Oddly enough, that which is not spoken or never heard, which is never written and carries no weight, packs the biggest punch of all.

CHAPTER 38

The letter lay on the glass table in the middle of my screened porch next to the sports section that proclaimed in World War Two victory font that the Rays had just swept the Yankees.

Garrett looked as if he'd sweated away most of the water in the bay and took another mouthful from his bottle. The *Tampa Bay Times* was scattered on the glass table that needed to be cleaned. The blind was halfway down, filtering the relentless sun, but you could still feel the heat from the ball of fire ninety-three million miles away. On the water there was an open bow boat with four young girls in swimsuits. One of them had a serious camera. I assumed they were from the marine institute that was around the corner.

"I don't know how you stand it," he said.

"You've got to be out before the sun and realize you don't set any personal best in the summertime."

"And swimming?"

"Even tougher. The pool and Gulf are too warm to get anything other than a leisurely workout."

"I don't think 'leisurely' and 'workout' belong in the same sentence," Garrett said. He glanced down at the table. "Where did you get the Copacabana ashtray? I don't recall seeing it before."

"I dunno. Picked it up along the way."

"You going to call Kittredge?"

"Did this morning. Left a message with his boy that our business is settled."

I propped my feet on top of the letter. A couple hundred feet off the west end of the dock a dolphin cleared the water. Then again. The girls in the boat swung around toward that direction. Camera ready.

"Nevis?" Garrett asked.

"Haven't a clue. I can't tell them apart from this distance." I wanted to ask if he really saw Nevis give me a boost into the boat, but that was a bridge you cross only once. A lone woman in a sailboat headed out to the vast waters of the Gulf. Neither of us spoke until she passed.

"Colonel called," Garrett said.

"You tell him we ran into the FBI and they look a shitload better than him?"

"I did tell him other agencies of our federal government were on the scene, but for an entirely different matter. He wasn't concerned or interested. Said that's the way it's going to be from now on."

"Versus how it's going to be in the past?"

"Don't even think we're even. 'Leisurely workout' is a classic."

The final chorus of "Run" by Collective Soul spilled out of my massive living room floor speakers.

"How does he want it returned?" I asked.

"Mail."

"As in, put it in a larger envelope, lick a Disney commemorative stamp, maybe one of Goofy since no one knows who, or what, he/she really is, and place in my box with the little red flag sticking up? Maybe set up a lemonade stand next to it?"

"I believe so."

"Ten cents a cup?"

"Make it five. Times are hard."

"Seriously."

"He said double wrapped was fine."

Double wrapped is an inner envelope marked classified placed inside a larger envelope and sent via a registered service. It is standard procedure for secret information. That was not the colonel's preferred method. He insisted on hand carried in a double-locked bag out of MacDill Air Force Base, which was standard for any material classified higher than secret.

We didn't say anything for a moment. I thought I knew what was coming and was already telling myself to let it go. I had become suspicious when Garrett told me the colonel wanted me to proffer a deal to Escobar. I told myself that I knew this is how the world spun and not to be surprised when I kept learning that lesson—crossing that bridge—over and over. There are invisible strings of random cords of folly that bind us all together, and the sooner we accept that, the closer we come to understanding.

"When did they decide this?" I asked.

"Said the guys up top just sent it down yesterday."

"Believe him?" I wondered who was "up" to send things "down," and where the hell their authority came from.

"Does it matter?"

"What's the official line?"

"Routine declassification of nonmaterial information no longer considered or deemed to be paramount to national defense."

"Freedom of Information breathing down someone's neck," I said.

"Most likely."

"And if they decided this a week earlier?"

"None of it would have occurred."

"Alternate history."

"Happens every day."

"Open it together?"

"You go right ahead," Garrett said. "I'm going to take an outdoor shower and try to cool down—I'm just generating heat. My flight is at 1:10. I got a car coming, save you a trip to Tampa."

"Appreciate that, Tonto."

"You can have Florida in the summer," he said on his way out the door.

"I'll take it," I said to my empty screened porch. "Every day."

I considered the faded and dirty white envelope under my bare left foot. *Dulles. Rusk. McNamara.* Once powerful men that sand swept away.

A pelican perched on one of the lift's pilings. My boat needed a good waxing. Double wax on the west side due to the direct sun. I wondered where the lone woman in the sailboat was headed. I hoped the girls with the camera got a good shot of the dolphin. The name "Collective Soul" was taken from Ayn Rand's *The Fountainhead*. Ayn—rhymes with "pine"—used the phrase to connote the mass of humanity that interferes with individualism. The group's founding member just liked the name; he wasn't really into Rand's "objectivism." Former Fed Chairman Alan Greenspan, however, was. He was part of Rand's inner circle in his youth. Married Andrea Mitchell. Good catch, Al. I heard the Larry Clinton band's rendition of "I Hear Music" from my speakers. A minor bandleader from a time when even the big names were forgotten.

My mind, like the world, was on shuffle. I wondered if anything would change once I opened the letter.

I got a knife from the kitchen and returned to the porch. I picked up the envelope and slit it open. I put it down. I picked it up. I glanced up as two Jet Skis churned up the water off my dock and assailed the air with their obnoxious roar. While I looked at the water and wished they would find another area to buzz, I reached in and extracted the letter. I took one last look at the drawbridge across the bay, caught a dolphin breaking the water's surface to my right, and read the letter.

It was dated February 8, 1961. From Allen Dulles, director of the Central Intelligence Agency, to Secretary of State Dean Rusk and Secretary of Defense Robert McNamara. I knew both secretaries came into power with Kennedy in January 1961. Dulles was a holdover from the previous administration. The transfer of power is always a dicey business.

The letter was "in response to the request by both of you for a perusal of agency's opinions on matters recently discussed." It provided a terse overview of global CIA operations. It also gave a dismal view of US objectives and failures in Korea and concluded that a single nuclear bomb at the onset of the war would have in all "calculable probability" greatly reduced the total number of dead, likely prevented further escalation, and resulted in a US victory. The agency's conclusion was that if the United States should find itself involved in similar situations in the future to not shy away from the "power of a single hydrogen bomb dropped in a heavily populated and industrial zone.

"Just as it did in the conclusion of the Pacific war," the letter concluded, "the bomb does not kill as much as it saves lives."

There was a sentence worth framing. I imagined Bobby McNamara by that point realized that he was no longer selecting Falcon transmissions.

But it carried little significance to me compared to what followed.

The letter went on to note strong dissent within the agency. Dulles warned that one tenured agent requested his "vociferous disagreement concerning the appraisal of atomic weapons as well as US policy that aggressively sought to manipulate and interfere with other sovereign powers" be recorded. He also cautioned that this individual was outspoken in criticizing the agency for its "hodgepodge collection of street thugs" that comprised Operation Pluto. Despite a "failed effort to reason with him," Dulles wrote that this "rogue thinker" was still loose. If the upcoming operation were not successful, "we could ill afford second-guessing and inside dissension" All parties, he wrote, would need "to support the decision."

Operation Pluto, I recalled, was the code name for the Bay of Pigs. Dulles was already covering his ass. He had likely talked Kennedy and his virgin cabinet into supporting the plan. The last thing Dulles needed, especially if it failed, was a strong voice of dissention from within his own ranks that proved Dulles wrong.

It didn't work. Dulles, as Mary Evelyn had pointed out, took the fall and his gold watch in November of that year. The tenured agent?

Theodore Wayne Sullivan. The man who died twice.

James Harrison's buddy.

I thought of the Bay of Pigs. April 17 19, 1961. A disaster, as the name would suggest. Fifteen hundred CIA- and mafia-trained "street thugs," thieves, rapists, and guns-for-hire couldn't overthrow Castro's 25,000 armed men. I recalled Garrett and my earlier conversation regarding Dulles and the second death of Harrison. I'd double down on my bet: Dulles was out to get Sullivan. I doubt that Rusk and McNamara knew to what extend Dulles would go to silence his critics. I assumed both men, Rusk and McNamara, knew not to ask too many questions. You really don't want to know what the head of the CIA has immersed himself in.

The letter concluded by stating separate reports would be forthcoming on Iran and the escalating tension in French Indo-China.

When I was finished, I picked up the empty envelope and opened it to place the letter back inside. As I did, I noticed that there was a second letter along with a handwritten note. I pulled out the handwritten note and marveled at the neat penmanship. It was from Theodore Sullivan.

Washington, DC, April 12, 1961

Dear Dottie,

If you are reading this, you have gotten my call, for I can bear it no longer.

I apologize that I did not place this in your hand. I am to be in the possession of neither letter. I know asking you to hide these letters is the act of a coward. So be it.

The first letter is self-explanatory. I stole it. It will bear witness to the diseased logic that infects men's minds. We cannot succumb to men of power and persuasion who have lost sight of humanity in their pursuit of political dogma.

After the agency exorcised me from Southeast Asia, both Jim and I, as you know, have been heavily involved in the Cuba matter and that brings me to the second letter.

I found it in his room at the Hotel Florida in Havana the day his plane went down. He only planned to be in the states for a few days and left most things in his room. I can only assume that Jim banged it out during his last night on that rickety Remington portable that he traveled with. I took it before other agents swept the site. Our mission was classified and anything in his room would have been archived with government documents. I assure you there was nothing of interest to you other than this letter.

As you know, I had fallen from grace due to my viral anti-aggression stance. However, I was soon to become an even more vocal dissident of the agency for its going to bed with the Outfit, the Chicago mafia, in order to finance Operation Pluto. I'm fairly certain you will know it as the Bay of Pigs. It is yet to occur as of this writing but will commence within the week and, I fervently believe, fail soon thereafter. The Kennedy brothers succumbed to the power of Dulles and made promises to the Mafia in return for their cooperation. Who knows what repercussions could result from such an alliance? Who can foretell what events being in bed with the devil will alter? Why is madness, so plain and simple, so excruciating hard to see? I have exceeded what I thought I was capable of, but I fear it is not enough. I have made monstrous enemies. Enough. To the point.

I am embarrassed to say that I breathe only by the allure of a common street girl. Jim and I spent our last night together at an expatriate bar called Sloppy Joe's. We were to depart the next morning. Jim, as always, excused himself early and retired, although he obviously hit the typewriter's keys before the pillow. I drank, as I often do, and ended up in a room and with a girl that I do not remember entering. In either sense.

I was in sorry shape the following morning.

I was supposed to deliver a diplomatic pouch to Miami. I always filed a flight plan, but I rarely adhered to them and had no such intention to do so on that day. Jim went instead.

Jim's plane did not go down in a summer squall. It was shot from the sky.

"A failed effort to reason with him."

It was I they were after.

I am so sorry,

Teddy

I blew out my breath. Francine barked next door. Did Sullivan ever come clean with Dorothy Harrison? Was I the first to know, half a century later? And what did I know?

That Sullivan was about to squeal his displeasure over the Bay of Pigs. Win or lose, Sullivan was prescient enough to know that doing business with the Mafia, and the agency's constant urge to orchestrate coups like high school musicals, was all very wrong. Sullivan needed to be silenced. Dulles whacked his own man, but got the wrong one. I wondered if things got too complicated and I stood tall if I, too, would someday fall from the sky.

I picked up the second letter. It was from Jim Harrison to his wife, Dorothy.

I read it.

I read it again.

I placed it gently on the table and for a long time I sat and stared out at the water, but I cannot remember anything I saw or heard.

Tinker Bell rang.

Time to drink.

CHAPTER 39

If I had a giant saltshaker, I'd sprinkle the coastline of the Gulf of Mexico and pour the whole damn thing down my throat like a giant margarita.

But I didn't. I headed to the hotel.

I grabbed a high stool in the shade of the white canopy that covered the bar and did my best to keep the world at bay. I had the choice bird-dog spot. My back was to the pink lady. The bar, boardwalk, beach, and Gulf of Mexico were stacked in front of me like French pastries at a Versailles picnic. The place was a smorgasbord of flesh as women competed to see who could clothe themselves the least. I just didn't need that shit today.

Kathleen had called and reminded me that we were attending the museum's fund-raiser the following evening. She said that she would meet me there, as she wanted to arrive early.

Neither of us fell for it. Our conversation had been blunt and was the only words that we had spoken to each other since my silent exit from her car.

The low afternoon sun burned the water into a blinding glare. Figures on the beach and paddleboarders in the shallow waters appeared as silhouetted shadows cut from black cardboard. A slight breeze whisked a translucent wisp of sand over the beach like a low-gliding ghost. One solitary lady stood at water's edge, and then she sat and stared out at the sea. Every time I go to the beach I see that: some cutout cardboard with their back to the noise and contemplating the great flatness. My spot on the west coast of Florida was not a location to me but a woman I loved and not nearly as problematic as the other one in my life.

My wide sunglasses blocked my eyes and my baseball cap was low over my face. For amusement I studied the patrons at the bar. I discovered a new species and dubbed them "drink holders." *Bibo obtineo*. They can't keep their paws off the drink parked in front of them. They need to retain some form of physical contact, usually a hand that delicately caresses the base of the drink. Maintaining the lifeline. I wondered if that sliver of contact was a culmination of their dreams and hard work. A reward for the days of their lives that they had traded away for money. It all seemed hollow, but that's what I wanted to see and that is what I would see. The hell with it. I stuffed another sliced lime into the Corona's long neck.

Fucking Escobar. He would have died rather than turn over the letter, but he wouldn't let Elvis die for it. Fuck Victor too, while I'm at it. Was lowering his gun when I shot. Knew it then, know it now. Then bleeding like he had all the time in the world to die. Just a terrible thing to witness—life losing The Battle and then "poof" like it was never there.

Gotta admit, though, it was sort of handy having old Victor and Escobar to kick around. It kept me from thinking about what's-her-face.

"She said I could find you here," the guy next to me said. I didn't know if he was even talking to me.

I didn't remember him moving in. Last time I checked there was a flabby guy camped out there with cheeks that looked like fishing weights draped under his eyes. Flabby had a gold chain around his neck and a diamond ring the size of my swollen left cheek. But he was gone. Maybe he died and they hauled his ass away. I just don't know.

My new buddy was an old guy, at least to be sitting at the bar. Not that I got anything against old guys sitting at the bar, it seemed like a fine retirement plan, but you don't see that very often. He wore a faded straw boater that looked like it had put in its share of years keeping the rays off his head. His skin, already a Caribbean brown, was tanned from a lifetime in the sun. He wore a faded red but clean short sleeve shirt with a palm pattern. He had on long pants and worn sandals. Nashville's latest twenty-two-year-old blonde diva gushed through the speakers sharing with the world her first love, first breakup, or first fuck. I couldn't keep them straight or figure out why anyone even cared. I'd drop a grand to hear the Chairman of the Board, but that era slipped out a long time ago.

I heard again from the seat where gold chain used to be but that was now occupied by the old man in the hat.

"She said I could find you here." My peripheral vision caught him as he stared at me.

"She say it once or she stutter like you?" I asked in an acid tone that would hopefully put him down. Here's a clue, bozo, if I want to talk, I'll start the conversation.

"Pardon me?"

I glanced at him and was met with a sincere and innocent look. What a jerk. No wonder I drink; at least then I have an excuse for my boorish behavior.

"Who said you could find me here?"

"Your friend, Miss Kathleen. Maybe you are not the right person. I am looking for a man named Jake Travis."

Chad dropped off another drink and I took a large sip of the greyhound and wished I had stuck with beer. But I knew it didn't matter; the bottle wasn't going to help me find any truths today. But, hey, no harm in trying.

"Where did you run into my friend?" I asked.

"She came over to see Miss Sophia today."

"Miss Sophia," I said and wondered where this was going and if I wanted to follow.

"Yes, sir. I work for Miss Sophia."

"And you are?"

"Alejo."

"No, I mean, what do you do for Miss Sophia?"

"I am their gardener. Been working for her and Mr. Escobar for three years now. But it all went bad and they hauled him off to jail just the other night. A terrible thing. Miss Kathleen has been there letting Miss Sophia cry on her shoulder. She is a fine woman."

I didn't know, nor did I care, which woman he was referring to. "Your ex-boss had a few legal issues. The world will be a better place with him behind bars."

"I understand that. He did have a fine taste in music, though. I don't think he was that bad, I really don't. I think he just got lost."

He never took his eyes off me and had an easy way of talking, as if nothing were of real concern to him. A pair of silicone tits so tight you could pop them just by staring moved off to his left. A blue star tattoo rested high on the right breast. Am I missing something here? My eyes ran from that. I glanced up at the screen just in time to see someone catch a deep fly to center. A dozen seats away a guy, a drink holder, who'd been staring at the screen as if the sand and the water weren't even there, pounded his fist on the bar and shouted "Yes!" when the little man on the television secured the ball in his leather glove. There's just a truckload of shit that I don't understand. I turned back to my stool companion.

"What brings you into my neighborhood?" I asked.

"Excuse me, sir?"

"What can I do for you?"

"Nothing."

"Then why do you seek me?"

"Just to tell you. Miss Kathleen thought you would like to know. But there is nothing you can do for me."

"Know what?"

"That I told Mr. Escobar and Elvis about the letter in the back corner of Miss Dorothy's house."

I reappraised my stool mate, but he was the same good and gentle man that I made him to be. He was probably north of eighty and was thin like he'd been thin his whole life, not frail because of age. There was an aura of calmness around him that was incongruous with the beach bar vibe.

"And how did you know about it?" I asked.

"I worked for Mrs. Dorothy Harrison for thirty years." He laid it down proud.

I shoved my drink away. It was too damn sweet. "You worked for her?"

"Yes, sir. I was her gardener."

"Alejo, right?"

"My friends call me Angelo. That is what Miss Dorothy— that is what I called Mrs. Harrison—always called me."

"Tell me, Angelo, what was she like?" I figured I might as well delve into the past; I'd certainly made a mess of the present.

And then a small smile as he—who was not really at the bar in the same sense as the others were, trying to torque their lives with alcohol and flesh—slipped even further into his quiet world.

"Those were the best years, Mr. Jake." He gave a slight nod of his head. "She was a fine woman and treated me just fine too.

There wasn't that much work to do, but we enjoyed talking to each other and would just sit on her front porch and visit with her neighbors. You got to understand, there was always people around her. That is just the way she was. She never wanted anyone to knock on the door. She said true friends just walk right in, and she had a lot of true friends. We had nice times. When the Lord wants, he can make good years. But she missed him. I could tell."

"Who?"

"Pardon me?"

"Who did she miss?"

"Oh. Her husband, Jim. He passed not long after they moved to Pass-a-Grille. But she missed him. I could tell, and she knew that I could tell."

"Did she ever have another man in her life?" I was already into the question before I wondered why I even cared.

"No. No, sir. We talked about that after I lost my Lucille and Rose. I did not mean to get into all this with you." He looked down. It was the first time he had dropped eye contact with me.

"I'm sorry about your loss. Who were they?" He had my full attention, which wasn't saying much.

He looked up, and if the sadness was there before, I didn't see it. I wished I hadn't blurted my question out so forcefully. I thought of Kathleen asking Sophia if her mother was still alive. I thought it came out too harsh, but my tone sounded egregiously worse.

"Lucille was my love. She died, along with little Rose, the day she tried to bring her into this world. I think Miss Dorothy cried as much as I did. No. No, that's not right. She cried even more. She and Jim could never have any children and she was looking forward to mine like it was her own."

"I'm sorry." It sounded even weaker than the first time I said it.

He gave me a dismissive smile. "It was all a long time ago. But you know, I always wondered what it would have been like to raise a little girl. For some reason, that's the thought I can't get out of my head." He leaned in just a little and brought his volume down a couple of notches. "I never should have told them about that letter."

"A lot of good came from that letter."

"You know, we never talked about it," Angelo said. "Except late that year Miss Dorothy told me the man who brought her the letter died. She wasn't a woman who carried her sadness, but she carried that for quite a few days."

"November 29, 1961," I said.

"That's right, but it's the day before that I remember."

"The day before Theodore Sullivan died?"

"That's his name. I can never remember it. Yes, sir. Miss Dorothy was in the Keys for a few days, and I worked around the house that day and her phone just rang and rang and rang. I didn't know if I should answer it or not. I don't know...it just didn't seem my place." Angelo leaned in even closer to me. "You don't think, do you, Mr. Jake, that that phone ringing, like an alarm clock in an empty house, had anything to do with Mr. Sullivan?"

"I can't see how." And then, because of my desire to not have Angelo dwell on what might have been I asked, "Did you tell Miss Dorothy?"

"I should have," he said. "I should have, shouldn't I?"

"I wouldn't give it a second thought." As heard my words I knew that he'd given it decades of thought. I wanted to change direction and remembered seeing an older man picking up sticks when I first went to the museum, and although I didn't get a good look at him, I'd make him any day for the old man sitting next to me.

"Do you ever go back to the old house?" I asked him. "It's a museum now, as I'm sure you know."

"No. It was just too sad after Miss Dorothy died." He looked away from me for the second time.

I let it go.

"Where do you live now?"

"Well," Angelo smiled at me and sat up even straighter, "in my mind, I guess, I am still there with Miss Dorothy and my Lucille. It doesn't bother me. I don't get much out of the noise of the world. Miss Dorothy used to swim at night out in the Gulf. She said that when she swam, she lost sense of time and Jim was there in the water with her. Said that all those days came back, and everything she ever knew or experienced was there in the water like it was just waiting for her. I don't do much swimming, but all my lost days stay in my heart and I choose where and when to live, and when I'm at the...I still live with my Lucille and work for Miss Dorothy. Yes, sir. That is where I live. Where I float and kick and the days aren't lost."

Chad circled back in front of me. "That not hit the spot, Jake?" My greyhound, in my bar space in front of me, had been largely ignored.

"A little sweet," I said.

"Make you something else?"

"I'm fine."

"Try it at home with fresh-squeezed red grapefruit, it's a whole new concoction. Not nearly as sweet."

"I'll do that." He moved on, sensing my lack of enthusiasm, and I felt bad for not talking more to him. Lord knows he's listened to me plenty of times, whether he wanted to or not.

"Did you ever love anyone else?" I don't know where it came from or why I valued this man's opinion, other than I was at that point where I would take anyone's opinion over mine.

"Oh no." Angelo shook his head. "You only love once in your life, or it is not true love. Miss Dorothy and I talked about that. If you are lucky, she said, love kisses you once." Angelo spoke as if he was reciting a deeply held mantra. "I am a lucky man. I carry memories that most people can only dream."

"Only thing is, that thing luck is an odd bird, Mr. Jake. Miss Dorothy told me once that she thought it took plain old luck to live to an old age. But when she got there she knew more dead people than living, and now that I'm there I know that to be true and I wonder what type of luck you call that."

Sweet or not, I needed a stiff one. I grabbed my drink and took a healthy swig.

"I'm glad you're happy," I said, not being able to come up with anything better and thinking how poor it sounded. Angelo looked at his feet, and I congratulated myself on screwing up such a simple rejoinder. "Angelo?" But his head was down for the third time, and for some reason it seemed the saddest damn thing, and I wondered if he regretted taking flabby guy's seat.

"After Lucille and Rose died, I never left these islands," he said with his head still bent. "When I was young," he said softly and then stopped. The bar noise was that much louder. I wished to hell that they all would just go away.

"When I was young," Angelo's voice came from down a long road, "I was afraid of dying before I had a chance to live, and now that I am an old man, I am afraid of dying without ever having lived."

It floated out as a melodic drift, the bastard child of music and words, and after that symphony of a sentence, I drained my glass. I wished there was more. But I had work to do. Angelo had sparked an idea, and when the stallion of opportunity comes galloping by, you've got to throw your ass on the saddle, *because it does not slow down.*

"If you do not mind," Angelo said as he looked back to me, "what was that letter about?"

"You said she never mentioned it again?"

"No, sir. I don't think she cared. I think she was trying to leave all that behind her."

"Did she assume there was just the single letter inside?"

"Yes, sir, for all I know."

"It wasn't about anything. Not anymore."

My turn to look away from him. A wedding party trudged through the sand, and one of the elderly guests was in a wheelchair. It was modified with large wide black tires, and the young man in a dark suit behind it leaned in hard, but only seemed to push it deeper into the sand.

"You want to see a little of the world?" I asked when I returned to him.

"Pardon me?"

"Would you like to travel?"

"It would be nice. I don't feel old. Fact is I feel pretty good. Lucille and Dorothy have been telling me I still got a long way to run. Listen to me." He gave a slight shake of his head. "You probably think I am an old man that has gone nuts."

"No, Angelo. I don't think you're an old nut. I think you're a young nut."

We both got a chuckle out of that, and then I gave him my plan and told him that he didn't have much time to think about it. He said he had been thinking about it for thirty years and asked if that was enough time. I inquired if I could do anything for him after he was gone.

"Not really," he said.

"Are your certain? I don't mind the least."

"Well, you could take care of Hadley III," he said. "She's old and stuck in her ways and probably be happier staying here. I could leave her with the neighbor woman, but she does not like Hadley bringing her mice and birds, and Hadley don't like her at all. Those two just don't hum the same song."

"And Hadley is?"

"Hadley III. I don't want to be disrespectful of the two before her. She's my cat. I appreciate it very much. Sure you don't mind?"

"No. No problem at all."

CHAPTER 40

It was the following evening and the second letter lay on top of the Copacabana ashtray where it had landed when it slipped out of my hands the previous day. I wondered if the letter found comfort resting on a relic from its own time and even though it was a total bullshit thought it worked for me.

Morgan decided to sail at night, and Morgan was very comfortable with the night. Garrett planned to ride shotgun. I told him I could use a trip myself. He told me that I needed to face my problems and not sail away from them.

What a chum.

Angelo stood beside me with a blue-and-white Pan Am luggage tag on his suitcase. I wondered where he had gotten the tag. That bird hadn't flown in a long time. His shirttail was tucked in, and he provided me detailed instructions regarding Hadley III. His excitement was tangible enough to scare the baitfish. Unlike when I met him sitting at the bar, I had a chance to see him moving, and his agile body was not close to his age. Angelo certainly still did have a long way to run. Apart from the excitement, he displayed no apprehension. No hesitation. Thirty years.

I put Angelo on the boat and bade farewell to Maria and Rosa. I told them I would be down in a few months to visit them.

Morgan assured me that his lady friend on St. Kitts insisted it was no big deal, even had a room awaiting them. That confirmed my belief that he had done similar acts in the past. As *Moon Child* pulled away from my dock, I got a glimpse of Angelo with Rosa on his hip. I thought how strange that when you think that life has forgotten about you it circles back in the most unpredictable and mysterious manner. I realized that I'd forgotten to ask Maria what she was thinking when she squeezed my hand as we faced Victor. I'd save it for my visit. Or not. I heard the main sail flutter and a dolphin blow.

I changed into summer slacks and a buttoned shirt. I picked up the second letter, I'm not sure why, and stuffed it in my right pants pocket. I fired up my eight cylinders and drove over the bridge to attend the museum fund-raiser with Kathleen. It was about a mile away.

A lesser man would have pedaled. But everybody's concerned about the environment and natural resources, so I wanted to abuse them as much as I could. Let Mother Earth know that I was once here and didn't give a damn. That way she knows that I feel about her the same way she feels about me.

People spilled out of the museum's front door and a small jazz combo performed in the side yard. I wasn't in the mood for the shoulder-to-shoulder, hi-it's-so-nice-to-meet-whoever-the-heck-you-are scene. I headed to the old car.

Dorothy Harrison's 1959 Buick, as Kathleen said it would be, was parked directly in front of the museum. The deuce and a quarter had its top down, and a pair of geezers stroked her fins like they were copping their first feel in junior high. I circled the car and ran my left hand over its silky massive skin. A 747 could land on her hood. I recalled my earlier sense of puzzlement that recent events can so quickly fade and be cataloged with those of the distant past. But this was the opposite. The feel of the steel, the hardness of the perfectly formed surface, brought the past up to me like a powerful force rising off the ocean floor. Those events that belonged long ago erupted through the surface and washed over me. As if they were drowning me in meaning and importance to my life, but I could not see why or what was required of me.

"You're not coming inside?" Kathleen's voice, once again, turned me around. She wore a black strapless dress that stopped just short of her knees and her hair was plastered tight behind her head. She looked like she was in the business of looking good.

"Crowds and I don't get along, and you've got a large one. A successful night?"

"We'll see, won't we?"

Oh boy. Here we go.

"Guess we will." Great Zeus, is that all I have?

"I need to be with the guests," Kathleen said. Her eyes were as level and as noncommittal as her voice. She turned and strolled away.

My left hand was on the deuce and a quarter, and I put my right hand in my pocket and felt the letter. It was like connecting two ends of a battery and completing a circuit. It hit me hard and just blew out of me.

My mind, junked with random thoughts that rendered it barely operational at times, and my emotions, which knew no leash, were now joined and focused to their greatest capacity as if the whole world had been poured into a giant funnel and the only thing that leaked out of the bottom was a single word.

Kathleen.

Kathleen.

Kathleen.

And she was walking away.

"Walk with me," I said.

She turned back. "What?"

"A short walk. Right now."

"I can't...not right now. Maybe in——"

"Walk with me."

I took two steps toward her and extended my hand.

"Walk with me."

An involuntary smile flashed on her face and then she erased it just as fast. We would be OK. But as I had informed her once and she had reminded me a few nights ago, "just OK" was for losers.

She took my hand and I led us to the park across the street. We sat on the same bench I had sat on after my first visit to the Gulf Beaches Historical Museum. I let her have the clean end.

I handed her the letter.

Dorothy Harrison never knew what her husband wrote to her the last night of his life. His words would speak for me. His letter would serve its intent, just in a different time and with different lovers. Sometimes we can do that, have lives that we've never known intertwine and affect our course. Everyone's into the future, but it is the past that drifts us like a leaf on the water.

"What's this?"

"It's Jim Harrison's letter to Dorothy, written the night before he died."

"How did you——?"

"There were two, make that three, letters in the envelope." I explained the first letter as well as Sullivan's handwritten note.

She asked, "Jim was shot down by either the CIA or a Mafia CIA team that was actually gunning for Sullivan?"

"Yes. But that's for later. Read the letter. And K?"

"Yes?" Another smile, but nothing involuntary about it. I had never referred to her as a single letter. I was making headway here. But I had done serious damage. *You can always go back to your books* was a little left of the heart.

I paused. "Nothing. Read it."

Her eyes left mine and she read the letter. She blew her breath out and read it again. She sniffled and stood and walked over to the dark hedges that were out of the glare of the light pole that was behind the bench. I went to her. She spoke before I stopped, her back still toward me.

"She never read it?"

"No."

"No one?"

"No."

We were silent for a minute. Her back rose and fell several times and I heard her breath shudder from her.

"It's for you, Kathleen. He wrote it, but it's—"

She spun around to me. Her face was moist and mascara streaked her cheeks.

"You do that, don't you? I noticed that you do that."

"I do."

"Do it now, Jake."

I put my arms around her shoulders and hovered my mouth over the corner of her mouth, and as her breath escaped I inhaled until I could breathe no more, until I had taken all I could and there was nothing left. Mother Earth would be pleased, for we wasted not a molecule of air.

My lips had only graced the surface of her lips.

I pulled my head back. "What I want to say is—"

"Jake?"

"Yeah?"

"Shut up."

I did.

Hotel Florida
Havana, January 4, 1961

My Dearest Dottie,

You'd be so proud, for I've secured a room with a window, which is not a given in this hotel. I have the symbolic spot.

I spent the evening with Ted at a rowdy expatriate joint called Sloppy Joe's. We were toasting the folly of our government's thinking, for by the time you read this our disastrous invasion of Cuba will have faltered.

I am sorry to be away so long. I have been increasingly aware of the compression of time and how fortunate we are to share the same time. It seems I get caught in events that are not me, yet extracting myself from such situations is not easy.

Do events change us or, like a creeping dawn, does life finally make its presence known and kill the false gods of our idealistic youth? And if so, how much of the day remains?

What alcoholic rubbish. I'll go again and leave nothing at the edges.

I risk my life. For what? A world that will never know I was here? To never again run my fingers along the curve of your hips? All I want is to hover my mouth over yours and to breathe in as you breathe out so that we share the same air. There is nothing I crave more than to take life from your lips and use it for my own lungs, my heart. To fuel my lust for you.

I am finished. A few months to tidy up loose ends and then I am home for good.

Know that when you swim in the Gulf, that I am the water that envelopes you. I am the tide that moves gently in and out of you, our rhythm one with the moon and stars.

And even when mine are gone, I will love you tomorrow.

Yours, forever

Jim

CPSIA information can be obtained
at www.ICGtesting.com
Printed in the USA
LVOW12s2105120117
520759LV00001B/108/P